D0378928

OF TIME and Change

a memoir

OF TIME

a n d Change

a memoir

FRANK WATERS

MacMurray & Beck
Denver

Published by:
MacMurray & Beck
1649 Downing St.
Denver, CO 80218

Acknowledgments are due and are gratefully made to the following: *The Frank Waters Foundation,* for the photographs on pages xvii, 12, 229; *Kit Carson Historical Society,* Taos, N.M., for the photographs on pages 47, 75, 102; *Bob Kostka,* for the photograph on page 133; *Eya Fechin,* for the photograph on page 168; *Anne Dasburg,* for the photograph on page 203; and *Dan Budnik,* for the photograph on page 252.

Printed and bound in the United States of America

1 2 3 4 5 6 7 8 9 10

Library of Congress Cataloging-in-Publication Data
Waters, Frank, 1902—
Of time and change : a memoir / by Frank Waters.
p. cm.
ISBN 1-878448-86-2
1. Waters, Frank, 1902– —Homes and haunts—New Mexico—Taos. 2. Lawrence, D. H. (David Herbert), 1885–1930—Friends and associates. 3. Luhan, Mabel Dodge, 1879–1962—Friends and associates. 4. Brett, Dorothy, 1883–1977—Friends and associates. 5. Authors, American—20th century—Biography. 6. Taos (N.M.)—Social life and customs. 7. Taos (N.M.)—Biography. I. Title.
PS3545.A82Z47 1998
818′.5209—dc21
[b] 98-26707
CIP

Of Time and Change cover design by Laurie Dolphin.
Cover photograph by Robert Miller.
The text was set in Weiss by Chris Davis, Mulberry Tree Enterprises.

Also by
FRANK WATERS

FICTION

Fever Pitch (1930)
The Wild Earth's Nobility (1935)
Below Grass Roots (1937)
The Dust Within the Rock (1940)
People of the Valley (1941)
The Man Who Killed the Deer (1942)
River Lady (1942)
with Houston Branch
The Yogi of Cockroach Court (1947)
Diamond Head (1948)
with Houston Branch
The Woman at Otowi Crossing (1966)
Pike's Peak (1972)
Flight from Fiesta (1986)

NONFICTION

Midas of the Rockies (1937)
The Colorado (1946)
Masked Gods (1950)
The Earp Brothers of Tombstone (1960)
Book of the Hopi (1963)
Robert Gilruth (1963)
Leon Gaspard (1964)
Pumpkin Seed Point (1969)
To Possess the Land (1973)
Mesico Mystique (1975)
Mountain Dialogues (1981)
Eternal Desert (1990)
Brave Are My People (1993)

CONTENTS

LIST OF ILLUSTRATIONS

FOREWORD

Reading *Of Time and Change* is like sitting with Frank Waters and listening to him tell rich and fabulous stories. One of Frank's greatest gifts was his power as a storyteller to involve the reader in the story. He also had that ability in his non-fiction, the skill to sketch out characters and their dramas and create living scenes. He blurred the distance between fiction and essay, a feat only the most accomplished writer dares.

In this collection of essays, Frank presents reminiscences of the time and changes he lived through. Again he draws on that extraordinary gift as he reveals episodes in the lives of the artists and writers who gathered in Taos in the 40s and 50s.

What an exciting time to live through! Before WW II the deeply religious (some would say mystical) roots of the place were fed by the people from Taos Pueblo and the Hispanic villages. Drawn by his desire to live in a place that throbbed with the spirit of the Universal One, Frank moved from Colorado to New Mexico. He found his unity with nature in Taos, at the foot of the sacred mountain.

Then came the war and the discovery of Taos by artists from the east coast and from far more distant places. It was a gathering of creative energy that is a landmark in New Mexican literary and artistic history, and Frank was in the middle of it. He was an integral part of the creative explosion that was taking place.

We are fortunate that Frank recorded his involvement with the artists who gathered in Taos during that watershed period. The essays incisively reveal an era that is gone. These revelations may not suit everybody's sensibilities. Frank is candid and truthful. You will find warts, wrinkles, and petty human foibles in Frank as well as in his compatriots. But you will also find much to satisfy your spirit in Frank's unique illumination of the time, the people and the place.

It's that honesty that makes this collection so compelling. Frank induces the reader to feel like a voyeur as he exposes the lives of the people he knew. There's an intimacy as we hear Frank's voice reveal the richness and, sometimes, the poverty of soul in the lives of world reknowned artists. In every single page we are with Frank as he moves back and forth in a time that shaped the lives of the Taos artists—a time that was also shaping the life and literature of Frank Waters.

In the last two chapters of the book, Frank widens his perspective to muse on the interconnectedness of Indian cultures whose ceremonies have kept harmony in the sacred circle of life. The Maya and the Hopi are related, for both groups have for centuries kept alive a humanistic religion that connects one to the Earth. It took the sympathetic heart and mind of Frank Waters to see this. In these chapters we feel his anguish as he witnesses a materialistic world bent on destroying the ancient cultures. Frank was a witness in his time of change, as we must be in ours.

Another gift that he possessed was his ability to teach. These essays reveal his constant theme: the interconnectedness of life on Earth and throughout the universe. As a writer Frank brought Native American thought to the forefront. In his novels and in his non-fiction books, he provided us glimpses into that Otherworld he sought.

Often we sat enthralled when Frank told stories. We sensed we were in the presence of a teacher who could guide us into that realm of higher consciousness we all seek, the Unity of Spirit that is the heartbeat of the creation. Today we have these essays, among his many works, as signposts for our path. The spirit of Frank Waters is still guiding us.

Rudolfo Anaya
Albuquerque, NM

PREFACE

Many of the following sketches are of the place that has been my permanent home for the last forty years, and of a few of my early intimate friends. Surely no more disparate individuals could be found than these who were drawn by an enigmatic destiny to share their lives in a small adobe village so different from their native homelands.

How little do we know one another. Certainly my character sketches are biased and incomplete, but I loved them all. Curiously interconnected for a short time in this temporal world, susceptible to the wind and rain of time and change, they have left upon me the mark of their passing.

It seems only fair that I first write something about myself to accompany what I've written here about them.

My mirror view is not an outline for a full autobiography, which I will never write. All the other persons I've known and loved, the places I've lived, and my diverse activities in many fields have been factually or fictionally reflected in my previous books. Instead, these rambling notes simply attempt to trace the thread of an inner life running beneath the landmarks of my outer life. Its course toward a still growing maturity of spirit had many lapses but was consistent. When it surfaced into daylight, it revealed what I thought were assurances of my early notion of an invisible Otherworld we simultaneously inhabit. What and where it was, I didn't know; but I experienced many ways it influenced me, as it did in other ways those persons I've sketched here. Perhaps it is this invisible reality that is ever working to achieve the interconnectedness, unity, and wholeness of all persons, places, and events everywhere.

Frank Waters, ca. 1927

1
A MIRROR VIEW

Seventy-six-year-old Chief White Antelope said it at break of day a century or more ago when he stumbled out of his lodge at the sound of rifle shots. His village of Cheyennes and Arapahos at Sand Creek, Colorado, was surrounded by white soldiers firing at frightened and fleeing men, women, and children. There was no escaping their total massacre. White Antelope, the first of his people to be riddled with bullets, stood calmly erect, arms folded, singing his death song:

> Nothing lives long,
> Only the earth and the mountains . . .

The wind and the rain of time and change prove the truth of his song. They alter our daily lives, wash away civilizations. Only the earth and its mountains, visible parts of an unseen whole, endure forever.

I first felt this as a child in Colorado Springs, Colorado, my birthplace at the foot of Pikes Peak. My grandfather Joseph Dozier was a Southerner who had come west in the early 1870s. He built a large house for his growing family along the stream of Shook's Run and became a leading building contractor.

My mother, Onie, was the oldest of his five daughters; and my father, Frank Jonathon, was a relative newcomer to the region. Although my younger sister, Naomi, and I were born in Grandfather's old house like all the children in the Dozier clan, we lived at first in a house of our own. It stood a block away on El Paso. The street ran parallel to the high embankment of the Santa Fe Railroad line and was reached through an underpass.

My father, with his dark skin and straight black hair, was of a different breed than the Dozier clan. We didn't know much of his background save that he was part Indian—Cheyenne. National prejudice against Indians was still prevalent, and my maternal grandmother was never quite reconciled to accepting him into the family.

One of his best friends was a vegetable huckster named Joe, a Cheyenne. Father often rode with him on his rounds. Sight of my father neatly dressed in a suit and polished boots as he sat on the plank seat of a rickety wagon beside an Indian huddled in a tattered blanket with moccasins on his bare feet always disconcerted Mother. She was even more upset by Father's frequent visits to the Ute encampment on the mesa.

The Utes had been moved to a western reservation; however, a band of them was permitted to return here to their former homeland every summer. Their smoke-gray lodges were shunned by respectable townspeople, but Father often took me there of an evening. He would squat down cross-legged in the circle of men around the cooking fire. With the long-bladed knife he always wore, even in church, he would cut off a pink slice of the steaming haunch and eat it, as did they, in his fingers. I waited patiently with the women and children for our turn at table.

The high peak rising above us was the Utes' sacred mountain. Looming prominently in their creation myth, it always had been a place of power, not only for the mountain Utes but for Cheyennes and Arapahos who had come in from the plains to deposit votive offerings at the many mineral springs. Later it became the beacon for white gold-seekers whose wagon sheets were emblazoned with the boast, "Pikes Peak or Bust."

Not until years later, in 1891, was gold finally discovered on the south slope of the fourteen-thousand-foot Peak itself. The "Cripple Creek Cow Pasture," only eighteen miles west and one mile up from sedate Little London, as Colorado Springs was familiarly called, quickly became the world's greatest gold camp. The pharmacist at our corner drugstore rushed up there one Sunday morning. Throwing his hat into a gulch and digging where it fell, he discovered the famous Pharmacist Mine. Jimmie Burns, a plumber, uncovered a richer vein from which he extracted enough gold to build a new Burns Theater. It seemed that everybody in town was getting rich and building ornate mansions in the elite North End of Little London.

Our east part of town was tidy and respectable but divided from the North End by the barrier of Cripple Creek gold. Grandfather, now a prosperous building contractor, finally succumbed to gold fever. One after another, he began to open unproductive shafts in the gold camp, down which he sank his business and everything he owned except his own home; and he kept urging my father to help him open still another working.

Occasionally I was taken up to the gold camp by Grandfather and Father on the spectacular Cripple Creek Short Line Railroad. Cripple Creek was everything that conservative Little London was not. It was a madhouse of activity and extravagant hopes. The muddy streets of Cripple Creek, the largest new town, swarmed with muckers, drillers, promoters and stockbrokers, ladies in long skirts and high button shoes, jostled off the boardwalks by painted prostitutes. Across the whole slope of Pikes Peak rumbled mule-drawn freight and ore wagons. Everywhere surface structures of great mines rose amidst open tunnels and shafts. All this activity, Father told me, was devoted to mining tons of rock from the Peak, grinding it into dust, and extracting a few specks of gold.

One day while playing with a handful of sand on the dump of one of Grandfather's mines, I had a strange experience of a far different nature.

In the bright sunlight every grain stood out with its distinctive shape, color, and texture. Then it happened. In an instant Pike's Peak took on a new and different meaning. I saw that it was composed of all these millions of grains of sand, which were mysteriously and precisely fitted together into one mighty, single whole—a sacred place of power, as the Utes regarded it. This momentary realization prompted the extravagant notion that all the mountains and continents in the world, like the grains in my hand, were also precisely fitted together to make a greater whole whose purpose and meaning were perceived by another world somewhere. The notion frightened me a little, but I never forgot it.

Late that summer Father took me to the remote Navajo trading post of *Hon-Not-Klee* (Shallow Water) in New Mexico. The post was an island in a vast pelagic plain, a thick-walled adobe with iron-barred windows. The trading room was full of trade goods: salt, sugar, coffee, canned goods, bridles and ropes, bolts of flowered gingham and brilliant velveteen. In back were our living quarters, storerooms for sheep pelts and sacks of wool, and a locked rug room piled with Navajo blankets and silver jewelry. Every day Navajos rode in: slim, arrogant men on horseback, women and children in springless wagons. Different in appearance from the Utes, they were much alike. I learned that they too regarded the land as their Mother Earth, and that it was bounded by four sacred mountains, one in each primary direction; these were places of power from which the land and people drew life and energy.

Bruce, the master of this outpost of civilization, was ill; and Father had come to help him manage the post. This was a natural life for Father. He belonged to the open sunlit plains, not confined underground in a dark granite stope. Bruce offered him partnership in the post, but it was no place for Mother. She recalled him home with Grandfather's urgings to help him in his mining ventures.

Shortly after his return Father developed double pneumonia and was brought down from Cripple Creek to our house on El Paso. In my bed upstairs I faintly heard his death rattle downstairs. The nurse came up. Without explaining what the sound was, she simply directed me to go to Grandfather's house on Bijou Street. I was twelve years old, but it was a long walk at midnight through the dark railroad underpass. At my repeated knocks Grandfather opened the door and without a word put his arms around me and led me inside.

So it was that my mother, sister, and I went to live in that nest in which most of the Dozier clan had been hatched and which still nurtured many of us. Besides us three there were two small children of one of my aunts, who was divorced and had gone away to open and abandon a series of chocolate shops in mining towns throughout the Colorado Rockies. For all three generations of us began a difficult period.

Lying in bed in my small third-story bedroom, listening to the wind of change whistling around the eaves and grieving for my father, I remembered him telling me that the Cheyennes' name for themselves, *Tsistsistas,* meant "like-hearted ones," people whose hearts were united as one. They got along without quarreling, just as we folks should on Bijou Street. Moreover, all the children of Mother Earth—plants, trees, birds, animals, and human beings—were members of one big family, so we shouldn't kill these others just for fun or other needless purposes.

Under the influence of my father I had rejected the Christian brand of religion taught in the Southern Methodist Church as we listened to the preacher's descriptions of white-winged angels in heaven and devils in hell herding sinners into vats of burning brimstone. I still had the notion of an invisible world somewhere where everybody and everything were somehow connected. My mother was then induced to enroll me in the Sunday school of the more enlightened Presbyterian Church. By Easter my classmates and I were declared ready for baptism in the church. That morning we were lined up in the hallway, waiting to be marched to the altar. As my last name began with "W," I was the last in line. For no conscious reason I bolted out the back door into the alley, and never returned to church. Nor have I ever been a member of any church or religious cult.

High school was no more rewarding. At Colorado College I enrolled in engineering, in preference to business administration or the classics. Soon I knew I wasn't cut out to be an engineer. Home life on a skimpy budget was trying. Our Shook's Run neighborhood was deteriorating, and the snobbish North End regarded me as "a kid from the other side of the railroad tracks." Everything conspired to make me feel utterly miserable, alienated from the world about me.

Near the end of my third year I quit school and left home as a paying passenger on Santa Fe Number 5. As the train drew out of the station, I glimpsed the gaunt house in which I had been born and lived for so many years. Behind it loomed the high, snowy peak on whose slope Cripple Creek was now an almost abandoned mining camp, pockmarked with glory holes, empty shafts, and the rotting timbers of gallows frames. The train was gathering speed now, and Little London of my childhood and disgruntled youth was left behind. Yet buried within me I carried my childhood conception of another world of unity and completeness invisibly connected to this one.

The influence of the place where one emerges into earthly existence can never be wholly eradicated. Even his natal hour stamps its influence, marking the intersection of space and time on him, his planetary world, and the pattern of the stars above.

So it seems to me that wherever I have since lived, whatever I have done, have repeated in some way my early thoughts and life in Little London.

My fledgling flight carried me to Casper, Wyoming, where I hitchhiked a ride with a truck driver to the booming Salt

Creek oil fields. Here I got a job as a roustabout in a gang laying a line of ten-inch pipe.

All Salt Creek on its desolate plain sprouted high oil rigs flanked with pumping plants and tool shanties. Everywhere swarmed men and trucks. It reminded me of Cripple Creek, the jackpot here being oil instead of gold.

That fall I met an aging old-time Westerner. He had been offered a home with his daughter in California, and with his savings he bought a little Star roadster to drive there. Having difficulty driving it, he persuaded me to drive him.

The long drive opened for me a wide and empty land sparsely dotted with villages and small towns. Puttering along at thirty miles an hour, camping at night off the unfenced road, we finally reached what old Mr. Garth remembered as the heart of Los Angeles—the shabby, historical Mexican plaza at the end of Main Street. Dividing our last few dollars, Mr. Garth drove on to his daughter's home in San Diego, and I rented a room in a squalid hotel on the plaza.

A few days later I discovered uptown the great modern Los Angeles and found a job. I was hired, strangely enough, as a junior engineer by the telephone company and sent down to Imperial Valley on the California–Baja California border. It lay in what was then known as the Colorado Desert because it was bounded on the east by the Colorado River. Years before, the river had been tapped, channeled west through the Mexican part of the desert, then diverted north into the American portion. With irrigation the barren wasteland produced such bumper crops of fruit and vegetables that Imperial Valley was proudly called the "Winter Garden of America." It reminded me of Cripple Creek and Salt Creek, its own symbol a round, ripe cantaloupe.

My job was to help expedite telephone service through switchboards overworked from growers demanding more trucks or railroad cars and from fruit brokers calling eastern cities to order diversions of refrigerator cars as the market rose and fell with the thermometer. I traveled throughout the valley and made a long trip down into desolate Baja California.

Mountain bred, I had never seen the desert before. And here I felt the full, shattering impact of its appalling emptiness and immensity. Tawny scorched rock mountains rearing from a sea of sand shimmering in the pitiless glare of the sun and reflected heat waves. Fantastic skeletal shapes of spiny trees. Clumps of weird cacti. A world of mystical unreality. Was the desert the beginning of the green world we know? Or were the earthly barren sands its end? Or was it both, completing time's circle?

This substratum of our earth must have awakened something within the substratum of my own self, for at night after work I wrote a description of an imaginary desert valley enclosed by a wall of rocky mountains, around whose circular rim lay the semblance of a gigantic lizard with a woman's face meeting the end of her scaly tail.

This fantastic description turned out to be the middle of my first novel. Writing for me was difficult, for my engineering course in college had included no classes in English or literature. I then contrived a beginning and an end of a story to enclose it. The novel was published, inept as it was, and was an instant flop.

Yet for all its obvious faults, as Thomas J. Lyon years later pointed out in his critical analysis of my writing, the book anticipated a theme in all my following books. I had projected here, as I finally learned, one of the oldest symbols known to mankind—the *uroboros,* the circle formed by a serpent biting its own tail. As interpreted by the eminent psychologist Carl G. Jung, it is a symbol of primordial unity, enclosing the infinitude of all space and time. The serpent itself, the Lizard Woman, linking the beginning and the end, symbolized timeless time.

Here then had emerged in conscious form my childhood apperception of a universal whole.

Transferred back to the head offices in Los Angeles, I was confined to a desk and pored over blueprints. It was too much for me. I finally quit and began a new life as a full-time writer.

For years I traveled aimlessly throughout the Southwest in a 1929 Ford coupe, carrying a sleeping bag, coffee pot, and frying pan, or living in hall bedrooms and cheap motels. I kept writing anything that could be sold. My first full-length books, of course, were about a mountain, Pikes Peak. When a chapter was finished, I sent the handwritten

Frank Waters and Frank Samora

manuscript to Naomi, who was married and living in Los Angeles. She typed and held it until the book was completed and ready to be sent to a publisher.

Indian pueblos became familiar to me. Each was then a little city-state whose people were self-sufficient, spoke their own language, and observed their own customs. All lived in a common secretive world little known to whites. Among them I made many close friendships that still endure. It was several years before I wrote my first Indian novel. Conception of it came in a curious way.

In the modern town of Taos, New Mexico, I happened to be in the county courthouse when an Indian from the nearby pueblo was being given a hearing for killing a deer out of season in the Carson National Forest. He was found guilty and fined. I thought nothing of the incident and walked out.

A few mornings later while I was shaving, I saw in the washbowl the images of three men: the regional Spanish head of the Forest Service, the blanketed Indian governor of Taos Pueblo, and an Anglo man whom I couldn't quite identify. They appeared to be arguing over the judgment upon the guilty Indian who had killed the deer in the mountains. Instantly the full scope of the novel took shape. After washing the breakfast dishes, I sat down to begin it.

The story didn't have to be contrived. Despite interruptions, it unfolded like a flower in its own inherent pattern. The words flowed easily from my old Parker pen.

The theme of the novel was another emergence of my notion of a universal wholeness and invisible unity, also traditionally believed by Indians to include all living things—the tall pine and corn plant, the deer, snake and eagle, springs and mountains. Hence, the novel developed the differences between the Indians' spiritual and the Anglos' pragmatic modes of thought.

But it also had a factual background, which expanded like the far spread of ripples from a stone cast into a still pool. The simple incident of that Indian killing a deer touched off the long-unresolved demand of Taos Pueblo for the federal government's restoration of the immense mountain wilderness surrounding its sacred Blue Lake. The novel followed the involved legal battle, presenting it as the Pueblo's constitutional right to religious freedom opposed to economic exploitation of the land. The book helped to enlist the general public's support of this view.

The controversy dragged on until Congress passed a bill in 1970 that awarded the Pueblo title to the land. My novel *The Man Who Killed the Deer* was a flop when first published in 1942 but was reissued, constantly reprinted, translated into foreign languages, and is still in print after nearly fifty years. The book has never seemed mine. It was born in a circular washbowl, another symbol of unity and wholeness.

During my early writing years other young American writers and painters were flocking to Europe for cultural nourishment. I didn't want to go, and never yet have gone. Instead I was drawn to Mexico, the heartland of Indian America once extending from Central America north into the American Southwest. We here are the tip of that submerged ethnic and cultural iceberg, utterly different in thought and feeling from Anglo America east of the Mississippi.

In this motherland I always felt at home. The same tawny deserts and blue mountains, the same native people rooted to their Mother Earth, the same soul beneath the facade of Christian teachings. One early trip revealed it all. Alone on horseback or muleback, I followed the course of the Sierra Madre, traveling from one remote ranchito to another. In every one a family shared with me their tortillas and beans, let me sleep with them on the earthen floor of their adobe hut, and found a young boy or older man who could be spared from their fields to guide me to the next. How friendly, warm, and hospitable they were. A "people of one heart." Wherever they were, in isolated ranchitos or *jacales,* in remote little villages, what remains of those years now is etched in my memory: dark, earthy faces in firelight, the stench of urine on every wall, the taste of roasted chiles, and the heartbeat of all the land—the clap of hands shaping tortillas and the dainty quickstep of burros on cobblestone streets.

It has always seemed strange to me that if Mexico's spirit of place revealed itself through my five physical senses, it also curiously stimulated a sixth sense of the influence of that nebulous Otherworld I believed existed.

This sense came in many ways: dreams, coincidences, and events ranging from the trivial to the extravagant.

One happening I remember only because of a woman's odd remark. Late one night I was let off a local train in the mountains at what an old guidebook had designated as the stop for the village I wanted to visit. The conductor had objected to stopping the train. He explained that the village on top of the mountain was very old and could be reached only by an ancient trail up the canyon. When the railroad line was built, an old mule-drawn streetcar had carried passengers up to the village from the depot. Now a new station had been built on the other side of the mountain, and a new road led to the village.

Sleepy, hungry, and too impatient to ride the long way around, I insisted on being let off the train so I could walk up to the village.

The former wooden depot was a crumbling ruin, and the streetcar rails had been removed. The moonless night was too dark for me to find either their trace or the ancient trail. Lost, and blindly groping through the thick brush, I felt a curious sixth sense guiding me to turnings I otherwise never would have found.

When at last I straggled into the small village, several men and an aged Indian woman were huddled together in the empty plaza. The men's surprise at seeing me was expressed in excited questions. "How did you find your way and get here safely?" asked one. "Didn't you see the piles of stones and little crosses as you came?" asked another.

Explained another, "They mark the places where others have been murdered by thieves. A dangerous way even nowadays and in daytime."

The old woman then let loose a torrent in her own *idioma*. One of the men tersely translated it. "This *extranjero* old soul. He remember the way." The remark I couldn't explain.

An extravagant fantasy occurred later. One afternoon in Mexico City I was riding in an upstairs seat on a bus traveling down the lovely Reforma. Abruptly, without warning, I found myself floating in the air high above. I could see myself sitting on the bus and the great traffic-jammed city spread out below. At the same time and not far away I saw Teotihuacán, the ancient Toltec metropolis of Mesoamerica. All its edifices stood out solid and unchanged—the towering pyramids of the sun and the moon, the massive Ciudela with its pyramidal temple of Quetzalcoatl, and crowds of people thronging the Street of the Dead and other temple courtyards. Simultaneous sight of these two great cities whose lifetimes were separated by more than a thousand years disoriented me completely. Then, just as suddenly, I was back in my seat on the bus again, not knowing who I was or where I was going. Not until the bus reached the end of its run did I remember my identity.

This was not the only time I experienced disassociation from my physical body but the only time so completely. It didn't upset me later. I had met a few poorly dressed and unassuming men who belonged to that class of *hechiceros, brujos, curanderos,* and shamans who made regular excursions into the metaphysical realm for specific purposes. There was nothing spooky about them. So I didn't worry about my own periodic deviations from the usual aspects of reality. They came unexpectedly and were uncontrollable but kept reminding me in various ways of that nebulous Otherworld, each incident seeming to open a crack wider the door to it.

The door banged shut when I was in the world of constant change. There is no need to write here of my activities during these many years in Los Angeles, in New York, a stint in the army during World War II before I was released to write propaganda briefs for the Office of Inter-American Affairs in Washington, D.C., and then in Santa Fe and Los Alamos. They were exciting years filled with many new and enjoyable experiences. But none of my successive jobs and hectic marriages held any conviction of permanency. I felt I was playing roles in which I was miscast, and I had lost the thread of my inner life.

Not until I finally returned to my permanent home on the slope of the Sangre de Cristo Mountains in New Mexico did I feel in touch again with the natural world. The old adobe and pastures lay just above the small Spanish village of Arroyo Seco and adjoined the reservation of Taos Pueblo. Mountains and Indians. The setting repeated the pattern of my childhood. My psychic experiences returned, but my fantastic notion of an Otherworld had been drastically revised by all the books I'd been reading.

One of the first was the published talks of Sri Ramana Maharshi of southern India, who died in 1950. He was commonly known as a holy man who expounded the truths embodied in the *Vedanta,* the ancient core of India's religious philosophy. My Sanskrit scholar friend Dr. Allan H. Fry in New York, however, did not include him in the direct line of Vedantic sages and seers. The Maharshi, he said, was "one of those birds the Hindus called *laimsas,*" or "wild geese," who by his own life achieved realization of the Otherworld, which he called the universal Self. Perhaps that is why he appealed to me.

The four primary volumes on Tibetan Buddhism by Dr. W. Y. Evans-Wentz were most influential. In one of my own books I had pointed out the many similarities and parallels between Tibetan Buddhist and Pueblo Indian ceremonialism. Dr. Evans-Wentz, when I became friends with him, found many more. After living many years in India and Tibet, he had returned to San Diego, California, and had begun a new book on the sacred mountains of the world. It included Cuchama, a mountain rising to the east on his immense ranch at the Mexican border. Cuchama was the sacred mountain of neighboring Indian tribes, and his book recounted their traditions about it. I helped Dr. Evans-Wentz with his book and, when it was published after his death, edited and annotated it.*

There was also Chinese Taoism, which gave the name of Tao to the one universal and enduring spiritual reality infusing every speck of matter and every organic cell with life and consciousness, another name for the Otherworld I had imagined.

The teachings of Georges Ivanovitch Gurdjieff, the mystic from Central Asia, I appreciated for their universal scope. Also important were the writings of C. G. Jung, the famous Swiss psychologist who discovered what he called the collective unconscious, a level below Freud's personal unconscious. Illuminating as his studies were to me, and to all mankind, I found they lacked the spirituality of Eastern teachings, which Jung could not accept. He maintained that self-realization was achieved by the personal ego experiencing itself as the universal Self, a process he called individuation. This postulation clearly showed the difference between the religious philosophies of the East and the psychological view of the pragmatic West.

Books, books. Dozens of such books. All revealing mankind's ages-old search for the Otherworld under different names, and by different disciplines. Yet there was too a constant flood of teachings by swamis and gurus, many of them American opportunists who had grown beards and were adjusting their teachings to popular tastes and pocketbooks, as well as mail courses on astral projection, practical yoga for health, wealth, and power, tarot cards, do-it-yourself kits of crystal balls and color charts of auric emanations. And with all this came widespread testimony from persons who had had the same sort of psychic experiences that I'd had.

All this was discouraging. The "black tide of occultism," as Freud had termed even the science of parapsychology, was sweeping Western civilization. And in it I had been caught for years. How could we pull out of it? Yet I still felt in it a hidden spiritual current I had not found.

It carried me to a changeless world within the world of change. I went to live for nearly three years among the Hopi Indians in northern Arizona.

The small Hopi reservation lay in the middle of the immense Navajo reservation. The Hopi pueblos were built on the tops of three rocky mesas rising from the sandy desert. One of them, Oraibi, dating from A.D. 1150 or earlier, was the oldest continuously occupied settlement in the United States. From their villages the Hopis always had descended to plant small *milpas* of corn, squash, and beans in the waterless desert soil, invoking rain with prayerful ceremonies. Here was an entire society that for centuries had lived in another reality.

Hopi Traditionalists still depended upon dreams, visions, prayers, and the appearances of spirits from the mystical past to guide their daily lives. Their abstract religious ceremonials always had confused rational anthropologists. So I had come here, under the auspices of a New York foundation, to record their creation myths and the meanings of their esoteric ceremonials.

I found the Hopis obdurate, secretive, and wary of a strange Anglo. The ice was broken for me when I met old Dan Qochhongva, a venerated religious leader whose father, Chief Yukioma, had been dubbed the "American Dalai Lama" and jailed for seventeen years by a government Indian agent for inciting Hopi Traditionalists to resist the incoming white people. Old Dan first viewed me with suspicion; then he relented. "If your heart is right you will have four important dreams," he told me. They came as he predicted, each just before a great ceremonial in the annual cycle. None of these ceremonials had I seen; I knew nothing about their meaning. Yet each dream symbolically initiated me into meaning. I understood each ceremonial when it took place. I have related these dreams in *Pumpkin Seed Point* and described the ceremonials in the comprehensive book I finally wrote, *The Book of the Hopi.*

John Lansa, who took me with him on a pilgrimage to a sacred shrine, and his wife, Mina, the *kikmongwi* of Oraibi, became my friends until they died. They were among thirty elder Hopis who freely contributed information in order to leave their children and grandchildren a written record of their people's traditional beliefs.

My long stay among the Hopis was one of the richest experiences in my life. Their communal life, spent in constant touch with dreams, spirits, and living symbols, restored my own belief in another reality.

Knowing that I lived in this enduring world of reality as well as the world of change, I kept wondering why I had never been able to maintain constantly my intermittent and momentary perceptions of it. A dream I had while living among the Hopis later showed me why. It is related in another book and is now repeated.

I was slowly climbing down a flight of stone stairs in the dark interior of what I thought was a pyramid. One flight terminated at a small landing, only to give way to another flight leading below. By light of a candle I finally reached the bottom, a subterranean chamber enclosed on all sides by solid dark walls.

Possessed by a growing uneasiness, I noticed embedded in the floor a great bronze slab peculiarly shaped like a rectangular keyhole. Looking at it more closely, I saw the engraving of an ancient head, Egyptian or Mayan, wearing large earrings of the same shape as the slab itself. Around this was a border or frieze of similar, smaller heads. Suddenly a voice spoke. "Don't just stand there and look! Why don't you pull it up?"

I stooped, took hold of one of the large earrings, and pulled. It was a handle for the massive bronze slab, which lifted easily, as if it were on hinges. Dimly revealed in the opening was a vast room. Just then I woke up.

At the time I thought the dream merely reflected unique Hopi shapes: the keyhole pattern of their doorways, the floor plan of their kivas, and every man's head with his square-cut hair falling down over his ears. Now it held the deeper personal meaning that there were depths within myself I was not yet prepared to enter.

All of us have been incarnated for our present existence in this material world to learn the lessons that will permit our entry into a greater, subtle world of the spirit for a longer residence. Obviously most of our human family hasn't been learning its lessons very well. We are divided into quarreling races, nations, religions, political and economic ideologies. A fragmented world rent with wars, suffering mass starvation, disease, mental illness. Prominent spokesmen preach the gospel that this fragmentation is a law of nature and will eventually spread throughout the entire universe.

Fortunately other spokesmen, including eminent Western scientists, assert that unification, rather than diversification, is the principle underlying the structure of the universe. Their modern views parallel those of ancient Eastern doctrines claiming that all life, mind, matter, and consciousness stem from one universal, spiritual source.

One of the greatest lessons I finally learned is that this source in which everything is interconnected in one harmonious whole—the nebulous Otherworld I had imagined so long ago—does not exist somewhere among the splendor of the midnight stars, but within ourselves. Nor does it lie far in the future. Realization of it may come slowly or suddenly with our conscious awareness of ourselves, others, and the world about us. Any event, a chance remark, even a handful of sand, anything that leads to a better way of seeing, doing, or being, may provide an opening to it.

I am a slow learner. Time and change have far surpassed my stumbling approach toward a fuller maturity of spirit. My present wife, Barbara, reflects the change. She is a psychotherapist who helps to relieve her clients' feelings of guilt and insecurity, shame, and lack of self-esteem. One of her best tools is hypnotherapy. She has cured men of years of smoking, stopped immediate pain, partially healed her own finger after it was crushed by a car door, and regressed clients under hypnosis into former lives. These modern methods surpass those of *curanderos* and shamans of a former era. And their use is widespread. They are telling us more about ourselves, expanding our realization of the great potential within us.

At my late stage in this era of world distress, I can only optimistically believe that the yeast of self-discovery is working to raise us all eventually to a higher level of consciousness.

---

*Editor's Note: Frank Waters and Dr. Charles Adams co-edited W.Y. Evans-Wentz's *Cuchama and Sacred Mountains* (Swallow Press/Ohio University Press, 1981).

2

THE TAOS CHARISMA

Places, like people, have their own distinctive characters. Some of them, small and remote as they may be, seem to be imbued with a curious charisma, an indefinable attraction, a compulsive magnetism. Taos Valley has always had it, despite the drastic changes it has undergone.

The setting of Taos Valley is justly said to be one of the most beautiful in the world. Driving on the old dirt road twisting up the steep side of the rocky gorge cut by the Rio Grande River, one emerges to confront the snow-capped peaks of the Sangre de Cristo Mountains embracing the flat valley floor of sage and chamisa, which stretches westward to still more blue mountain walls.

Taos Pueblo huddles at the foot of the close peak, its Sacred Mountain. The Indian founders settled here five hundred or more years ago. With sun-baked adobe bricks, they built the two main buildings four and five stories high, their terraces mirroring the shape of the Sacred

Mountain rising above. Deeply religious, the people made ritual observances to help maintain harmony between mankind and all the forces of nature.

The most northern and eastern of all pueblos, its influence extended to tribes on the Great Plains, which acknowledged its spiritual power. Taos Pueblo in turn became the only pueblo in which the men wore their hair in long pigtails, Plains fashion.

The long Rio Grande eventually became the corridor up which Spanish soldiers and settlers from Mexico came to colonize the new province. The Spanish rule was harsh. Indians were enslaved to labor for the Crown and the Church. In 1680 a widespread revolt organized by Popé, a medicine man in Taos, succeeded in killing most Spanish missionaries and settlers, the survivors fleeing back to Mexico. Twelve years later a new wave of conquest subdued the tribes and recolonized the country.

For a century and a half there was little change in the life of Taos Valley beneath the veneer of Spanish rule. The principal community of Spanish and Mexican settlers, Ranchos de Taos, blended with the landscape, and the lives of the people conformed to the rhythm of nature.

In 1847, after the United States took over the land from Mexico, the arrival of Anglo settlers prompted another revolt. It occurred in Taos. Indians and Spanish alike resisted the invasion of the new alien Americans by murdering the newly appointed governor, Charles Bent, and a dozen other Anglos. American troops quickly put down the rebellion, bombarding Taos Pueblo, killing 150 insurgents, and hanging fourteen of their leaders.

There followed another change in the persona of the valley. Don Fernando de Taos, which now housed most of the American settlers, became a noted frontier town of the American West. All the usual types of characters swarmed in. The gold-mining camp of Twining, established up Hondo Canyon, lasted only until Mr. Twining was found to have appropriated the profits of the major mine, and the veins in other mines petered out. Horses provided the only transportation, and horse handlers of every kind swarmed in the plaza. Many had come to round up wild horses, which they broke and sold to army buyers for cavalry mounts. Later arrivals were horse dealers and cowpunchers who were hired for work on the ranches being established. And in the motley crowd of newcomers who lived by their wits were the ever-present gamblers.

This frontier aspect lasted until the beginning of the Second World War. When I arrived in Taos during the late 1930s, all these colorful characters still lent distinctive life to the growing town. Although none of them hesitated to turn a trick when expedient, they were far from being regarded as disreputable. They had hard-rock honesty, loyalty to their own code, and could be depended upon in a pinch. I was proud to be trusted as their friend.

Long John Dunn was the acknowledged leader of the gambling fraternity. He dealt games in a room on the plaza adjoining La Fonda hotel. Tall and thin, somberly dressed, austere and taciturn, he could have stepped forth from Bret Harte's pages.

He had wandered into New Mexico from Texas after some dispute with the law, and engaged in several activities to support his growing family. One of them was driving a stagecoach from the Chile Line railroad to Taos. The John Dunn Bridge across the gorge of the Rio Grande still bears his name and supports many tall stories about him. He then depended upon the more lucrative career of dealing blackjack and draw and stud poker. Long John was no chicken-shit gambler, but a seasoned professional from the heels up.

When open gambling was prohibited by law in New Mexico, Long John promptly informed the governor that as a professional gambler for years, he had supported his family and paid taxes on his income. New Mexico had no right to abolish his respectable profession and deprive him of his livelihood. And when the sheriff padlocked his front door, he continued dealing hands to players entering the back door.

His wife was a small and cheerful Spanish woman, and his oldest daughter a brilliant chip off the block. She had gone to school in Chicago, made a career for herself, and a successful marriage. Long after Long John died, I looked forward to her annual visits.

Another popular gambling spot was on the north side of the plaza, opposite Long John Dunn's place. It was run by Curly Murray, an accomplished horseman, dealer in horses, and czar of all slot machines in northern New Mexico. Of medium height and deceptively slight build, he was *muy hombre*—hard as nails, sharp as a knife. An experienced card dealer, his place at the table when he was away was taken by a good-looking young woman adept with cards as he. There was no nonsense about her. She was cold as a fish, impervious to advances made by admiring swains.

I had met Curly Murray in Mora, where I'd been living in the old Butler Hotel before moving to Taos. I've related fully elsewhere an incident that occurred there. Briefly, the half-Cherokee man I name Ralph was then helping old Mrs. Butler to run the hotel in return for the privilege of running gambling games at night when she had gone to bed. One court day when lawyers, litigants, and politicians who came monthly to hear impending cases were being served lunch by Ralph in the hotel dining room, Ralph conked the district attorney over the head with a water pitcher. Confronted by the sight of him on the floor, with blood spurting from his cracked skull, Ralph dashed out into the road, hired a car to drive him to the railroad line, and hopped a freight train.

Living in a rented two-room tourist cottage, I was then working on a book in Colorado Springs. When Ralph telephoned me at midnight, I picked him up and brought him home. Here I kept him for a week, listening to radio reports. The district attorney Ralph had conked on the head was still in the hospital, and a warrant for Ralph's arrest had been issued.

Answers to Ralph's letters to friends in several Colorado mining towns indicated prospects were good for him to find a job there dealing cards. So I drove him over La Veta Pass to Fort Garland and left him to catch a train to Durango, Colorado. I didn't return to Mora as I had planned, for I was known to be Ralph's close friend and didn't want to be questioned. I moved instead to Taos, renting Spud Johnson's house for the summer.

Letters from Durango, Silverton, and Ouray came in Ralph's scrawled handwriting and signed with his alias, J. R. Smith. He always asked for money. The few dollars I sent him were not enough. When a desperate plea for a large amount came, I went that evening to Curly Murray's place. He was there, dealing blackjack. I stood at his right shoulder and said in a low voice, "A friend of ours in Silverton is in a pinch and needs two hundred dollars immediately." Curly, without looking up, and continuing to deal with his left hand, reached into his cash drawer and handed up a roll of bills.

No comment. No questions asked. No receipt necessary. That's how it was with all these men.

The gathering place for freedom-loving souls on Saturday nights was Mike Cunico's, a mile south of town on the Santa Fe road. The large building enticed us all to kick up our heels. To the left of the entrance extended a long, crowded bar. Beyond it was the large dance floor, crammed with the sporting crowd, townspeople, and a scatter of tourists dancing to the blare of an orchestra. And to the side was the smoke-filled room presided over by dealers of poker, blackjack, and roulette. The place was always packed, and the bedlam could be heard a mile away.

Mike Cunico directed activities from his station at the entrance. A broad-shouldered, muscular man, he had been a cowpoke who excelled at calf roping, steer bulldozing, and bronco riding at rodeos. He won acclaim as Western champion. Quiet and with a friendly smile, he was liked and trusted by everyone in Taos.

A year or two later an obstreperous customer provoked a quarrel with him when Mike asked him to leave. Mike didn't argue. He threw the man out, then shot and killed him. Defended by one of the best lawyers in the state, he was freed in court but lost his business and the town's goodwill. His place closed, and he moved up to high country above timberline to raise cattle. After a severe winter blizzard froze the feet of his cattle, he lost the entire herd.

For many years he visited his son, who had converted his building in town into a tourist curio shop. When I occasionally saw him there, I reminded Mike of the late Saturday night when I rang the bell of his living quarters after his place had closed. Dressed in a long nightgown, he opened the door. I mumbled, "Mike, I've got to have a hundred dollars before Monday morning. The bank is closed, and I don't know where else I can get it."

"You can have it, Frank. Wait here." He went back into his bedroom, returning with a fat roll of greenbacks.

During Saturday night gatherings at Mike Cunico's, Rebecca James was conspicuously present. Strikingly handsome, she habitually dressed in a black cowboy shirt with white buttons, and black trousers tucked into black cowboy boots. Accentuating this dark outfit gleamed the smooth wings of her platinum-white hair. She constantly smoked cigarettes in a long holder and sipped domestic absinthe.

Becky was the daughter of Nat Salisbury, a New York theatrical producer. Needing a lead for a play with a Western setting, he had chosen a virtually unknown actor, William Cody, and given him the stage name of Buffalo Bill. Following the successful run of the play, Buffalo Bill had gone West, learned to shoot a Sharpe's rifle, and gained fame by helping to decimate the millions of buffalo blackening the Great Plains. The rest is history. Salisbury organized and conducted the famous Buffalo Bill's Wild West Show that toured America and Europe.

Becky didn't ride on the coattails of her father's reputation. Now married to Bill James, member of a rich Denver banking family, she lived in a gracious adobe. A natural artist, she painted exquisite little oil landscapes unobtrusively rivaling the large paintings of her friend, the renowned Georgia O'Keeffe. Becky was also adept at stitching *colchas,* a native New Mexico art. Becky shunned the rest of the town, allying herself with the sporting clique. Her engaging monograph, *Introducing Eighteen Ladies and Gentlemen of Taos,* is now a collector's item.

Frances Martin was just as unique. Living alone, she was for years the only land broker in the area. She didn't sell lots and houses in town, dealing only in ranches, great expanses of grazing land, and stands of timber. Much of the land lay in former Spanish and Mexican land grants whose titles were obscure or had been contested since American occupancy of the Territory of New Mexico. Frances's work required a thorough knowledge of history, legal ramifications, and water and mineral rights. This paperwork research she conducted in a small combination office, kitchen, and bedroom in an old adobe building on a side street off the plaza. It was backed by her intimate knowledge of the land itself. Driving in her old car across plains and into mountains, she knew every watercourse, could tell at a glance that a stretch of grass was overgrazed, estimate the board feet and worth of a stand of timber. Tanned and weathered, she looked like a storied Earth Mother.

Frances too was a maverick without social contacts in town, but always in close touch with all the ranchers, cowboys, and workmen who often depended upon her advice. When Taos expanded and changed into a tourist resort, she retired and moved with a companion to a secluded house and garden in southern New Mexico, where I still occasionally see her.

Doughbelly Price was the one who sold and rented houses in town. He was a small, compact man who might have been born wearing a large battered Stetson, open vest, unkempt trousers, and scuffed cowboy boots. What he'd done before he arrived, I don't remember, he fitted so well his present job as the first real estate agent in Taos. His listings were read in the weekly *El Crepusculo* newspaper, which I was editing. Every day we ate lunch together, perched on stools at a short lunch counter. The tiny restaurant was an oasis for any connoisseur of the one superb dish native to northern New Mexico and seldom found anywhere else—a "Bowl of Green," fresh green chiles and pinto beans.

It was Doughbelly who popularized the adjective "Silk Stocking" for the beautiful modern homes being built. There was of course no Silk Stocking neighborhood with Silk Stocking houses apart from the scatter of small old adobes housing less affluent occupants. But the name indicated his effort to find roofs for other working stiffs like himself. His honesty and humor showed in his listings. He didn't mince words. One of them might read:

> FOR SALE. Tourist cottage up Taos Canyon. Three rooms partly furnished. But cheap. You might look at the plumbing. Water pipes freeze easy up there.

His reliability was never equaled by the later horde of transient get-rich-quick salesmen eager to grab any available building for a quick sale. Everybody knew and loved him. And when he died, his funeral was the largest ever held in town. In the traditional cowboy funeral march to the cemetery, his boots and Stetson were hung on the horse pulling his coffin, and following this came a packed crowd of townspeople from all sections. It was the end of Taos's frontier era.

The town's emergence as a renowned art center really began about the turn of the century when two painters, Blumenschein and Phillips, straggled into the remote, mountain-ringed valley. Here was the place to paint! Aspen groves in full color and blanketed Indians!

Other painters arrived, the First Seven, the First Eight, bringing their families. It was easy to understand their attraction to this relatively unknown and primitive adobe village of Don Fernando de Taos. It was set in an incomparably beautiful landscape, presenting an aspect of biblical times, with simple Spanish villagers tilling their small fields and colorful Indians walking in from their pueblo. Here the new Anglo residents found a peaceful, slow tenor of life that far outweighed the lack of plumbing and other material comforts. They too succumbed to the living spirit of the land.

It was Mabel Dodge Luhan who officially "discovered" Taos, drawing to it a host of famous visitors from all over the world. Perhaps no other small town in America prompted so much writing about it. But it soon showed a negative face to many observers who began to debunk its so-called romantic aspects. The foibles of its best-known resident, the famous "Indian-lover" Mabel, were gleefully exposed by the press. The glamor of the D. H. Lawrence cult was badly tarnished. The clouds of alleged mysticism that hovered over the Pueblo's Sacred Mountain were dispelled by gusts of laughter from New York and Hollywood. The representational art of the pioneer painters was discounted as old-fashioned, and the horde of new painters was seen as opportunists sporting berets and turning out picture-postcard paintings by the dozen. Adobe houses with outdoor privies began to go out of fashion. Older residents were chided for trying to maintain a pseudo-primitive lifestyle. Taos, in short, came to be known as a haven for misfits, escapists, pseudo-artists, and individualists of all kinds. Much of what was written about it was healthy criticism. More of it was bitter, pseudo-sophisticated, and slightly tinged with envy.

Taos soon outgrew these negative views and entered a new phase of its ever-changing existence. The change began at the end of World War II with a new influx of Anglo residents. Prominent among them were avid promoters of new business ventures who saw this poorest county in the state as a ripe field for development. It was thinly populated by impoverished Spanish subsistence farmers living in primitive adobes on a few acres of land. The entrepreneurs began buying up these home sites, forcing many of their owners to leave Taos and seek work elsewhere. The cheap labor of those who remained was a lucrative human resource ruthlessly exploited by those who regarded Spanish, Indian, and Black workers with the same arrogant superiority.

So began Taos's entry into the era of commercialism and modernization. I have never disputed the prevalent opinion that New Mexico politics is among the most corrupt in the nation. Taos was not exempt. Corruption termited every phase of its community life. Politics was the major industry.

The fastest-growing, central part of the state was becoming predominantly Anglo and Protestant. The northern section, with Taos in the center, remained the last stronghold of the Spanish-Catholic element. Rivalry between them was bitter. Soon after I arrived, I developed a pet theory of how Taos partly achieved a balance. It was as if the Anglo merchants and Spanish *politicos* had made a secret deal. "You let us run all the major businesses," said the Anglos, "and we'll let you control all the political offices and schools." So it was. The most lucrative business houses were owned by Anglos, while Spanish *politicos* filled all the town and country jobs—councilmen, sheriffs, policemen, clerks in the county courthouse, and commissioners of every kind. The schools were operated with such militant Spanish-Catholic domination that most Anglo-Protestant teachers and pupils were forced to leave.

The balance between these opposite forces was not always maintained. Our little schoolhouse in Arroyo Seco leaked water so badly that money for a new roof was appropriated. What resulted was merely a new layer of tarpaper. In Taos, streets were continually paved and torn up, water and sewer lines laid only to be replaced, community buildings remodeled constantly, the face of the plaza repeatedly changed. No one objected. It was clearly understood that the purpose of all such projects was not to achieve permanent improvements but to give jobs to voters of the political party in power.

One leading lawyer was brought to court with fifteen charges against him for claiming property obtained by bribing courthouse clerks to falsify records. All charges were dismissed by the judge by reason of a technical error.

The unbreakable hold exerted by the Anglo merchants was first demonstrated twenty or more years ago when increasing traffic began to be a problem. At one corner of the plaza two main streets intersected. One was a section of the only highway running between Santa Fe and Denver. The other extended east through Taos Canyon to Raton. There was no alternate route for interstate travel, and both local and through traffic was delayed by jams at the intersection.

A meeting to discuss the problem was held in the county courthouse. All segments of the community, Indian, Spanish, and Anglo, crowded the hall. Informed speakers pointed out how bypasses around similar towns had alleviated traffic congestion without decreasing business. But the plaza merchants were adamantly opposed to any bypass around town, fearful that a truck driver might want a midnight cup of coffee and thus deprive the town of ten cents. Year after year the subject came up. A traffic light at the intersection increased the jams as traffic backed up for blocks. The governor of New Mexico was delayed once while riding a horse in the summer fiesta parade; he swore he'd remedy the situation. Nothing happened. And every year the state Highway Department offered a new route around town. But nothing was done for many years. The Taos bypass boondoggle today is no longer a problem; it is accepted as an incurable travesty of community management, a state highway disgrace, and an interstate joke.

Taos kept growing. Supermarkets; condominiums; fast-food joints; hamburger and taco stands; chain stores; filling stations; a hundred or more art galleries, most of them little more than souvenir shops; countless bed-and-breakfast places; real estate agents swarming everywhere.

As the town changed into a tourist resort, commercial exploitation changed the aspect of the surrounding mountains. Taos Ski Valley, located up Hondo Canyon on the site of the old mining camp of Twining, was developed by an aggressive, vociferous Swiss-German promoter. He persuaded the bureaucratic Forest Service, which controlled the land, to build a new highway up the canyon and to keep it open at public expense. From the start it exerted undeniable snob appeal. Approaching the inexpressibly beautiful high mountain valley, one confronted a sign announcing, "Achtung! you are now leaving the American sector." And as one entered the German sector there appeared a jumble of Bavarian ski lodges and great resort hotels whose restaurants offered après-ski cocktails and continental cuisine priced beyond the means of most "local yokels."

The locals, who lived on little farms in Valdez Valley downstream, were not impressed. For Taos Ski Valley, growing into a town itself, did not have a waste-treatment plant adequate to handle the sewage draining into the Rio Hondo, once a famous trout stream. Despite protests by downstream residents and local and environmental committees, the Ski Valley successfully delayed action for years.

Today Taos regards it as the region's most valuable attraction, drawing winter as well as summer tourists. The Ski Valley is not only increasing its capacity to handle thousands of skiers a day but planning new lifts up the mountainside and on top a new restaurant and still more ski runs. Already under construction are a hundred condominiums on nearby private land. Also projected is a highway through the mountains to the ski area at Red River.

What has been the reaction of Taos Pueblo to this violation and destruction of its ancient Indian earth? Dedicated to helping maintain the balance between men and nature, even aiding the Sun itself to make its daily journey in the sky, it too has bent to the winds of change.

Some years ago the Pueblo was split into opposing factions. Older members were adamantly opposed to admitting electric and telephone lines into the reservation. The younger men clamored for the right to have radios, TVs, washing machines, and all the modern conveniences of their Anglo and Spanish neighbors. Denied seats on the governing council, they organized a "Young People's Revolt." It was squashed for the time, but the underlying dissension and unrest continued.

The decisive change of values came in 1970 when Congress restored to the Pueblo the forty thousand acres of mountain wilderness surrounding its sacred Blue Lake, which had been illegally taken by the federal government in 1906. Soon afterward the Pueblo was awarded $1 million restitution for land in Taos preempted by early settlers. Overnight, as it were, the impoverished Indians found themselves potentially the richest people in the valley.

Their elders were dying off or losing power. The younger men who took over management of the Pueblo now ran it as a business institution. Educated, enterprising, and aggressive, they manifested at once a militant anti-Spanish and anti-Anglo attitude. All roads into the reservation were closed to outsiders. No more picnics at the mouth of the Lucero, where we all, Indians, Spanish, and Anglo, used to gather. No longer could I ride horseback across the reservation from my house at Arroyo Seco. Tourists and townspeople alike were charged admission when they entered the Pueblo, even for dances customarily open to the public. Additional fees were charged for taking snapshots. This was Big Business, but how big no one knew, not even the residents of the Pueblo.

Nor was this enough. The Pueblo filed suit against the residents of Arroyo Seco, most of us living along El Salto Road, which divided the village and the Pueblo Reservation. The dirt road itself, claimed the Indians, was the property of the Pueblo, and all Arroyo Seco residents were to be obliged to pay annual rental fees for access to their property. As the road for years had been kept open by the county for the school bus, the suit included the county of Taos. At the same time, the Pueblo filed suit against the town of Taos for payment for use of alleged Indian-owned streets and properties. The suits are still pending.

How all this is affecting the ordinary residents of the Pueblo was revealed by a recent book that quoted statements of many of the people. They recounted numerous instances of theft and vandalism, rapes and murders, alcoholism and drug addiction. With the adoption of Anglo clothes, values, and customs, traditional Indian life is vanishing. Some Indians appear uncertain about their roles.

Council members violently denounced the book, and some of the persons who were quoted and photographed claimed they had not given permission for such use. Yet much of what was written reflects a tragic attrition of the traditional beliefs that had been preserved for centuries.

Taos Valley, then, has been swept by the same wind and rain of time and change that has afflicted the entire country. The town of Taos itself has undergone many eras and periods. Like an individual person, it has worn different personas or masks. And yet its charisma, that indefinable magnetism, kept drawing more people. It still does, despite the region's engulfing materialism.

What do its thousands of visitors expect to find here? A curio-shop owner tells of a woman tourist who entered her shop and inquired, "I want to meet Kit Carson. Do you know where I can find him?" The shop owner answered immediately, pointing out the window. "There he goes now! I just saw him passing by. He's probably going to the plaza."

Taos. The magic of the word. What timeless spirit does it embody? Could it be that of the Pueblo's Sacred Mountain, unchanged by all the changes that have taken place around it?

3
THE CHIEF

Tony Lujan of Taos Pueblo was my closest Indian friend. He was more than six feet tall, massively built, with a face dark as mahogany. His black hair hung almost to his waist, and he braided it into two pigtails entwined with ribbons of two colors. Although he wore a suit on his infrequent trips to New York and Washington, he always wore a blanket over it. It was a superb Chief robe of pure bayeta. The material for it he had bought at the Thieves Market in Mexico City during one of our trips. Made of two colors, dark blue on one side and brilliant red on the other, it made a regal robe.

Tony spoke his own native Tiwa, fluent Spanish, and fairly good English, but couldn't read. This didn't disconcert him when in a large hotel dining room he was handed a menu. He would study it—upside down—for several minutes, and then with perfect composure ask the waiter, "What is good you say?"

There are few men like him left today; they don't have the stature and hawk-like faces still occasionally seen among northern Plains tribes. Most of them have died, giving way to a new generation, aggressive, pragmatic, and self-conscious of being Indians in these days when Indians are clamoring for equal rights in our national life. The great old men of the past knew exactly who they were, without making a fuss about it.

Tony's appearance and inborn dignity amply provoked the title of "Chief" given him by white people everywhere out of New Mexico. Pueblos don't have chiefs as do the plains tribes, and Tony was not a chief. He was never elected governor of the Pueblo, never an officer, never a member of the council. For he had left his Indian wife and, breaking tribal law, married a white woman, a rich woman, Mabel Dodge Luhan, with whom he lived in their Big House on the edge of the reservation. He was not ostracized from his pueblo, however, and his loyalty was undiminished. He attended ceremonial functions and several times went to Washington, D.C., to plead the Pueblo's cause.

I met him while I was living in Mora and driving out to several pueblos to attend their ceremonial dances. He invited me to visit him at home, where I eventually met Mabel. She was, as everyone knew, a rich, internationally known, and controversial woman I was hesitant to meet. Her warm friendliness dispelled the image I had of her, and we developed a close friendship.

Mabel and Tony

I once asked her why Tony's last name was spelled with a "j" and hers with an "h." "Oh," she replied, "I used Tony's 'j' for my post office box."

Save for Mabel's friends, Tony was not generally liked by the Anglos in Taos. Businessmen regarded him as an ignorant, lazy Indian supported and spoiled by a rich wife and driving around in a big car when he should have been walking or riding a broomtail nag. Tony ignored their traditional Anglo prejudice against Indians. He owned several large fields and employed his nephews and other young Pueblo boys to plant and harvest crops of corn and wheat. From the modest profits he helped to provide for the needs of his extended Pueblo family.

Mabel was dependent upon his love, solidity, and ever-present sense of his inner self. This didn't deter her from frequently inviting Anglo friends for dinners or visits as house guests. Tony, becoming bored with their constant talk, talk, talk, would rise from his chair, wrap his blanket around himself, and stalk out, saying, "I go Pueblo now."

There was never a doubt of the bond between me and Tony. We hit it off from the start, and I loved him as an elder brother or uncle. Throughout the years I've had many other loved Indian friends among several pueblos: Valencio Garcia, a religious leader of Santa Ana; old Dan Qochhongva and John Lansa, Hopi Traditionalists leaders; José Tafoya, the cacique of San Juan Pueblo; Pete Concha and Tony Reyna, governors of Taos Pueblo; Joe Sun Hawk; Albert Martinez; Frank Samora; and more. Some of them entrusted me with a little of their tribal beliefs and wisdom. My friendship with Tony was far different.

We both carefully avoided any mention of his pueblo ceremonialism, which was sealed by traditional secrecy, and his own religious beliefs. Actually, we talked little, for there seemed to exist a silent communication between us. It always seemed to me that he was like an iceberg of which only the tip emerged as his surface self. He was profoundly intuitive, accepted the presence of invisible spirits as a matter of course, and possessed good medicine. "He got the power," another Indian friend confided to me. This Otherworld streak in him—or rather his casual acceptance of another larger and mysterious reality in which he also existed—jutted out when least expected and lent an edge to his comfortable character. For he was so intensely human, with so many profane faults and weaknesses, I can hardly recall our many experiences together without laughing. All of them were fun; but some of them, like Tony himself, contained an element of inexplicable strangeness.

During the winter of 1940, if I remember exactly, we made a trip to New York. That fall I had returned to Los Angeles to spend the winter and was bombarded by letters from Mabel. She had gone to New York where she occupied a tower apartment on the twenty-fourth floor of the One Fifth Avenue Hotel overlooking Washington Square. Now she was lonesome for Tony, worried about leaving him alone in Taos, where he was probably drinking with some of the Pueblo boys. She kept insisting that I drive him to New York for a visit. As I had never been there, I took the bus to Taos, picked up Tony in his car, and we started out.

It was late January during a deep snow. The first night we stayed in a drab motel on the outskirts of Amarillo, Texas, and ordered a bottle of scotch. With it the Negro porter brought two scrubby call girls to keep us company. Becoming bored with them, we paid them for their time, sent them home, and finished the bottle.

Early next morning, suffering hangovers, we started out again, only to discover in Oklahoma that Tony's ring was missing, a large, clear turquoise mounted in hand-cast silver that had been given him by a Navajo medicine man. Assuming that he had left it in the motel—whose name we didn't remember—I telephoned Bob Gribbroek, an artist in Amarillo, asking him to pick it up and mail it to us in New York. Tony was certain he would get it back. The Navajo medicine man had told him the stone belonged on his hand; whatever happened, it would always return to him.

The weather was so frightful I told Tony we would drive south through Tennessee, where it would be warm and sunny, with flowers blooming. Instead, the Mississippi was frozen over by the worst cold spell in years, and Memphis was blanketed with a pall of black smoke. We continued east through the great Smokies to Highway 1 leading north to New York. All along the way we passed cars stalled, driven into snowbanks, or overturned. Tony beside me sat beating his little drum and singing the Eagle Song, invoking with his small buckskin medicine bag the Powers to protect us.

New York! As we emerged from the tunnel under East River, it burst upon us in the evening with an explosion of lights and sounds. I could not read the signs of many branching streets in the falling snow. Utterly confused, I stopped the car. A traffic jam piled up around us immediately: cars honking, drivers shouting and cursing, lights flashing. Tony remained unperturbed, softly beating the little drum in his lap. "Don't worryin'," he said quietly. "Help comin'. I send for him."

There sounded a knock on the window. I rolled it down to hear a voice ask, "Now, what are you two boys up to?"

It was absurdly unbelievable—a Hopi Indian dressed in the uniform of a New York City police lieutenant! Unsnarling the traffic jam around us, he got into the front seat with us. "You want to go to One Fifth Avenue, hey? OK. I'll take you there!"

It was that easy. When we arrived at Mabel's tower apartment, a letter awaited us from Bob Gribbroek in Amarillo. He and the manager of the motel had ransacked our room thoroughly without finding Tony's ring. Mabel was disconcerted at its loss, but Tony was not worried. "That stone got the power. It come back to me. You wait and see."

Mabel at the time was reviving the famous evenings she had held in her 1913 salon at 23 Fifth Avenue. She seemed to know everyone of importance, and many of her old friends invited us to their apartments for dinner: Alfred Stieglitz and Georgia O'Keeffe; Roy Howard of the Scripps-Howard newspaper chain; Eve and John Young-Hunter, the portrait painter; the anthropologist Elsie Clews Parsons; and the Freudian psychologist Dr. Brill. Others came to visit: Thornton Wilder, Wyndham Lewis, John Collier, a host of famous persons. It was a great privilege for me to meet all of them.

The weekly salon gatherings were something else: throngs of people coming to talk furiously and drink copiously. The high expense, I understood, was being met by Vincent Bendix, who had just invented a new helicopter he was endeavoring to finance. There were seats for 70 people, and one night 120 came. It was necessary to lock the door to keep out the crowd massed in the hallway, but all evening the avid curious kept beating on the door.

In such crowded gatherings Tony was distinctly superfluous. I suspected that Mabel had induced me to bring him to New York so we could spend these evenings outside by ourselves. Not that I minded baby-sitting him, as it were, in this fabulous city I had never seen before.

Our first hangout was in Greenwich Village at the Rendezvous Club, whose sign of a rampant stallion had intrigued Tony. We were eventually kicked out because the manager refused to sell us a bottle of scotch at nominal cost, and we refused to buy drinks at the usual price.

We then went to the large Savoy Ballroom in Harlem. All the Blacks were fascinated by Tony in his red blanket and treated us royally, dozens of them coming to our table to shake his hand. The manager gladly provided us a bottle of scotch so that we didn't have to pay the exorbitant price per drink. I danced with the percentage girls while Tony obliged by going up on the orchestra platform to beat the drum. A bit under the weather, we were finally escorted out to a taxi by a group of his laughing admirers.

In contrast to this warm welcome in Harlem occurred one of the few incidents where I saw Tony embarrassed. We were walking down Fifth Avenue when a woman, coming out of a doorway, bumped into him. Backing away, her face livid with rage, she shouted at him, "You big, ignorant lout! Why don't you go back to your wigwam where you belong?" The incident distressed Tony beyond all measure. Although neither of us mentioned it, he brooded upon it all day.

He kept complaining of a severe backache due to a slipped disc but refused to go to a doctor. In Greenwich Village, however, we ran into Romany Marie, a gypsy fortune-teller whose grizzled husband, she said, was an excellent osteopath. As he did not have a license to practice, he received patients in the dreary back room of their apartment. Here he worked on Tony's broad back several times, taking cash in payment for each treatment. For the first time Tony "felt straight." The doctor then advised Tony to have the hotel manager install a wood support under the mattress of his bed. So, much to Mabel's annoyance, carpenters came up to saw boards to fit his bed.

One morning Mabel exclaimed to Tony, "Frank's been taking you out to eat, and you know he doesn't have much money. Now, today you must take him to lunch. Spend your own money."

We picked at random a large Swedish smorgasbord on Madison Avenue. After having a drink, we walked to a large revolving table and helped ourselves to chunks of lobster, iced shrimps, chilled green salad with a choice of dressings, and assorted rolls. As we finished this with another scotch, I caught Tony's eye. We returned to the revolving table. This time we filled our plates with delicacies we had ignored before: slices of cold red salmon and beef, asparagus spears with dressing, and a bit of potato salad flanked with radishes. To accommodate this, we had another drink.

When we finished, the host came up smiling. "I see you gentlemen have worked up an appetite for our splendid lunch. Now, what may I have brought you—an order of our special Dover sole; some really excellent red snapper; or a small dinner steak, if you prefer?"

Tony groaned assent. "Got to have another drink."

"Of course! Your favorite scotch."

It came, and with it the sole. In due time the very nice man, as Tony called him, appeared again, rubbing his hands together. "Ah. And now to finish off a splendid meal, you must have some lingonberries imported from Sweden, with a Napoleon brandy. Yes, indeed!"

Tony's glazed eyes brightened. *"Ai. Como no?"*

Late that afternoon we staggered back to One Fifth Avenue, where we were met by Mabel. "You must have had a good lunch after all this time!" she said caustically.

Tony dragged out his wallet, empty and flat as a pancake. "Got nothin' left!"

That sumptuous lunch was the last hearty meal Tony was to have for several weeks. For now, in February, it was necessary for him to take the train back to Taos. This was his year "to work for the Sun," being confined to his kiva for forty days, wearing only breechcloth, blanket, and moccasins of Indian make, eating only natural foods, observing the traditional prayers, recitals, and rituals necessary to give strength to the Sun for his daily journey. How he grumbled at having to leave the comforts and luxuries of New York!

A week or so later I drove Mabel back home to Taos. It was necessary then to make an appointment to see Tony in a house near his kiva. After we had been kept waiting for some time, an attendant brought him in, seating himself in the room as a chaperon. Tony looked thinner, sallow, and tired. There was nothing to say; but he nodded gratefully at the fresh lettuce and green onions, and a packet of laxatives we had brought. In his eyes was a faraway look that couldn't quite focus on our presence. A few minutes later he was led back into the kiva to continue his work for the Sun.

His forty-day immuration in the kiva ended in mid-April. Once home again, he began to look alive. The First Inter-American Conference on Indian Life to be held in Pátzcuaro, Michoacán, Mexico, was scheduled to begin soon; and we made preparations to drive there. U.S. Commissioner of Indian Affairs John Collier, who was directing the conference, had named Tony as an Indian delegate. He had also recommended that the King Features Syndicate in New York commission me to write two feature articles on the conference, which would help to pay part of my expenses there.

Before driving Mabel back from New York, I had cleaned out the car thoroughly, hoping to find Tony's lost ring. Now, before leaving for Mexico, Tony and I again emptied the dashboard compartment and looked under the seat cushions, without finding the ring. Nevertheless, we set out in high spirits. Another carful of delegates followed a day behind us. They included Emma Reh, an ethnologist, driving José Tafoya, and a couple of Navajos and Papagos.

Pátzcuaro was no longer the charming old lakeside town I had seen a decade before. It had grown immensely in size and significance as the home of Mexico's President

Cárdenas, who had built a great new resort hotel on the edge of town. Here the conference was held. No reservations had been made for us, and we stayed in the old Ocampo Hotel in town.

The ten-day conference was not exhilarating. It was really a political convention. Nearly three hundred delegates from North, Central, and South America milled around the rooms and corridors, reading 1,100 pages of prepared papers. Among them were only twenty-five Indians, ostensibly brought only for window dressing. "All talkin', doin' nothin'!" said Tony. Bored and listless, he and I, with the other few Indians from the United States, sat on the *portal* listening to a couple of guitar players singing old Mexican folk songs. Even Mabel didn't get a word with John Collier, who continued politicking, hidden from sight in a closed room.

Mabel finally broke our boredom with her usual dispatch. "You're moping because you're not getting any attention. Now, come on. We're getting out!"

It seemed to me that she was speaking more for herself than for Tony and me. For a woman who most of her life had been the center of attention, it must have been galling to be so completely ignored here.

Taking José Tafoya with us, we drove west to Uruapan into the *tierra caliente*. Coming back we stopped at an old village where the best serapes in the region were woven. It was evening of the *Día de la Plaza*. Several hundred people filled the torchlit plaza, two circles revolving in opposite directions, the women on the inside, the men outside. We all were charmed by the red, black, and pink serapes displayed by many vendors. Tafoya bought two for fifteen pesos apiece (about $2.50). Tony was miffed, for in Uruapan he had bought two for twenty-five pesos apiece. Then, parading in the outer circle, I saw an old barefoot man wearing one of the most beautiful serapes I'd ever seen. It was muted brown in color, with a red design and a long fringe that must have required many days' work. It had no *boca,* or mouth, being an unbroken weave. I went up to him and offered to buy it. He refused, saying it was not for sale but *para usar,* for use. After two or three more revolutions of the circle, I again stopped him, only to be refused again. On the third attempt he followed me to the edge of the plaza to bargain for it. Tony stepped up, declaring the serape old, worn, and ragged. Nevertheless, I offered to buy the wearer any new serape he picked out in exchange for the one he was wearing, and he picked out one for fifteen pesos. This, on top of Tafoya's purchases, made Tony jealous. So after an hour's dickering in a shop he bought for twelve pesos another serape priced at sixteen pesos.

Driving back late at night, Mabel and I indulged in extravagant fancies. She projected a time when the whites would be gone and all Mexico taken back by the Indians. I had heard of an extinct volcano nearby, the Cerro de Paracho. So I said jokingly, "Why not? The very land will erupt and spew out all the Spanish and us Anglos. I can see now one of these old volcanos erupting fire, brimstone, and lava, right here!"

Tony turned around from the front seat, disturbed and angry. "Don't talkin' like that! Or it happen sure! Words got more power than you thinkin'!"

Curiously enough, just a few miles from where we were, and just three years later, the newborn volcano of Paracutin sprouted in an empty cornfield. It grew swiftly and with an explosive eruption destroyed several Tarascan villages, forcing the people to abandon their homes. I don't take the blame for this phenomenal catastrophe, but I've never forgotten Tony's admonition. Back home in Taos, the three of us settled into our separate routines. Except for an occasional dinner, I saw little of them. During the midsummer Santa Ana fiesta I wandered one evening into a hall where a public dance was in progress. The place was crowded with tourists in costume; a Spanish orchestra was playing; dancing couples filled the floor. Then I happened to see Tony standing against the wall, looking out of place, disconsolate, and not amused by the goings-on. He glimpsed me at the same time and beckoned. I followed him out the door. "Comin' with me. I got drink for us," he said.

We walked into the parking lot and got into his car. Fumbling with his keys, he unlocked the glove compartment to take out the little pint bottle of whiskey.

"Ai-ai-ai!" His ejaculation of surprise and delight filled the car. "It jump right to my hand! Comin' back to me just

like I sayin'! That ring got the power all right!" He withdrew his hand to show me the large turquoise and silver ring that had been mysteriously lost for months.

That fall, broke again, I went to Hollywood. Here my loyal agent, Rosalie Stewart, somehow got me a job as a writer with a shoestring motion-picture company turning out quickie cowboy-Indian thrillers. A month later Mabel and Tony arrived to visit Carl Hovey and his wife, Sonya Levien, the top-notch screenwriter for Fox studios, on their large estate at Malibu Beach. Beautiful as it was, with its private beach, there was nothing for Tony to do. I had no car to drive the many miles up the coast, and rarely was Tony able to get to Hollywood to visit with me.

One of these times, I took him to the office where I was working. The producer was a Jewish entrepreneur from New York who had never seen a live Indian. Confronted with one in his blanket, he inquired if Tony lived in a wigwam. "Got good house!" said Tony. "Do you still hunt with bows and arrows?" Tony's back stiffened. "Got good rifle. .30-30!" Another question. "Well, you still have horses, don't you?" Tony smiled. "Lots of horses. Big bunch!" "What do you do with them?" "Nothin'," said Tony. "All Indians got plenty horses!" The producer frowned. "Tell me, in your younger days perhaps, did you ever scalp a white man?" Tony rose. "White people good people. My friends. I don't scalp Frank." Drawing his blanket about him, he said curtly, "We goin' now," and turned toward the door. The interview was less than satisfactory to all of us. Certainly it did little to reassure the producer that I could turn out authentic scripts of Indians beleaguering wagon trains before they were rescued by a band of brave cowboys, and I was soon fired.

One Saturday the doorbell of my small apartment rang. I opened the door to see Tony. Raising one finger, he led me to the curb outside. "I buy car for you. With my own money. One hundred dollars."

There it stood. A vintage Ford sedan painted grass green, with paper cutouts of mermaids, bathing beauties, and pin-up girls plastered on windows and doors. "Now you come to see me anytime. Bring me in to see you. *Ai, ai!*" He puffed up with pride.

The next day I drove into a filling station and went into the men's room while the tank was being filled with gas. When I came out the attendants were standing beside the car with solemn faces. "What's the trouble?" I asked. One of them answered slowly, "We've been wondering. Can you tell us what makes this thing run?"

The car lasted for a few weeks after Mabel and Tony had gone home. Then I gave it to a newly married young man who was working the graveyard shift in a factory and had difficulty getting home by streetcar so late at night. When I finally returned to Taos in a newer used car, Tony said nothing; but I knew his feelings were hurt because I hadn't driven there in his generous grass-green jalopy.

Mexico! Tony loved Mexico. It was still Indian country, and he fitted into it perfectly. He, Mabel, and I drove down there again; and wherever we stayed, Mabel had a room to herself, Tony and I sharing another. She always retired early to read in bed, leaving us free to roam around.

One night in Mexico City we wandered into a drab *barrio* containing sordid *cantinas* and the *casitas* of Soiled Doves, and entered a squalid *pulqueria*. The room was filled with Indians and Mexican peons barefoot and dressed in filthy white *camisas* and *pantalones*. Stepping up to the crowded bar, we ordered the usual drinks, milky pulque or powerful clear mezcal. After a time I became aware of a feeling of tension, of resentment against us; and we were gradually being forced down to the end of the bar.

Tony, stolid and imperturbable, seemed to be enjoying himself. He had struck up an acquaintance with an Indian by making a sign with his hand. Strangely enough, the Indian responded with another. They began to converse in the old sign language once common to all tribes in the United States. How this Indian in Mexico happened to know it was a mystery to me, but it was a pleasure to watch their quick, poetic gestures. They were interrupted when we were given a push to the end of the bar. The Indian uttered a low exclamation. I now understood what was happening. We two well-dressed, rich strangers were being forced to the back of the room to be robbed and probably knifed. Quick as a wink the Indian plucked Tony by the sleeve and led us toward the door, Tony's massive shoulders shoving men out of our path.

The Friday *Día de la Plaza* in Toluca was one of the biggest native markets in Mexico. The plaza was one huge mass of Indians squatting on the ground in front of their displays of flowers, serapes, pottery, fruit, and vegetables; and they were flanked on all sides by stalls of still more wares of every description. Tony loved it all. He wandered about, smelling a bunch of flowers, examining the weave of a serape, the texture of pottery, pricing every item. I held my breath, fearing he would see something he liked. Then would begin a noisy squabble that would draw a crowd. For Tony liked to bargain, and bargaining for Indians was a battle of will and wit. He would deride the quality of the object, offer half the price asked for it. The seller would lower it a bit, but not enough. Then his friends would intercede. Voices would rise from a chorus of angry muttering. The seller, a poor Indian, desperately needed to sell a piece he had worked for weeks to fashion. Tony could well afford to buy it for twice its worth and give it away when he returned home. But he would stand his ground with indomitable stubbornness. This day, luckily, he was content to stalk about, enjoying himself. What a picture he must have been to these smaller people, a massive, dark-faced figure swathed in his regal Chief blanket. A squatting woman timidly plucked at my trouser leg. "*Por favor,* señor," she asked, "can you tell me whether your friend is a man or a woman?"

The surprising question recalled to me with a start how much he reminded me of a woman when after washing his hair he would sit in the sun to dry it. The long, thick fall covered his shoulders, hung almost to his waist. Fluffing it dry, he would part it in the middle, then braid it into two pigtails entwined with ribbons. Just like a woman leisurely making her morning toilette.

But even an empty plaza in the morning he enjoyed to the full. As he sat down on a bench, a dozen small boys would come running to polish the boots he was sporting at that time. He knew them all, which ones had shined them last, those whose turn had come. So there he sat while a *camacho* worked on his shiny boots. Basking in the sun, listening to the sounds of the late-awakening shops, admiring the brilliant flowers, smelling the distinctive smell of Mexico. *Ai-ai-ai. México. Viva Mexico!* To a little cantina he would go for a tequila and a chat with the bartender. Then he would come back to another bench in the plaza to have his already shiny boots polished by another *camacho*.

Mabel, Tony, and I once were stuck for a couple of days in an auto camp in a jungle clearing near Tamazunchale. This was the *tierra caliente,* hot and tropical, with banana, mango, and papaya trees and thick jungle growth. Trying to read and to escape the swarms of mosquitoes, Mabel stayed inside her thatched-roof hut. Tony and I wandered around outside, watching the brilliant butterflies and parakeets, looking at the beautiful, flamboyant trees with their bright red blossoms and the blue-blossoming plumbago vines, listening to the high queer calls of the *gilguero*, or clarinet bird. Then Tony busied himself preparing some large gourds he had bought. All afternoon he sat peeling off the thin dried skin, tediously poking loose the pulp and seeds inside with a piece of wire. Back home the *guajes* would be fitted with wooden handles, painted, and decorated with feathers. Dance rattles for the young men. His sweaty face beamed pride.

Mabel grew bored. "Why can't we get ON! Anywhere!"

So we took off for a little mountaintop village nearby, of which we had heard. Xilitla. First we had to cross a soap-green river. There was no bridge. We had to wait an hour for some Indians to pole us across on a rude ferry. An argument began. Tony balked. "Road no good. Not goin' anywhere!" Mabel was always more adventurous, and now she was bored. "Yes, we *are* going."

And go we did. The uphill road was steep, with so many dangerous sharp turns that we couldn't see an occasional truck approaching at breakneck speed until it was almost upon us. "Sound your horn!" demanded Mabel. Tony, at the wheel, shrugged. "I see 'em comin'," he said. "You can't see around a curve or through the mountain!" insisted Mabel. "I knowin' anyway!" repeated Tony. He would take some curves at high speed, driving in the middle of the road. Then, approaching another sharp turn around a high cliff wall, he would drive off to the side or stop. "Car comin'!" And sure enough, one would wheel around the obscured turn.

Xilitla was a hospitable village among coffee *fincas*. The family who took Mabel in to rest and quiet her nerves could not give her a cup of tea but made her coffee. Tony meanwhile struck up acquaintance with several men and bought some skins of the kinkajou, a small, monkeylike animal of the raccoon family.

On this same trip he and I went to a village that may have been Xatla, a little plaza surrounded by a few huts. Here we were welcomed by the people bringing Tony presents of seed corn, herbs, and *guajes*. Observing that I smoked, they brought me little bunches of fresh-dried leaves of home-grown tobacco. This *punche*, powerful as the kick of a mule, I carried home to present to the Pueblo council, which invited us both to a meeting.

Tony casually mentioned that he would like to buy a few parrot feathers. As none were available, we were asked to return that night. The news had spread by the time we returned. A large fire had been lit in the plaza, around which all the men were sitting. The gathering, in contrast to our morning welcome, was formal and solemn. One barefoot Indian after another would step forth and offer Tony a feather. In the light of the flames, he would carefully inspect each, its quill, color, luster. Then the interminable dickering began for those he accepted. For centuries, long before the Spaniards came, this trading had gone on. The hundreds of parrot skeletons found in the great kivas of prehistoric Pueblo Bonito up north, and all the parrot feathers still worn in the sacred dances of contemporary pueblos, came from these jungles of Mexico.

Mexico! *Viva México!* These were Tony's best days. They ended, as all days must. There were no more trips anywhere. His long, thick hairbraids shrank into short, thin pigtails. He lost his resonant singing voice. His twilight years he spent sitting with his Indian family at the Pueblo or at home listening to nasal cowboy songs on the radio or TV. I was married and busy working. Only occasionally did I see him at home or bring him to my house to doze under the cottonwoods.

Mabel died on August 13, 1962, at the age of eighty-three, and was buried in historic Kit Carson Cemetery. Tony, the same age, failed rapidly. A motherly Indian woman cooked his meals and did the household chores. In the afternoons a few boys from the Pueblo sat with him, beating a drum and singing, or listening to the interminable Western music on the TV. Their company did not alleviate his loneliness. They would open a bottle of scotch and drink until Tony fell drunkenly asleep. Then they would put him to bed.

The end came five months after Mabel's death, when he was taken to the local hospital. The last time I visited him there, on a Saturday afternoon, he was dying. Oxygen tubes were in his nostrils, and his labored breathing sounded throughout the room. His dark, broad face was sallow and gaunt; out of it his great black eyes stared blankly. When I sat down on the bed beside him, they lit with recognition. For a long time we clasped hands in silence.

The room was filled with his family members and Pueblo friends who stood or squatted on the floor, heads bowed. One could feel the texture of their thoughts, their prayers. Then I rose and left the room.

He died the next morning, on Sunday, January 27, 1963, about one-thirty. At nine o'clock one of his family telephoned to tell me of his death and to ask me to come to the Pueblo right away. The Indians had immediately removed his body from the hospital and carried it to the Pueblo. Apparently a brief ceremony had been held for him. When I arrived, his body was being carried to the graveyard in the shadow of the crumbling bell tower of the old church that had been destroyed by American howitzers a little more than a century ago—the jagged tower that Mabel said looked like the snag of an old tooth. It was followed by a procession of blanketed men and women filing to the open grave.

There were no other Anglos present for the burial. According to custom, his body was wrapped in his red-and-blue Chief blanket. The large turquoise and silver ring that had mysteriously disappeared and reappeared shone on his hand. His full-beaded turquoise moccasins had been put on his protruding bare feet. The body was now lashed with ropes and lowered into the grave. There was no coffin, no box. He was simply returned to his Mother Earth.

It was a bright, sunny morning. The silence was broken by a burst of gunfire. The traditional annual weapons inspection was taking place in the nearby plaza, where men and youths were presenting their firearms and bows and arrows. It seemed fitting that the reports of their old muskets, modern shotguns, and rifles sounded the last farewell to him who had been at heart, if not by name, a true Chief.

4
SOMETHING ABOUT MABEL

For years I've been plagued to write "something about Mabel." The apparent assumption was that I knew a bit more about her than those hundreds of others who have written about her. Mabel and Tony were intimate friends of mine for almost twenty-five years. I lived for a time in two of their houses in "Mabeltown," went with them on two trips to Mexico, and saw them in New York, Los Angeles, and Tucson, so there was ample opportunity to see Mabel in many of her various moods.

The thought of adding to the reams already written about her repelled me, perhaps because we seldom write about those we love and know intimately. This reluctance is not encountered when we write about one known only from published books, articles, letters, autobiographical writings, and opinions from interviewed friends. Such an objective study presents a full-figure character against his or her background. But it lacks eye-to-eye, intuitive, personal contact. Unconscious empathy or antagonism is replaced by a rational balancing of the subject's positive and negative qualities according to the biographer's own value judgments.

This is true of the two biographies and many commentaries written about Mabel. All the facts of her colorful and controversial life are well known. Emily Hahn's *Mabel* is a recital of her faults and foibles. *Mabel Dodge Luhan* by Lois Falken Rudnick, which may not be surpassed, was compiled from her exhaustive research into 1,500 pounds of papers Mabel left to the library of Yale University. It fully documents her childhood in Buffalo, her years in Italy, establishment of her salon in New York, relationships with three husbands, and her move to Taos.

This comprehensive account of Mabel's active years is judiciously impartial, analytical, and written from the viewpoint of Ms. Rudnick's own intellectual, metropolitan, and cultural background. Definitive as it is, I find too skimpy Ms. Rudnick's coverage of Mabel's last twenty-five years in Taos. As she told me during a pleasant evening we spent together in Mabel's reopened Big House, Rudnick had never been in the Southwest and knew nothing of Indian life until she made a brief visit to Taos. Here, she gained a fleeting and casual picture of that small town and nearby Indian pueblo whose reputation had spread worldwide. She did not experience the impact of the ancient, indigenous culture that was Mabel's obsessive concern during the last part of her life.

I didn't know Mabel during her active years when she was motivated by what has been called her sexual drive, feminine wiles, and mental will to dominate everyone she knew. I knew her only during her later, more passive years when an aspect of her hidden inner self revealed itself only to be obscured again by her individual ego. This is what interests me more. Hence, these comments will contribute little to the continuing squabbling about her. They simply reflect my gradual awareness of this neglected aspect of her complex character.

I met Mabel in Taos, where I was renting Spud Johnson's house in Placita for the summer. I had been living in Mora, just over the mountains. Tony I had met at several pueblo dances downriver while I was there. He had invited me to visit him, but I'd never gone. This I mentioned to Spud when he returned to town and wanted to reoccupy his house. He promptly took me to Tony and Mabel's Big House, where they were giving a big party that afternoon.

The Big House was swarming with guests. In the large tiled dining room, an orchestra of Spanish musicians was playing. Food and drinks were served in the crowded living and sun rooms. And outside on the *portal,* Indians were dancing and singing to the beat of a belly-drum. In this crowd, I met Mabel. She was a rather short and compactly built woman with one of the loveliest voices I had ever heard. She dispelled my uneasiness at being an uninvited stranger by her warm friendliness. There was little for us to say among the swarming guests. I left without seeing Tony, who was singing outside.

Back in Placita, I gave up the house to Spud, packed my few belongings, and drove back to Mora. Here, I moved in to stay a few days with Fran and Ed Tinker in their small adobe outside town. A week later, however, Tony and Mabel drove there to see me.

"Spud tells me you don't want to stay here in Mora and that you haven't found another place to live in Taos," said Mabel. "Come on back. I have a small empty house just back of Spud's you can have if you fix it up a little."

Her surprising offer I couldn't refuse. On the day I arrived there, Mabel invited me to lunch. For something to do, she got out a copy of the ancient Chinese book of divination, the *I Ching*. This early translation by James Legge simply showed the six lines of the hexagrams not separated into their two trigrams. To represent the six lines someone had made for her six small sticks, three of which had been marked with a dividing line and three of which were unmarked. To obtain an oracular pronouncement, Mabel explained, one simply threw the sticks, observed the hexagram shown, then read its meaning in the text of the *I Ching*. This Mabel did after silently asking a question. Then I, in turn, threw the sticks and obtained the same hexagram. The *I Ching* was new to me, and the text was so full of archaic Chinese allusions, I could make no sense of it.

This was irrelevant. For as I read into the book, unbroken yang lines often changed into broken yin lines and yin lines changed into yang lines; it was possible for each hexagram to change into another for a total of 4,096

(64×64) transitional stages, representing every possible condition or relationship in the world.

What seemed significant was that I had thrown the same hexagram as Mabel against the odds of 4,096 to 1.

Today, I wish I knew which hexagram we both obtained, what image or relationship it represented, and the psychological meaning of this extraordinary coincidence. Oracularly, it may have foretold my long, close friendship with her. Or perhaps it may merely account for my recalling the incident here.

At the house in Placita, I repaired the loose window frames and installed a wood stove. The following spring, when Myron Brinig bought and modernized the house, Mabel let me have the huge studio room above the garage of the Tony House on the Pueblo reservation. Dorothy Brett lived in the one-room Studio House nearby, and we shared an outdoor privy.

Mabel's life in the Big House seemed simple and pleasant. She was served breakfast in her room at promptly six o'clock while Tony ate leisurely in the big kitchen before going out to his fields. Then she was up and about, seeing that things in Mabeltown ran smoothly. There was always a succession of cooks and maids in the house and two permanent Spanish men for work outside. José looked after all living things, the dogs and horses, vegetable garden, and orchard. Max made all the needed repairs in the various buildings, driving around in a big truck with a dog whose patient expression matched his own.

At Mabel's house: Eve Young-Hunter, John Young-Hunter, Mabel Dodge Luhan, and Spud Johnson

Every evening Mabel invited someone for dinner. Those who came most often were Spud Johnson, who kept her accounts and published the weekly *Horse Fly*; Rowena and Ralph Meyers, the grizzled Indian trader; Eve and John Young-Hunter, the English portrait painter; Myron Brinig, a popular New York novelist of the time; and various Taos artists taking turns at her table. Never invited were members of the business community and town officials. Their omission created in them a deep, repressed resentment, which in later years emerged in a movement to run a road through her property; this would have destroyed the Big House. Fortunately, it did not happen.

John Evans, her son from her first marriage, came infrequently with his wife, Claire, and their children. He was handsome and charming, and had held several important business and government positions, but had retired to their home in Maine. I enjoyed seeing him, though their visits were short. He and Mabel did not get along, perhaps because they were too much alike.

Mabel's gifts to the town included its first hospital and a bandstand in the plaza. To the Harwood Library she gave sets of rare first-edition books, a collection of Persian miniature paintings and Spanish *santos*, and yearly donations of popular books. Few people knew of the money, food, and personal help she gave to needy families. As Claire Morrill wrote, "Her reticence was somehow reserved for her virtues."

If Mabel was impervious to what people thought of her, Taos was always slightly in awe of her. This held true even during a time when she was receiving medical attention for a condition that might have embarrassed anyone else. Driving through the crowded plaza, she would suddenly stop the car, leave the motor running, and dash into the nearest shop or restaurant. Everyone hastily cleared the way for her. It was a distinctly understood imperative that Mabel had to go to the bathroom.

During one of the two trips I made to Mexico with her and Tony, she was surprisingly adaptable. Late one evening when we were walking in the upper plaza at Pátzcuaro, I was struck by the somber mystery of the huge church belltower looming high in the darkness. "I'd like to climb up inside it and see what it's like," I murmured.

"Why don't we? Let's go!" she said instantly.

So we fumbled our way through the dark church to a steep, narrow flight of stairs, and climbed steadily up into the lofty tower beset by bats and roosting pigeons. How eerie it was, but how beautiful the view when the lights of town and of Janitzio on its island far out in the lake finally spread out below. For a rather heavy woman, sixty-one years old and dressed in skirts and flimsy slippers, the climb must have been arduous.

A few years later, when Tony and I visited her in New York, I later drove her back to Taos, Tony having taken the train a week before. Throughout the South, she always chose to stay overnight in the "tourist homes" found in every small town and village. They were old family homes with rooms for rent, a common bathroom down the hall, and no coffee available in the morning. Had Tony been with us, he'd have insisted we drive on to a modern hotel in the next large town. Mabel, so used to having breakfast in bed, accepted these discomforts and inconveniences as a matter of course.

We arrived in New Orleans on the evening of the town's first showing of the lauded movie *Gone with the Wind*. The Old South had come alive to welcome it. Confederate flags hung from every balcony and rooftop. Crowds of costumed people swarmed through the squares and streets, ladies in lace and crinoline, gentlemen in frock coats and top hats, every woman a Scarlett O'Hara, every man a Rhett Butler. Every seat in the theater had been long sold, of course. This did not deter Mabel. She barged into the office of the manager and cajoled him into selling her two tickets. The seats were in a back row whose view of the screen was partially obstructed by a tall pillar. Mabel promptly moved us down to center seats. And now began a battle of wills.

The ticket holders for the seats arrived to claim them. When Mabel refused to budge, the head usher came to oust us. A small crowd gathered in the aisle; the picture was soon to start. The manager arrived to expostulate. "You sold me tickets to seats from which we couldn't see," Mabel said quietly. To his indignant protestations and threats to evacuate us by force, the angry muttering of the audience, and my own embarrassment, Mabel was deaf.

She sat there silently, hands folded primly in her lap, exerting the will that had so enraged D. H. Lawrence.

Such displays of combative self-assertiveness were rare. At home she was generally relaxed, sure of herself and her place in the world. How different she seemed from the self-portrayed Mabel in the four volumes of her *Intimate Memories:* a woman of contradictory moods and desires, selfish, willful, contriving, and demanding. There was a great rift between them I couldn't understand. She had loaned me the books and followed my reading with a curious interest. From one volume to another, she told me additional details about incidents and persons recounted in her writing. They were most frank, for she didn't spare her own role. It was as if she wanted everything, good and bad, to be known about her eventually.

Mabel's openness is reflected in 183 letters she wrote me between 1939 and 1960. Some of them were short notes delivered by hand while I was living in Taos. Others were long letters mailed to me in New York, Washington, D.C., or Los Angeles. All were undated, handwritten in ink on white manuscript paper in a flowing, bold script as if dashed off impulsively and without reservations. She also gave me her complete medical history and a dozen or more unpublished articles she had written for Arthur Brisbane when he had suggested she do a syndicated newspaper column.

It was not enough for her to reveal everything about herself; she desired to be fully understood. Deep below her revealed surface, I sensed an unknown part of her that had always endeavored to emerge into upper consciousness. My intimation of this threw into focus all I had read of her past life. She became at once more intensely personal and vastly impersonal, as if she had been acting out the same universal role we all are blindly following.

Mabel's admission of being "nobody in myself" leaves no doubt that she became aware early of her incompleteness. Her primary approach toward discovering what she lacked came when she met Dr. A. A. Brill. Brill was a Freudian psychologist, the first to translate Freud's writings into English and the first to practice in America. Soon after his arrival in New York in 1921, Mabel consulted him. Off and on for the next twenty years she consulted him as an analyst and a friend. He came to visit her in Taos, and when I was in New York with Tony, Brill invited us to dinner at his home.

Almost coincident with Mabel's introduction into psychology was the beginning of her interest in the mystical teachings that Georges Ivanovitch Gurdjieff had brought from Central Asia. To propound them he established the Institute for the Harmonious Development of Man at the Chateau du Prieure, Fontainebleau, near Paris. Mabel was impressed by his teachings and by Gurdjieff himself when he came to lecture in New York in 1924. She introduced him to Tony; and, as she told me, he took one look at Tony in his Chief blanket and hairbraids and said to her, "What a clever woman you are! You have broken the mold!"

Unfortunately, Mabel became briefly infatuated with Jean Toomer, one of Gurdjieff's followers and loaned him $14,000 for use by the institute, which she later learned had been misspent. This cut short her contact with Gurdjieff. Still, she continued to correspond with Orage, another disciple, and to follow the gradual spread of the Gurdjieff movement. As late as 1949, when Gurdjieff was preparing to publish the first volume of his objective writings on the world and man—the mammoth *All and Everything*—Mabel received letters from Lord Pentland in England requesting that she share in the expense by buying one of the expensive copies of the first edition. Whether she did or not, I don't know. Nor when or from whom she received a typescript draft of Gurdjieff's first section, *Beelzebub's Tales to His Grandson, an Objectively Impartial Criticism of the Life of Man.* This rare manuscript she gave me with the terse comment, "Here, this will probably interest you!"

Forty years or more later, the Gurdjieff teachings are no longer regarded as a hodgepodge of Asian mysticism and occult practices put together by a master charlatan. They have established their philosophical and psychological values. Gurdjieff centers have been founded in all large cities. I myself find his imaginative view of mankind's evolution most instructive.

A few years ago I was privileged to visit Madam Olga de Hartmann in her home in New Mexico shortly before her death. Her late husband had composed the music for all of Gurdjieff's celebrated dance "Movements," and both of them had accompanied Gurdjieff on his flight from Russia, through Turkey to Europe. Soon after I met her, I watched these therapeutic Movements, derived from ancient ritual dances in Central Asia, performed in a private school in Arizona. The dancers were teenaged men and women charged with criminal acts and prostitution; they had been released to the school to reform or to be sent back to detention homes or face prosecution. Vigorously "dancing" without moving from their places in line, sweat dripping from their bodies and running down their faces, hoarsely chanting meanwhile, one of them sobbing incontrollably, they were giving release to long-repressed emotions and feelings of guilt. I have never experienced such a strong emotional impact. Such physical as well as mental exercises were required of Gurdjieff's pupils.

Mabel, of course, could never have submitted to such discipline. I doubt that she ever intellectually comprehended the systems of either Freud or Gurdjieff for attaining realization of her inner self, nor the spiritual teachings of many world religions she had read. Her approach to any subject or situation was never mental but emotional or instinctive.

When Tony and I visited her in New York, she was reviving the famous evenings held in 1913 in her salon at 23

Fifth Avenue. To them came old friends, psychologists, anthropologists, artists, writers, publishers. I was impressed by seeing for the first time the world of wealth and power they represented. "Take a good look at it," Mabel told me. "It's falling to pieces. I know. I was part of it."

At home she had collected a great library of books on philosophy, psychology, and world religions, many of which she loaned me. "But don't believe any of them," she cautioned me. "You've got to discover your own truth within your inner self."

Yet if she had not assimilated their teachings, she must have gained from them an objective view of her outer world. She had become convinced that Western civilization had reached a dead end like other civilizations of the past. A decadent, dying world in which she had been trying to play a part, always feeling unrelated to it. "The world," she wrote, "is an alien place to nine-tenths of those who live in it or who appear to live in it but who merely go through the motions . . . as though they were alive throughout." How strange this sounds, coming from one pictured as a social butterfly flitting from one salon to another.

She had resolved, as she told me, to record its false values and superficial attitudes, its materialistic greed and corruption, as Proust had recorded his time and world in his voluminous *Remembrance of Things Past,* without sparing her own faults and foibles. This illuminating statement of purpose reveals her *Intimate Memories* to be more than the writings of an egotistical exhibitionist, as they often have been regarded.

Today, a half-century later, her belief that our materialistic Western civilization, threatened by a nuclear holocaust, faces collapse or a drastic change in values is a major theme widely expounded. We must give her credit. Although her measure of objectivity didn't draw her inward, it led her to reject the outer world of appearances. There kept growing within her the desperate need to break away, to find a place where she could start living at last.

The break began one winter evening in 1917 when she rode the stage into Taos. One quick look in the snowy twilight was enough. She surrendered immediately to the remote, almost primitive village that became her permanent home until she died forty-five years later. One event followed another. She fell in love, for the first time, with Tony Lujan, an Indian in the nearby Pueblo, divorced her third husband, Maurice Sterne, and married Tony. Together they built on the edge of the reservation the adobe Big House of seventeen rooms, which drew visitors from all the world. Mabel began to live at last.

From the first, she was entranced by the life in Tony's pueblo. "Little by little," she later wrote, "I found out that every interpretation of Indian life by a white person from the most ignorant villager up to the most learned archaeologist or anthropologist, was rationalized from a false premise, the standpoint of his own white psyche. . . . There has never been written any true version of the Indian spirit. These people, one race from North America down through Mexico, Yucatan and Peru in South America, have never been known by any of the white people."

She viewed their life, contrary to the materialistic life of white people, as geared to universal realities—the living earth, the fructifying sun, the invisible forces of all life. This intimate relationship of man to the universe enabled Indians to survive as tribal societies through centuries of genocide by the incoming whites.

Taos townspeople could hardly believe Mabel had actually married a blanketed Indian. Nor could they believe the marriage would last long. Each time she left on a trip to New York, they would wisely assert, "This time she won't come back." And every year the rumors spread that Mabel was finally going to get rid of him.

Another thing difficult for Anglos to swallow was Mabel's so-called mystical view of their Pueblo neighbors. Indian women were reliable maids who worked for a few dollars a day. The men were considered excellent gardeners. They straggled into town ridiculously wearing blankets in winter, white sheets in summer, and sloppy moccasins instead of shoes. A people dirt poor, generally illiterate, buying cheap scraps of meat from the butcher and cadging a pint of whiskey from their friends. That they were highly evolved spiritually was pure bosh! Especially Tony—that lazy Indian—driving around in a car and supported by a rich white wife. As for Mabel, if she believed so strongly in Indian life, why didn't she move out to the Pueblo, cut her own firewood, draw water from the stream, and cook her own meals in the fireplace?

Knowing herself incompetent to interpret Indian life, Mabel drew others to Taos. With them she hoped to instigate here a rebirth of the dying Western civilization from the body of Indian culture. Among them, of course, was D. H. Lawrence, in Mabel's view the greatest living writer. He and his wife, Frieda, lived for short periods on a mountain ranch that Mabel gave him. Lawrence savagely resented Mabel's will to dominate him and, ill with tuberculosis, fled to Mexico. Although he admitted that neither he nor any white man could identify himself with Indian consciousness, he predicted that the cosmic religion of the pueblos, although temporarily beaten down by Anglo materialism, would see a resurgence and "the genuine America, the America of New Mexico" would resume its course.

This is the theme of Lawrence's great novel *The Plumed Serpent,* published in 1926. It was laid in Mexico. In it the government of Mexico is overthrown, Roman Catholic churches are closed, American industries are expropriated, and the ancient Aztec religion of Quetzalcoatl, the Plumed Serpent, is resurrected. This is the book Mabel wanted him to write, springing from their condemnation of the materialistic Western civilization and their belief in the resurgence of Indian culture. Though the book was not laid in

Taos, it transported Taos Pueblo and everything Lawrence had learned about its Indians to Mexico. It is all there—their dress and customs, dances, songs, the very drumbeat.

Lawrence's novella *The Woman Who Rode Away,* published about the same time, repeats the same theme on a smaller scale. The wife of an American mining engineer in Mexico rides horseback into the Sierra Madre. She is captured by the Indians of a remote pueblo and sacrificed by their priests in a secret cave. Awaiting the knife, the woman silently assents to her death, a symbolic sacrifice of her white culture to that of the Indians. The pueblo was again Taos Pueblo. Even the sacrificial cave was that which lies in the cliffs behind my own back pasture. These are both wonderful, evocative stories. And in each of them, the leading white woman is clearly Mabel.

That same year, a friend of Mabel's induced the famous European psychologist C. G. Jung to visit Taos. Mabel was away when he arrived, but he met and talked with Mountain Lake (Antonio Mirabal), a religious leader in the Pueblo. As recorded in his autobiography and *Collected Works,* Jung found the Indians' life "cosmologically meaningful" in contrast to "our own self-justification, the meaning of our own lives as it is formulated by our reason." He believed the preservation of their secret beliefs gave "the pueblo Indian pride and power to resist the dominant whites. It gives him cohesion and unity, and I feel sure that the pueblos as an individual community will continue to exist as long as their mysteries are not desecrated."

Still another important man Mabel persuaded to visit Taos was John Collier, a social worker. He arrived in the mid-'20s. His talks with Mabel and his visits to other pueblos with Tony convinced him of the importance of preserving Indian life. He worked with them to help defeat the infamous Bursum Bill, just introduced into Congress, which threatened all Indian land holdings. His interest in Indian welfare continued. Becoming executive secretary of the Indian Defense Association, he finally succeeded in being appointed commissioner of Indian Affairs in 1933, when Franklin D. Roosevelt took office as one of the great presidents of the United States. Collier's first move was to put through Congress the Indian Reorganization Act, designed to grant cultural, religious, and economic freedom to all tribes. Controversial as it was, it gained him the reputation of being the best Indian commissioner in the nation's history.

In 1940 he organized the First Inter-American Conference on Indian Life. It was held at Pátzcuaro, Mexico, and attended by delegates from the United States, Tony being named as a delegate, and all the twenty countries of Latin America. A permanent Inter-American Indian Institute was established, with Collier as president. The United States then created by executive order its own National Indian Institute, but Congress refused to appropriate funds for its operation. It was quite clear that prosperous Anglo America was not going to be drawn into any movement to rejuvenate Indian life.

Mabel's activities evoked some of the most harsh and humorous criticism in her career. Her chief function, it was remembered, always had been that of a catalyst, bringing together disparate persons to see what happened and to attain goals she couldn't achieve herself. As Maurice Sterne, her third husband, stated, "Mabel had no vitality or creative power of her own. She was a dead battery; she needed constantly to recharge with the juice of some man, though she might leave him dead in the process." Yet her "compulsion to meddle" in other people's lives, as in the cases of Lawrence and Collier, resulted in some of their outstanding achievements. And she was aware of an underground current that broke surface fifty years later when Congress finally restored to Taos Pueblo, for religious purposes, clear title to the mountainous area surrounding its sacred Blue Lake. The Pueblo's poor tribal members, once derided, are now potentially the richest people in the valley. Countrywide, the racial antipathy between the red and the white is gradually breaking down. The Indians, now called Native Americans, are asserting their rights; and we are realizing the soundness of their religious beliefs.

Mabel's extravagant ambition to achieve a resurrection of Western civilization from the body of Indian culture was a failure. She realized she was not cut out to make wide political and social reforms in her outer world. She retreated into herself, still aware of the old feeling of being "nobody in myself."

Who was she, anyway? She began writing her *Intimate Memories.* It is amazing how quickly, in such a short time, the four long volumes emerged in her loose, flowing script—the first volume published in 1933, followed in quick succession by the others in 1935, 1936, and 1937.

There is a great break between the first three volumes and the fourth. *Edge of Taos Desert,* the last, is the fulcrum of the series. The writing is warm and personal as she recounts her life in Taos.

How different it is from the preceding three volumes, Mabel herself explains. "In the other volumes of these *Memories,* I have written more like an anthropologist than a human being. I wrote observantly and coldly like one recording his findings, having returned from an unknown island, telling about an undocumented race of beings. . . . Never mind the blame and the shame, the hurts and regrets, the burned fingers and angry looks. I know what it cost us all and I know what it has been worth. Particularly, I know that it was a preliminary exercise for an eventual self-realization."

How this finally came is recounted in the most revealing and moving chapters of *Edge of Taos Desert.*

During her years in Taos, Mabel learned much about surface pueblo life, but it had a subterranean depth she had never penetrated. What religious belief gave the Indians their "cosmologically meaningful" perspective, as Jung called it? The rituals in their underground kivas and their pilgrimages to the sacred Blue Lake were closed to all outsiders. Everything about their religious beliefs was a guarded secret. Even Tony refused to say anything about it. With her compelling curiosity to discover the secret that made Indians tick, Mabel found herself facing a locked door.

I can well believe that she was confronted with the equivalent of what Zen Buddhists call a *koan,* or insoluble riddle. The purpose of such a riddle, they tell us, is to make a seeker realize there is no intellectual solution to it. When the seeker finally reaches this impasse, a simple incident is enough to reveal its meaning. It can be triggered by a word, a touch, anything. But one must be ready for such an instant realization. So it must have been with Mabel's fruitless efforts to discover the hidden mystery of Indian belief.

Her awakening, self-realization, or whatever we choose to call it, happened during a trip to the mountains with Tony and a group of his Indian friends. One night she became ill. One of the Indians gave her a drink of "good medicine," which most likely contained the hallucinogen peyote. In *Edge of Taos Desert* Mabel recounts her feelings as she lay listening to the Indians singing outside her shelter.

> Beginning with the inmost central point in my own organism, the whole universe fell into place. . . . On and

> on into wider spaces farther than I could divine, where all the heavenly bodies were connected with the order of the plan, and system within system interlocked in grace. I was not separate and isolated any more. . . .
>
> The singing filled the night and I perceived its design which was written upon the darkness in color . . . and composed of a myriad of bright living cells. These cells were like minute flowers or crystals and they vibrated constantly in their rank and circumstance, not one of them falling out of place, for the order of the whole was held together by the interdependence of each infinitesimal spark. And I learned that there is no single equilibrium anywhere in existence, and that the meaning and essence of balance depends upon neighboring organisms holding together, reinforcing the whole, creating form and defeating chaos which is the hellish realm of unattached and unassimilated atoms. . . . How this flash of revelation worked out into fact and substance took twenty years of living to be proved a reality.

These were pages of beautiful and meaningful writing. They echoed the insight of Eastern sages. To give words to the wordless has always been man's highest endeavor. And here was Mabel's attempt to record a transcendental glimpse of her ultimate completeness of being and the secret of Indian religion. This was the psychological climax of Mabel's life.

It was not strange that few of her book reviewers and critics mentioned this spiritual experience. A rational, practical people, we are inclined to ignore all such nonrealistic excursions as flights of fancy into the realm of the mystical or the occult, the dark and dangerous mysterious. We are committed to the reasoning, intellectual faculty of our dual nature, as other peoples throughout the world have been polarized to the intuitive.

Yet even in our Anglo culture there always have been aberrant individuals who have experienced totality, the Peak Experience, as it's called. Most of them hesitate to talk about it for fear they will be considered abnormal, having succumbed to an illusion, or will be made fun of. Also the experience does not last, for, as Zen Buddhists assert, it can be maintained during their daily lives only by those who dedicate themselves to strict religious discipline.

So it was with Mabel. The realization of completeness that replacing her long feeling of being "nobody in myself" must have lasted for a time. But the lifelong domination of her personal ego asserted itself, and her expanded awareness began to fade.

I was working in Washington, D.C., during the war years, and then in Los Angeles. When I returned to Taos late in 1949 to edit the weekly newspaper, I noticed the change in Mabel. It may have been accounted for by her advancing years; she was now nearly seventy. But she had lost much of her great vitality and sharp perceptiveness. Of the five guest houses in Mabeltown, the Pink House, Two-Story House, and the Studio had been sold or rented, and the Tony House had deteriorated too much for occupancy. Mabel had bought and modernized a small adobe, the River House, downriver at Embudo where she and Tony could spend quiet weekends.

It was well known that Tony had a mistress in Arroyo Seco or Arroyo Hondo. Mabel apparently ignored this, but now occurred something that worried her more. Millicent Rogers had arrived in Taos, buying and restoring an old hacienda south of town. Commonly known as the "Standard Oil Heiress," she had been left great wealth by two husbands and maintained other homes in Jamaica and Virginia. Furnishing the hacienda with excellent taste, she hung in it a notable collection of French Impressionist paintings. Meanwhile, she became romantically fascinated, as had Mabel, with the Indians at Taos Pueblo. Taking several of them along, she drove throughout the Southwest, buying Navajo blankets, Zuni and Hopi kachinas, pottery, artifacts, and handicrafts. Also she acquired Spanish colonial items of historical value. Her large collection is now displayed in the Millicent Rogers Museum, located on a beautiful estate just outside Taos.

To work on her house Millicent employed several Indians, including a young man who had returned from war dissolute, alcoholic, angry, and violent. She became infatuated with him, paid all his successive debts, and took him with Brett to Jamaica. Upon their return, and in late afternoons after work, all these Indians sat in the house drinking and cutting slices from the huge roast beef always available. How pleasant it was for Tony to join them! Not until late at night did he return home, well fed and smelling of scotch. Mabel ate a solitary dinner and went to bed seething with anger and jealousy.

She was still the grande dame of Taos. Millicent could not have challenged her prestige, nor did she wish to. Still, they had little to do with each other, and Millicent unwittingly had struck at Mabel's Achilles' heel—Tony.

One afternoon Millicent telephoned to ask me to call. I found her a beautiful, sensitive, and sensible woman. She came to the point immediately. "I want to talk to you, for I understand you're one of Mabel's and Tony's closest friends. She thinks I'm trying to steal Tony away from her. How preposterous! What do I want with an aging Indian when there are so many young and attractive men of every kind? He isn't invited here; he just comes, and I have nothing to do with him. Nor can I control the boys' eating and drinking; I have my dinner served in my own room. I don't want to hurt Mabel, nor offend Tony. What can I do about this dreadful situation?"

Mabel already had made up her own mind. "I can't stand this any longer," she said. "I'm going to get rid of him—this old man so infatuated with Millicent that he comes home drunk late every night! He's never here. Let Millicent have him for whatever he's worth to her. Judge Kiker will get me a divorce."

I looked at her drawn, pale face for a long time in silence. It was no use telling her of my talk with Millicent. Nor did I have the right to remonstrate with Tony. If Mabel did divorce him, he would simply go back to the Pueblo to live with his own people, perhaps depending more upon Millicent for daily amusement. No, I didn't worry about Tony. It was Mabel's distress that concerned me. Her confidence in me demanded all the honesty I could summon to reply haltingly, "That is the pattern you followed most of your life, Mabel. Years ago you broke it—'broke the mold,' as Gurdjieff told you—by marrying Tony. It gave you a new life. You can't go back now to the old, outworn pattern after all you've achieved. I think, Mabel, you should stick it out, distressing as it is."

She gave me one long, searching look from comprehending eyes. Then she turned away and went into her bedroom without a word.

Things straightened out somehow. Millicent died of tuberculosis. Mabel and Tony were still dependent upon one another, but their relationship no longer had the close intimacy of the past. And, more significantly, Mabel lost all interest in Indian life and religion.

How this change affected her had a parallel in what happened to the noted sinologist Richard Wilhelm, who had translated and interpreted the ancient Chinese *I Ching* and *The Secret of the Golden Flower.* Wilhelm, living and studying in China for many years, had submerged his intellectual European background and entered wholly, mind and heart, into the spirit of Chinese metaphysics. Psychically, wrote Jung, this resulted in an essential rearrangement of the component parts of his psyche. At the completion of his task, Wilhelm returned to Europe and reverted to his native German culture. Jung termed this *enantiodromia,* the process by which yang goes over to its opposite pole, the yin. Wilhelm's feeling for everything Chinese turned negative, resulting in his spiritual and physical illness, and death.

I seldom saw Mabel and Tony after that; I was working in Los Alamos and Nevada during the atomic test series. On the few occasions when I was in Taos, I visited them in the new two-story house Mabel had built on a nearby hillock. Completely modern, it was drastically different from her old Big House. The upper story was one huge room with picture windows on all four sides; but it had no access save an outside staircase, and no bathroom, and was thus unsuitable for living quarters. The downstairs lacked the charm and graciousness of all the other houses Mabel had built. The living room was large and comfortable, but the small alcove kitchen didn't have the hominess of the one in which Tony and his friends used to sit over coffee, joking with the cook and maids. Between it and the living room ran a narrow hall off which opened two bedrooms and opposite bathrooms. The house always gave me the uncomfortable feeling that it somehow repeated the pattern of the hotel suites and apartments she had occupied in the past. Here Mabel spent her last years.

My visits with her and Tony were saddening failures. Both were drinking too excessively to talk intelligently, and Mabel was becoming senile.

The end came when Mabel died on August 13, 1962, at the age of eighty-three. I was living on the Hopi Reservation, doing research for a book at the time, and was not present at her funeral.

There are many contradictory versions of how and where she was buried. This one I like best. Some years before, Mabel had invited me to dinner with the grizzled trader Ralph Meyers and his wife, Rowena. When Meyers walked in, he proudly announced that he had just bought a burial lot in the historic Kit Carson Cemetery. "You'd better buy one too, Mabel. There's not many left."

Rowena remembered this too when, upon Mabel's death she went to see Jack Boyer, who managed the cemetery for the Masonic Lodge. Mabel had neglected to buy a lot as Ralph had suggested, and there were no more available. "But Mabel has done so much for Taos; she must be buried there instead of in the newer cemetery across town!" pleaded Rowena. "Can't you please find a place for her?"

"Ralph was buried in the last empty lot," replied Boyer. "It's in the corner, as you know. There may be room for Mabel between his grave and the fence, but it would be a tight squeeze."

"That's all right," said Rowena. "I know Ralph would be glad to move over a bit to make room for her."

So here Mabel was laid to rest. A woman who had focused all the social, radical, and art movements of her generation; who had helped to change the tenor of our time; a legend in her own life span.

To me this international role mirrored her egotistical outer persona, concerned with the material world of appearances. If my view of her here reflects any measure of objectivity, it is an attempt to show that she, like all of us, embodied two selves. Their conflict is the great theme of all philosophies and religions. "Who am I?" We each, consciously or unconsciously, ask ourselves this ultimate question.

And yet in long retrospect I see her more personally than abstractly. I remember her lovely voice, the horseback rides, the fun we had with Tony on our trips to Mexico. And best, as an intimate friend whose private virtues have outlasted her public faults in the memory of those like myself who knew and loved her.

5
LEON GASPARD'S SHADOW

My book *Leon Gaspard,* which first appeared in 1964 and was reissued in a greatly expanded second edition in 1981, is not the authentic biography it often has been taken for.

It was conceived as a cooperative effort by Gaspard and me to present an informal monograph of his selected paintings and sketches illustrated by some of his tales and anecdotes. His stories were famous; he told them at every gathering. That they were manifestly untrue made little difference to his spellbound hearers. Exotic, exaggerated, and highly colored as his paintings, each was artistically recounted in the same manner Gaspard composed a painting—focusing on its dramatic background, emotional content, and sensual detail, without regard for the factual incident or character upon which it was based or which suggested it.

I was happy to write these tales for him, arranging them in a chronological sequence that followed his remarkable career. Gaspard was a loved friend of many years, then aging and failing in health. His last ardent wish was to leave a book presenting him as he wanted to be remembered. To be remembered and appreciated! The cry of every human heart.

Yet shortly before he died, when my manuscript was in the hands of the publisher, I belatedly recognized that too many of his tall tales were refuted by historical fact. It was too late to withdraw and revise the manuscript. Also, it would have broken my ties with this dying old friend. And so I let the book go to press—a collection of tall tales and wishful longings portraying Gaspard not only as he wanted to be remembered but as he always wanted to be.

In retrospect, I'm glad I did so. For while confronting the untruth of many of his stories, I discovered for the first time his efforts to conceal an inner life as tragic and frustrating as his outer life had been rich and rewarding. Gaspard, like each of us, had his shadow. Light and dark, image and shadow, we reflect both the man we want to be and the man we really are. It may be a moot question which is the truer man, for we are all at heart what we want to be. This is particularly true of artists, like Gaspard, whose vision of life seldom coincides with actual realities. The differences supplement rather than detract from either view.

These intimate notes pieced together after his death, then, present the shadow aspect of the Gaspard he tried to hide. I hope they supply another dimension to an immensely human and complete man.

Standing: Tony Lujan, Mabel's cousin, Mabel Luhan, Frieda Lawrence, Frank Waters, Leon Gaspard, Evelyn Gaspard, Malcolm Groefflo
Front: John Young-Hunter, Angelino Ravagli, Eve Young-Hunter

Let me now record some facts and observations that must be included in any later documented biography of him.

As related in the book, Gaspard was born in Vitebsk, Russia, in 1882. He derived his French name from his Huguenot great-grandfather, who had immigrated to Russia. His father, Maxime, was a retired army officer who traded for furs in the Siberian steppes. His mother, Zyra, had been born in Moscow and had been a brilliant pianist. There were five children: Leon, Joseph, Zahar, Esther, and Anna, all equally talented. Leon as a young boy used to steal down to the Jewish village or ghetto of Pisquachik where he made his first sketches.

Omitted from the book at Gaspard's request was the fact that his mother was a Jewess. Evidently his father, Maxime, his sister Esther, and his brother Zahar resented his fascination with Pisquachik as an expression of his Semitic heritage. But Leon's mother, to whom he was closely attached, secretly taught him to read Yiddish and encouraged him to learn the Hebrew customs and religious traditions of her people. This teaching enabled him to read in its original language *The Paper Bridge,* a long narrative poem by Frug depicting the life of the poor Jewish people Gaspard met in Pisquachik. A copy of this poem carefully wrapped in oilcloth Gaspard secretly carried next to his heart during much of his life.

To me the title of Frug's poem is psychologically significant. The bridge is one of Gaspard's favorite motifs.

Over and over again it appears in his paintings—narrow, delicate Chinese bridges; broad, teeming causeways over the Volga and Dvina Rivers; bridges of every kind. They are not only the bridges between Europe, Asia, and America that he repeatedly crossed but the bridges between the racial dominants of his own character: Jewish, French, Russian, and American.

So an inner conflict began in childhood, tormented him throughout his life, and continued unresolved to the day of his death: his wish to conceal his Jewish ancestry, although he secretly cherished it.

Pisquachik profoundly affected his life and paintings. It may have been a ghetto attached to Vitebsk, which must have been largely Jewish itself. It is the birthplace of two other Jewish men of worldwide distinction: Immanuel Velikovsky, originator of the theory of cosmic catastrophism, who was born there in 1895; and Marc Chagall, the artist often called the first Surrealist, who was born there in 1889. His great paintings always depict his memories of Jewish provincialism in Vitebsk—the same cows and chickens, fiddlers and festivals that appear in Gaspard's earliest sketches. But in them somewhere also appear those numinous symbols and archetypal images rising from the unconscious, which lift his art from regional to universal dimensions.

Gaspard claimed that in 1897 when he was fifteen years old, he first studied painting with Chagall under a local painter named Julius Penn, and that both young men courted the same girl, Bella, who later married Chagall and accompanied him to Paris. These assertions must be doubted. For in 1897 Chagall was only eight years old, and he must have worked under Penn much later than Gaspard. In 1907, Chagall went to St. Petersburg, entering the Imperial School of Fine Arts. From 1910 to 1914 he lived in Paris, and not until 1915 did he return to Vitebsk and marry Bella. The couple remained in Russia for eight years, Chagall in 1919 executing in Moscow the mural paintings, sets, and costumes for Granovsky's Jewish State Theater.

Another of Gaspard's entrancing stories of his youth related his close friendship in Odessa, where he went to study art, with the writer Maxim Gorky and the singer Fyodor Chaliapin. Both of his friends, allegedly young and uneducated, were working as stevedores at the docks. Their close friendship was broken when Gorky and Chaliapin, both barefoot, walked to Kharson on the Black Sea to hunt better jobs. This story had to be deleted from the book when I ascertained that Gorky was twenty-six years old and already renowned as a writer in 1894 when Gaspard was only twelve, and that Chaliapin, twenty-one, was singing in St. Petersburg.

More discrepancies appear in Gaspard's account of his formative period of art apprenticeship in Paris, where he arrived about 1900 when he was eighteen years old. La Bohème at the turn of the century, the great era that gave birth to modern art! Paris in the springtime of his youth!

What wonderful stories Gaspard told: of living in garrets, of the struggle of a young artist to learn his trade, of meeting everyone of consequence in the world of art—painters, writers, musicians, sculptors, poets. Extravagantly, he included as his friend the great painter Chaim Soutine, a child of about seven in 1900.

A half-century later in Taos, Gaspard told another whopper to an art student named Walter Bailey, later a staff artist for the *Los Angeles Herald Examiner.* According to this story, Puccini refused to submit his opera *La Bohème* for production until he had obtained Gaspard's criticisms. Bailey, in his review of my book in the *Herald Examiner*'s issue of January 10, 1965, bitterly indicted me for not including the story.

The reason was obvious. The first performance of *La Bohème* was given in the Teatro Reggio, Turin, Italy, on February 1, 1896. Giacomo Puccini was then thirty-eight years old. He already had composed three previous operas, including *Manon Lescaut,* and was so famous that he was hailed as the successor to Verdi. Gaspard at that time was only a fourteen-year-old boy still living in Russia, without musical training, who had not yet gone to Paris to study art.

What was Gaspard's background in Paris, where he arrived in 1900?

First studying in the Academie Julian and then with Eduard Toudouze, Gaspard finally selected as his master the immensely popular Adolphe William Bouguereau. He described the relationship between a master and his apprentice as almost equal to that between a father and his son. Gaspard dutifully prepared Bouguereau's canvasses, cleaned his brushes, swept out the studio, helped Madame Bouguereau with her marketing, and carried messages to Bouguereau's beautiful young mistress, *la belle* Suzanne. Bouguereau amply repaid his apprentice's devotion. He taught Gaspard how to paint and sent him out to make the quick sketches of Paris by which he achieved his first success.

Entrancing as his picture is, it must be looked at more closely. Indeed, this whole crucial period of Gaspard's life needs considerable research if his biography is ever written. For one thing, the well-known art critic Thomas Craven excoriates Bouguereau as a strict academician who aped the outmoded classicism of Rome and celebrated the "cult of prettiness." Bouguereau's pupils he regarded as the most worthless Bohemians of Paris. For another thing, Craven asserts that Bouguereau's favorite and most outstanding pupil was Henri Matisse. In his celebrated exhibit of 1905, Matisse and a group of other Bouguereau students were labeled "Fauves," establishing the new Fauvist school of art. Gaspard's name is not mentioned. Nor, curiously enough, did Gaspard ever mention Matisse in his reminiscences.

Another more serious lapse of memory occurred during Gaspard's detailed account of his marriage. The young couple was too poor to afford a wedding reception.

Bouguereau rose to the occasion. He gave the wedding dinner in the new and imposing Hotel Lutetia, which opened its dining room that night in honor of Gaspard and his bride. Everyone of note was invited; no expense was spared to make it a gala event Gaspard could never forget.

This story for me was the straw that broke the camel's back. Gaspard had approved the story as I had written it when I discovered that Bouguereau, becoming seriously ill, had left Paris for his home village of La Rochelle and died there on August 18, 1905—more than three years before he allegedly gave the wedding party for Gaspard on December 31, 1908.

I immediately confronted Gaspard with these facts and several pertinent questions. Was it true that a dying man of seventy-five had maintained as a mistress such a lively *cocotte* as *la belle* Suzanne? Did Gaspard remember nothing of his loved master's illness and departure? Had he not gone to his funeral at La Rochelle? And how could he now explain the wedding party, whose opulence and many guests he had described in careful detail?

Gaspard was embarrassed and surly. I was embarrassed and a little angry. The manuscript was in the hands of the printer. To correct it would necessitate holding up the press until I could rewrite the chapter, but I could get no information from Gaspard save that someone else must have sponsored his wedding reception. Disbelieving the whole yarn, I pulled a name out of the hat. "Was it Krecke?" Alfred Krecke, whom he had briefly mentioned, was a wealthy merchant from Ghent, Belgium, who came often to Paris and had bought several of Gaspard's sketches.

"Yes! It was Krecke! I remember now!" answered Gaspard at once. So Krecke I made it, embroidering his whopper with one of my own.

What wishful thinking, what great need, insisted on this and other fanciful stories like it after so many years?

Gaspard's early bride was Evelyn, the daughter of Mrs. Eugenia Adell, an extremely wealthy American woman who had brought Evelyn and her twin sisters, Irena and Irma, to visit Paris. Gaspard fell in love with Evelyn at once. According to Gaspard, Mrs. Adell objected to their infatuation on the grounds that he was a poor, struggling artist who would never be able to support Evelyn in the manner to which she was accustomed. To break their attachment, she took all three daughters on a tour of Europe, announcing that they would return to America from Italy. A short time later, Evelyn returned to Paris alone from Italy and married Gaspard.

This story may be true. But it seems strange that a circumspect woman like Mrs. Adell would let a young daughter return alone and destitute to Paris, and refuse to attend her wedding. There seems no doubt now, in view of what happened later, that the Adell family objected to the marriage because Gaspard was Jewish. Eve Young-Hunter, the wife of English portrait painter John Young-Hunter, later told me that during an early trip to Paris they had seen a painting of Gaspard's signed "Leon Gaspard Schulmann." Evidently Gaspard at that time was painting under this name. Was it his mother's maiden name? And why, after his marriage, did he drop the "Schulmann"?

In any case, we can easily divine his growing inner conflict. The compelling desire to be a great artist and, opposed to this, the equal need born of his sensual nature to achieve wealth, comfort, and social standing. Certainly the conflict was not alleviated by Evelyn, who had known nothing else.

After a trip to Russia with his young bride, Gaspard returned to Europe to develop the sketches he had made. They were an instant success, showing for the first time the Asiatic color sense that was to make him famous. His success was interrupted by World War I. Enlisting as a French aerial observer, he was shot down and carried to a base hospital where he was not expected to live. According to Gaspard, Evelyn now abandoned him and returned to her family in America because she could not bear to watch him die. A strange time to desert a husband! One suspects instead that her family induced her to return to America at the outbreak of the war in the hope of breaking up her marriage to Gaspard.

Gaspard recovered, however, and sailed to rejoin her. Evelyn was living with her family in Great Barrington, Massachusetts. What happened there, Gaspard never would say. Obviously there was a family squabble, the Adells refusing to accept him as a son-in-law. Gaspard, ill and needing a long recuperation, left for New York. Evelyn went with him, severing her last ties with her family.

Aided by George D. Pratt, head of the Pratt Institute of Art, Gaspard achieved instant recognition in America. Too ill to follow it up, he lived for a time in the art colony at Provincetown, Massachusetts, and then moved to Taos, New Mexico. With vigorous life in the open, his health returned. He worked hard, shipping his paintings to galleries in New York, Detroit, and Los Angeles, where they sold well, fetching high prices. Gaspard was made as an artist.

Now began the fruitful years. In 1921 the couple sailed for China. Leaving Evelyn alone in Peking, Gaspard traveled across the Gobi Desert, through Mongolia into Tibet, most of the way on horseback. The trip took two years and four months. Out of it came his most wonderful stories of high adventure and romance, attested to by his paintings in glowing color. Yet there are many details about this trip that can be questioned.

Gaspard could never trace on a map his route beyond Urga. And knowing Evelyn and her frugal nature, I cannot possibly imagine her staying alone in the expensive Wagon Lit Hotel in Peking for more than two years! Moreover, Gaspard kept recounting the close friendship he had formed with Somerset Maugham in Canton. These stories I did not include in the book, as he could never explain when and why he went to Canton in southern China during his one trip to northern China.

Returning to Taos, the couple built a large, two-story, Byzantine-style house, with barn, corral, sheep pen, and pigeon lofts, on thirty acres of irrigated land. In 1932 they made a trip to Europe and to Morocco, Tunisia, and Algeria in North Africa. From all these trips they brought back massive furniture, Oriental rugs, and tapestries for their house.

Here Gaspard settled down at last, painting the scenes he had seen during his travels. Taos was a famous art center, drawing people from all over the world. He could meet them as a mature and successful artist, an urbane world traveler, and at the same time indulge his love of simple outdoor life. What more could a man desire?

I first knew him during these years. What dinner parties, what picnics! And how he loved it all, this top side of his hour. And so did Evelyn. She was a small woman, usually dressed in Oriental silk gowns and hats, which she designed and sewed with impeccable taste. She was a woman pert of manner, sharp of tongue and humor, with a mind of her own. I always enjoyed her. But underneath their life ran a deeper, darker current.

Soon after World War II, when I returned to town after a long stint of war work in Washington, D.C., I met Evelyn in the plaza. She rushed up to me and grabbed me with both hands. "Frank! You're back! You must come to see us. Tomorrow. We will have some of that tea we brought back from China!"

Late next afternoon, I knocked on the door. Evelyn opened it with a cold, unrecognizing stare in her eyes.

"You said for me to come. I . . ."

She interrupted my stammer. "Yes, of course! You've come to see the studio." She took me not to Gaspard's studio upstairs but to her own studio downstairs. Here she showed me countless bolts of imported silk, satin, and brocades, and several designs she was working on. Then, escorting me to the door, she said sharply, "That will be one dollar, please!" I forked over the dollar and left, very much perplexed.

What had happened, Gaspard later explained, was that she had been thrown by a horse and was not quite the same. There was more to it than this. Through the years, Evelyn had grown to resent Gaspard's Jewish birthright that had alienated her from her family. This resentment intensified when her mother died, leaving her no inheritance from the vast estate. Not that the Gaspards needed money. In addition to a comfortable bank account, they had hidden in the house a considerable sum in cash. Still Evelyn blamed Gaspard. "When I die, you're not going to get a cent of my share of the money!" she told him. "You'll only marry a Jewess and fill the house with Jews!"

Gaspard felt cut off from the roots of his being. Only when he was out in the barn alone did he take out from beneath his shirt the little oilskin-wrapped copy of Frug's poem, *The Paper Bridge,* to read with love and joy. How he must have grown to hate Evelyn's domination through these years of loneliness and torment! When she developed diabetes, it was worse. He went nowhere, and he stopped painting.

Gaspard's closest friends were John and Jim Karavas, two Greek brothers who owned La Fonda Hotel, where he had formerly played chess. Jim's wife, Noula, was a small, delicate-boned woman who always dressed beautifully in exotic costumes patterned after Greek styles; Gaspard's portrait of her is one of his best. They had one son, Saki, whom the Gaspards virtually adopted after Jim died. Gaspard bought him a car, and every day Saki took Evelyn for a ride—her only outing.

During their rides, Gaspard insisted, Saki always bought her ice cream or candy to hasten her death. For she allegedly had repeated to him the complaint that had become an obsession with her. "I'm going to give you my one-half share in our house, Saki. Otherwise when I die, Leon will marry a Jewess and fill the house with Jews!"

So it dragged on until 1956. One day Gaspard stopped by the hotel to see Saki. Talking of various things, they visited almost a half-hour. Then Gaspard casually mentioned that Evelyn had died in her sleep that night. Saki, horrified, found that her body was still lying in bed, and that Gaspard had not notified the undertaking parlor or made any provisions for her burial. Saki promptly arranged to have her buried in one of his own family's plots in the cemetery and paid for the marker on her grave. The evening after the funeral, Gaspard took Noula to the movies.

It was during the following year I came to know Gaspard best. He was seventy-five years old and alone for the first time in that great, cold, and musty house still bestrewn with Evelyn's clothing. His pictures had been returned from the galleries and were stacked upstairs, unseen and unsold. His health was failing, and he had not found a doctor to help him. For the first time in his life, he was confronted, as we all are in our time, with the realization that he too would die. He was frightened. So throughout that fall and winter, I drove up from Santa Fe, where I was temporarily working, to spend every Sunday with him. Martha Reed, a dress designer in Taos, usually came over, too. We were his only friends.

During the morning, he worked on our portraits in the kitchen. Then we had vodka and stories, finished off with a huge borscht. Those wonderful stories of high adventure and romance in Asia, which pictured the Gaspard he wanted to be, the Gaspard he wanted remembered! I grew to love him in this effulgent twilight of his life. For Gaspard died that winter, man and artist. Everything after that was an anticlimax.

He was obsessed by two worries. One was the lack of recognition given to him at the same time contemporaries from his student days in Paris were now acclaimed worldwide as masters. The other worry was more immediate. Saki had left on a trip to Europe without coming to tell him good-bye. The reason Gaspard gave was that the ungrateful, greedy boy had gone to deposit in a foreign bank the $40,000 in currency that Evelyn had hidden in the house and given him before she died.

Saki was an old friend of mine, too. When he returned, I suggested to him that he try to patch up the differences between him and Gaspard, who was failing fast. Saki also had heard the story of the $40,000 and indignantly refused. "I'll never speak to him again as long as he lives! Neither will my mother!" Saki was pure Greek.

A year later, on September 22, 1958, Evelyn's prophecy came true. Gaspard suddenly married Dora Kaminsky. Of orthodox Jewish faith, she had been born in New York of Lithuanian and Georgian parents and had studied art in the Educational Alliance School and the Art Students' League. In 1944, she had come to Taos on a short visit and met Gaspard. Recently she had returned, married to her second husband, Michael Klein, a painter and a compulsive drinker.

The couple lived several miles out of town; and as they had no car, Dora was obliged to walk back and forth carrying groceries through the snow. There was not a ready market for either of the Kleins' work. Faced with extreme poverty and Michael's drinking problem, Dora divorced him and married lonely Gaspard.

She was a short, plump woman of fifty, energetic, extremely vociferous, and aggressive. The marriage was good for Gaspard. For the first time, he had someone of his own faith to talk to; there was no longer any need to conceal Frug's poem. They had everything in common, including now a mutual belief that Saki had stolen that hidden $40,000.

Their accusations spread rapidly throughout town, reaching the ears of Saki. He promptly went to a lawyer, George T. Reynolds, who called Gaspard and Dora on the carpet. Gaspard on that day, February 13, 1959, signed an endorsement to the effect that "Saki Karavas has never stolen anything from me or my previous wife. I certainly haven't ever accused him of such a thing."

Two months later the Gaspards sailed on a honeymoon cruise around the world. Upon their return Dora energetically set about selling Gaspard's pictures. A shrewd and clever manager, she refused to let them be handled by dealers or local galleries—at one-third commission—and converted Evelyn's old studio into a gallery. Then, hiking the prices of the paintings, she let it be known that they could be seen by those interested. No tourists, no pikers, please! Her consummate salesmanship worked. Wealthy admirers, collectors, and dealers began to call, not only to admire the paintings but to view the immense Byzantine house framing them so perfectly, the Chinese tea and Russian *pirogies* the guests were served, and the fascinating stories Gaspard told them. Paintings sold at still higher prices until the Gaspards set a limit to their annual sales in order to avoid excessive income tax. The restriction boosted the demand still more. Gaspard's eclipse was over.

Taos's reception of Dora as the new Mrs. Leon Gaspard was not an unqualified success. She was too talkative and aggressive for most of Gaspard's old friends, and they began to mutter the phrase "from rags to riches!" The town had treated her rather shabbily during her earlier days; and Dora, chip on shoulder, aggressively delighted in giving everyone their comeuppance. Few townspeople were welcome to call. The consensus was that the Gaspards knew which side their bread was buttered on; they restricted their hospitality to visiting wealthy patrons.

Gaspard, I'm sure, was not uncomfortable about this. The vaulting ambition of his early youth had returned to haunt him—but with a tragic switch. Then his desire had been to *become* a great painter. Now it was to *have been* one of the great painters who had ushered in modern art. Clearly, he was not a Cézanne, a Picasso, a Marc Chagall, nor any of those abstract painters now so widely known as innovators of drastic new styles in art. He was Leon Gaspard, an objective painter with a style and a palette of his own, whose work had been internationally recognized. Yet every time he picked up a newspaper or magazine article announcing the sale of a great painting for a million dollars or the "discovery" of a new master who had died unknown, he was irked because his own work was not placed in the same category.

The extent of such feeling cannot be measured. Perhaps no creative artist achieves the full measure of his talent. Yet his overriding ambition, his sense of frustration, can be alleviated by his acceptance of the inescapable fact that he has done what he has been able to do with his own nature and his own talent. No man can measure himself against others; he can only take his own.

This Gaspard was unable to do. For sixty years he had been a successful painter. His work had brought him all the comfort and pleasure his sensual nature demanded—freedom to travel all over the world, a comfortable home in quiet surroundings, peace and freedom from financial worry, the friendship of rich and famous people. This was his law of life, a dictate of his own nature, that he had instinctively obeyed. He was a jovial, gregarious, outgoing man—an extroverted man of action, as his paintings suggest. He was not an introverted man who could have remained an obscure painter in Paris, living in poverty and developing a style to portray on canvass an inner vision of life.

We discussed this during his last year when we were alone in his upstairs studio. This was not often, for Dora was usually present, guiding the conversation. Yet Gaspard remained disconsolate, speaking often of dying and not being remembered. To be remembered and appreciated!

A book would do it. A monograph of reproductions of his paintings, illustrated by a short text containing the stories that had delighted his friends for years. That was how this project came about. It gave him a new lease on life as we reviewed his stories and paintings, and found in Paul Weaver of Northland Press a warm, capable, and enthusiastic publisher. Then, as I have recounted, came my discovery of several discrepancies and his strange request to delete from the manuscript every mention of his Jewish background. I felt that this evisceration was abetted by Dora, who as a sharp manager believed it might be prejudicial to the sale of his paintings. She was adamant, even to the point of insisting that I delete every reference to her own Jewish background and her two previous marriages.

It was an awkward, unhappy time broken by a pleasant evening. I was suffering a brief and unhappy marriage myself when we were invited to dinner with Gaspard and Dora to celebrate the end of our work on his book. Paul Weaver had driven over a few days before to show us proofs of the book and carry back some additional sketches. Now everything was settled, and Gaspard was in a jovial mood. Dora served dinner in their big living room in front of the fireplace. We had vodka and vermouth without ice, as he liked it, and hors d'oeuvres, followed by one of his own turkeys and his favorite rosé wine. Afterward we sat listening to him retell his stories. This warm evening was the last time I saw him alive.

Early next morning, Friday, February 21, 1964, there was a fresh fall of snow. Gaspard got up late, feeling fine, and ate a hearty breakfast. Then he went out to feed his sheep, chickens, and pigeons. At ten o'clock, he stumbled on to the back porch and collapsed with a heart attack. Dora telephoned the doctor, who came with an ambulance and took him to the hospital. Then she called us.

There now happened an unfortunate, unhappy incident. My wife, Rose, answered the telephone and was told, "Tell Frank. Don't you come over. Stay away."

Perhaps Dora was distraught. Or perhaps now, at this crucial time, she gave vent to a dislike of Rose, who was her exact antithesis: generous, outgoing, and impulsive, but extremely jealous and quick-tempered.

Thinking of no one but Gaspard and wondering why Dora had not accompanied him to the hospital, I rushed to their house, loaded her into the car, and headed for the hospital. On the way we met Rose in her own car, angry because Dora had told her to stay away. The road was icy; her car skidded in front of us and ran off the road. Seeing that Rose had safely stopped it, I continued on to the hospital with Dora. We were not allowed to see Gaspard. He was under treatment, and we were advised to come back later.

Worrying about Rose, I drove Dora to our home where we found my wife seething with anger. As we settled down to restore our equilibrium with a cup of coffee, the telephone rang. Gaspard was dying. We all rushed back to the hospital, arriving a moment after he died.

Dora, strangely enough, was the coolest of us all. It had been Gaspard's wish to be buried on his own property in a plain pine box, without being embalmed and without a public service. This desire presented insuperable difficulties. It was a weekend. We would be unable to secure men to dig a grave in the frozen ground and build a plain pine box until Monday. Also, the director of the funeral parlor refused to keep the body without embalming it or to conduct the funeral without a coffin. I persuaded Dora to buy a simple coffin, which I selected, and to allow Gaspard's body to be embalmed. I then picked out in his apple orchard the site for his grave.

Two days later, on Sunday afternoon, a number of us—his closest friends, fellow artists, and neighbors of many years—gathered in the large Byzantine *sala* of his home. I made a few sincere remarks in English to pay him our sincere and profound respect. Eliseo Concha from the Pueblo gave a prayer in Tiwa. At the graveside stood two more Concha boys, Joe giving the final prayer and Pete singing the traveling song.

Back in the house, Rose served everyone from the huge roast and cakes she had brought; and we left Dora with Arthur and Cecily Church, two of Gaspard's close friends who had driven down from Colorado Springs. That evening we drove back. The Gaspard house was dark; Dora was out with the Churches. Then in the snow we walked out to Gaspard's final resting place for a last farewell.

One would have thought that was the end, but the anticlimax began immediately. Dora began to revise the text of the manuscript already set up in type. Every day I received exorbitant demands to change stories, incidents, sentences, words. To comply with her demands would have meant virtually rewriting the whole book. I accordingly wrote her a sharp letter refusing to make any more revisions. The text was not her biography of Gaspard and it had been eviscerated enough. I was more shocked when she wanted to include a foreword to be written by the director of a museum I'd had unfortunate dealings with; this I also refused.

Meanwhile, Paul Weaver was having trouble about the paintings. They had been carefully selected, for full-color reproductions were costly. Some of them were owned by collectors who had loaned them, signing releases for their use. Dora now began to make substitutions, two of which created a nasty tangle.

Some months before his death, Gaspard had sold two paintings for $9,000 to a wealthy oil man and art collector of Oklahoma City named Eugene B. Adkins. The buyer had paid a cash deposit of $1,500 and secured Gaspard's signature on a formal contract of sale. The paintings were to be reproduced in the book, Adkins giving Weaver a release for the purpose. Upon Gaspard's death, however, Dora raised the prices of all his paintings again and refused to honor Adkins's contract.

The matter was further complicated when Adkins sent the balance of $7,500 to Jane Hiatt of the Village Gallery in Taos, through whom he had bought the pictures. Hiatt was not only a thoroughly dependable dealer but had been a close and trusted friend of Gaspard's for many years.

Shocked at Dora's action, she refused to accept her commission and turned the check over to a lawyer to hold in escrow.

Weaver was tearing his hair. He already had made color plates of the two paintings, but dared not include them in the book until the dispute over their ownership was settled. Adkins was also in a stew. He fully appreciated Weaver's predicament. But not to be done out of the pictures he had paid for, he took legal action. A writ of replevin was issued on June 9, 1964, and Sheriff Uvaldo Sandoval removed the paintings from the Gaspard house. Upon Dora's release of them to Adkins, Weaver was notified that he could include them in the book as originally planned.

Weaver immediately drove to Taos to carry back other Asiatic paintings he had carefully selected. Dora refused to let him have them and substituted inferior paintings. One of them was reproduced in the book with the title *Navajo Women.* It showed two full-figure Navajo women, one carrying a baby in a cradle board. Ostensibly it had been painted from life in the Navajo country. Yet nothing about one figure—the shape of her face, her hands, her stance, beaded moccasins—was Navajo. It was our friend Martha Reed, who had posed for Gaspard in his studio. Another unfortunate selection given Weaver was a black-and-white sketch of a dance at a pueblo, entitled *Gaspard's Last Sketch.* It was an inferior copy of a full-color painting entitled *Corn Dance at Santo Domingo.* Both were reproduced in the book.

Nor was this the end. Just before the book went to press, Weaver sent Dora a set of final galley proofs. In the text I had added a short paragraph regarding Gaspard's untimely death. It briefly mentioned that on the night of the funeral, Rose and I had walked out to his grave. Dora now demanded that Weaver delete the reference to Rose. Holding up the presses, he telephoned me immediately. I refused to allow the deletion on the grounds that the text had been copyrighted in my name and that any change he made in it would be a breach of contract. He heartily agreed and so wrote Dora.

In November, the book came out. Its favorable acceptance promised a still wider recognition of Gaspard's paintings. Dora, paradoxically, criticized the book roundly and threatened to sue me for the cost of Gaspard's coffin. Also, she blamed me for having buried Gaspard in his own orchard. Fearing this would lower the potential value of the property, she transferred his remains to the public cemetery.

Another incident reflected her combative mood. She and Gaspard had given a small painting to Geraldine Harvey, a schoolteacher at the Pueblo. She, in turn, had given it to her boyfriend, who before he died had sold it to an art dealer in Santa Fe. The dealer had then resold it to Manuel Berg of the Blue Door Gallery in Taos. Dora, upon finding this out, was furious. She claimed that the painting had been given to Harvey upon the condition that it could be recalled when needed for showing in an exhibition.

Berg alleged that no deed of gift specifying the restriction had been drawn up. Moreover, he claimed that Gerry had known her boyfriend to be an alcoholic in debt to numerous persons, and that she had given him the painting without any restrictions. Gerry, indebted to Dora for having taken her on a trip to Spain, confirmed Dora's allegations. Hence, both of them instituted suit against Berg for repossession of the painting.

Then, surprisingly, on May 2, 1965, scarcely fourteen months after Gaspard's death, Dora married in Las Vegas, Nevada, young Belford "Paco" Blackman. She had been twenty-six years younger than Gaspard; now, at the age of fifty-seven, she was almost that much older than Blackman. Soon afterward, they left for a year's Hilton Hotel tour of Europe and the Near East. Dora could well afford it. She reportedly had found the $40,000, which Evelyn had hidden under the mattress of a bed.

Returning home, Blackman established his own private apartment downstairs and converted Gaspard's studio upstairs into his library. In the spring of 1967, just three years after Gaspard's death, Dora sold the house to Mrs. Duane Lineberry in town. Gaspard's old friends were not pleased to learn of the sale. They had hoped that Dora with her more than ample funds would establish with the old house and its thirty acres a community foundation or art center of some kind for young artists, like several other homes in town. Now they feared that the Lineberrys, who owned two motels in town, would convert it into a third business venture.

Dora was not disturbed. She shipped all of Gaspard's paintings to the Maxwell Galleries in San Francisco, which issued an impressive brochure of nearly fifty full-color reproductions and announced a retrospective exhibition of his work, marked at still higher prices. Then Dora and Blackman left town to establish residency in Hawaii.

Events and changes continued almost too quickly to follow. The Lineberrys resold the house, without its Oriental furnishings and the thirty acres of land; and the new owner converted it into an art gallery. Dora later returned and bought back the house, for what purpose no one knew. Occasionally she lived in it between solitary trips to Europe and the Near East. On rarer occasions Blackman came with her for a brief visit, then returned to the separate residence he had established in California, while Dora left for another extended trip abroad.

Meanwhile, the growing appeal and sale of Gaspard's paintings received their greatest impetus when Fenn Galleries in Santa Fe, with the cooperation of Biltmore Galleries of Los Angeles, held a retrospective exhibition of more than sixty paintings and sketches. For this special showing a representative full-color catalog was issued to art collectors, critics, and buyers throughout the country. Listed prices ranged up to $42,000. This great event drew more than 1,200 people. Gaspard's work at last had achieved the success he had wished for and deserved.

Dora died in Phoenix, Arizona, on February 24, 1977; while her husband, "Paco" Blackman, was said to be living mainly in Greece. He subsequently returned to Taos and reopened the house, erecting a large sign out in front:

GASPARD HOUSE MUSEUM
Old Mansion of the Famous Russian-American Painter

The sign announced as well the tawdry, tragic, and macabre last chapter in the history of Gaspard's home. The museum was not a success. One stray visitor, let in by a housekeeper, found it stripped almost bare of furniture, the dusty floors littered with papers, cigarette butts, empty beer cans, and Coke bottles. In the kitchen sat Blackman, ill, mentally confused, and penniless. The fortune he and Dora had derived from the sale of Gaspard's paintings had been spent. But at her death, she had left him this house, its furnishings, and still more paintings. What had happened to them?

Blackman apparently had sold some two hundred paintings to the Kennedy Galleries in California. When the galleries failed to live up to the contract, Blackman filed suit. The court ruled that the contract was void and ordered the unsold paintings placed in the trusteeship of a Santa Fe bank, pending an appeal. The ownership of still more paintings, which Blackman had assigned to the Fenn Galleries in Santa Fe, also came into legal dispute.

Blackman now signed another contract with S. R. Koman, an art dealer in Winchester, Virginia, giving him all the unsold paintings, the Gaspard house and furnishings, and the right to operate the house as a museum for five years. In return, Blackman was to receive $18,000 a year for eight years and would be allowed to live in the guest house. Also, a debt of $75,000 owed to Koman by Blackman was to be forgiven. Soon after signing the contract, Blackman reportedly borrowed $20,000 more from Koman in return for an addendum selling the "family collection" of Gaspard paintings.

Litigation over the contract began early in January 1981. Blackman alleged that due to his "physical and emotional infirmities and his desperate, confused, and deteriorated condition," he was not aware of the terms of the contract he had signed. Koman presented proof of the payments he had made, asserted that Blackman was destroying the house, and expressed doubt that it could ever be operated as a museum. The court on May 1 ruled that Blackman had sold the house and paintings under the terms of the contract.

The tangle of lawsuits was finally unsnarled by a settlement agreement on July 15. Under its terms Blackman moved out of the guest house and accepted $100,000 as full and final payment. Koman was assigned ownership of the house and paintings. He forgave all of Blackman's debts, including interest and damages, and agreed to pay the fees of the five attorneys hired by Blackman.

Forrest Fenn then acquired all available Gaspard paintings and bought the house from Koman to convert into a gallery. A "Gaspard Weekend" celebrated these acquisitions. A retrospective showing of Gaspard paintings and sketches was given in the Fenn Galleries in Santa Fe on the evening of October 23, 1981. This was followed next evening by the opening of the Gaspard Gallery in Taos. Large crowds packed both galleries. Despite its great opening, the Gaspard Gallery was not a success and was soon closed.

Today, years later, an evil spirit seems to hover over the big, garish pink Gaspard house; or at least it appears to carry a jinx. Unlike the former homes of Harwood, Blumenschein, Brett, Fechin, and Mabel Luhan, the Gaspard house has remained empty and unused much of the time.

It seems to me now that if Gaspard's stout spirit could return to Taos for a brief visit, he would be greatly amused by all these changes, events, and hijinks that have taken place during the last twenty years. He would relate them himself after carefully crossing his new cowboy boots and lifting his tumbler of vodka and vermouth colored with a dash of red wine. Events would bear little resemblance to the actual earthly happenings. They would be humorously transformed into exotic, melodramatic episodes that would hold us, his listeners, spellbound. *Como no?* He ran his mortal race with his own nature, time, and talent. No man can do more.

6

THE BRETT

To write about Brett the painter seems to be difficult for most commentators casually acquainted with her work. They always wind up writing about what to them is more impressive—her English lineage and her friendship with D. H. Lawrence. And indeed her family pedigrees alone are notable enough to fill pages.

Her paternal grandfather was Viscount Esher, Lord Chief Justice of the Court of Appeals and Queen Victoria's Master of the Rolls. Her maternal grandfather, a Belgian, put Leopold I on the throne and became his ambassador to the Court of St. James. Her own father, Reginald Baliol Brett, the second Viscount Esher, was Queen Victoria's personal adviser and was believed to be the power behind the throne of Edward VII. Her younger sister, Sylvia, became Lady Brooke, the Ranee of Sarawak. Without going into other ramifications, we can let the Ranee sum up the situation: "Being a child of the brilliant Reginald was like being related to the *Encyclopedia Britannica.*"

The Honorable Dorothy Eugenie Brett was born in Mayfair, London, on November 10, 1883. No child could have been more imprisoned in the lap of luxury, surrounded by maids, footmen, butlers, the very air tinctured by the perfume of her illustrious father's rose-tipped cigarettes. Brett rebelled from the start against the stuffiness of her milieu.

A delicate-looking but stubborn child, she took dancing lessons at Windsor Castle with Queen Victoria's grandchildren, was presented at court to King Edward and Queen Alexandra, and was escorted at age fifteen by Winston Churchill to her first court ball. Brett endured these social functions with growing resentment. She scorned being a "lady," snubbed her escorts, cut off her hair, and dressed like a boy.

What had gotten into her to make her such a maverick? "As a child one has a dream about life. As one grows up and out into life one tries to make the dream come true," she once said. "All of life is this endeavor to live that life of the dreaming child. What do we know of this strange and wonderful journey, from what to where?" Whatever her dream and journey, if she ever knew it, it may have begun with the Yellow Indian.

She saw him when she was taken by her nursemaid to Buffalo Bill's Wild West Show at the Crystal Palace. Trembling with excitement, she watched the doors of the arena open. Out rumbled the stagecoach behind its galloping horses. Then came the pursuing Indians, whooping and

Dorothy Brett

yelling, firing their guns, feathers in their warbonnets streaming as they raced around the arena. One of them, bareback on a pinto horse, rode at first sight into her undying memory. Seventy, eighty years later, she could still vividly recall his naked, slim young body painted bright lemon yellow. A creature of the wild, of limitless space and untrammeled freedom, he flashed everywhere like a lightning streak of lemon yellow before her. Like an archetypal image emerging from her dark unconscious to constellate the dream-image she was to pursue for a lifetime.

About this time Brett began taking drawing lessons from a woman her father engaged to paint her portrait. From then on she was seldom without a sketch pad. "The whole family ridiculed my unceasing cry to be an artist," she recounted. "To them this would be absurd and would also be a loss of social position. How could I convince them I didn't care a rap for their 'Social Position'? I wanted to be free."

Not until 1910, when she was twenty-seven years old, was she permitted to apply for entrance to Slade School of Art. Its director told her they didn't want people from her class because the Slade was a school for serious artists. On the strength of her drawings, however, he admitted her for a probationary six months. Her work proved acceptable, and she studied there for six years. Establishing her own studio in Earl's Court, she developed a new circle of friends who were creative like herself—Katherine Mansfield, John

Middleton Murry, Aldous Huxley, Bertrand Russell, and Virginia Woolf. During this time she casually met the man who was to have the most influence on her life—D. H. Lawrence.

A few years later she again met him and his buxom German wife, Frieda, with a group of friends in the Cafe Royal in London. The ornate, red plush cafe was hardly a natural setting for the small, red-bearded novelist who was shocking the public with declamations against the prudishness and the materialism of the time. The son of a poor collier, forever restless, he and Frieda had wandered through Europe to Australia, frugally living on his small royalties. He was then induced to come to Taos, New Mexico, by Mabel Luhan. The small mountain village and the nearby Indian pueblo captured his imagination. So now in the Cafe Royal he described it as the place for all of them, writers, painters, and freedom-hungry souls like himself, to escape from the shackles of a corrupt society and begin a new life. The commune they would establish would be named Rananim.

If Lawrence's listeners were momentarily sparked by his enthusiasm, Brett completely succumbed to a fatal fascination for him and his idealized Rananim. And though the other members of the group discreetly backed out of the scheme, Brett finally in 1924 accompanied the Lawrences to Taos. Thereafter, until she died more than a half-century later, her name was indissolubly linked with that of Lawrence.

There is no need here to recount her association with him as one of his "Three Fates," as Frieda, Mabel, and Brett came to be known, nor to detail her first years living in a log cabin on Lobo Mountain, close to the ranch Mabel gave Lawrence; here Brett learned to cook, to ride a horse, and to fish. It has all been told in Mabel's *Lorenzo in Taos,* Frieda's *Not I, But the Wind,* and Brett's own *Lawrence and Brett, a Friendship.* All these books, with a thousand magazine articles, newspaper interviews, and gossip columns, have portrayed her as a historical character in the cast of a literary drama still assiduously quoted, misquoted, and paraphrased. That she has almost escaped it, as well as the clutches of her genealogy, is due in part to that Yellow Indian of her childhood.

For here he came alive in the Indians of Taos Pueblo, dark, vital men swathed in blankets, singing as they plowed their fields and cleaned out their irrigation ditches. Mabel's big husband, Tony, was one of them. Often he brought some of the younger men up to help work on the ranch. In the evening they would build a big fire, beat drums, and dance beneath the pines. How beautiful, wild, and barbaric it was in this hinterland wilderness of America! Brett was free at last.

And she was painting steadily—painting Indians. As she later said, it was only then that she really began to paint. Her distinctive style emerged, and her paintings became more fluid and dynamic as her intuitive understanding of Indians developed. She finally had found the terms of her permanent appeal.

I met her in 1937 when I arrived in Taos. A wispy-haired woman of fifty-four, she held out a tin ear trumpet, which she called Toby, to catch my voice, for she had begun to lose her hearing while attending the Slade School. The Lawrence bubble up on Lobo had burst after he had spent portions of only a few years there. Still restless and rootless, he had gone to Mexico and Italy, where Brett had accompanied or joined him. Then he had died in Vence, France, and his ashes had been entombed in a shrine on Lobo. He was now one of the phenomenal literary figures of our time, and Brett still deeply venerated him.

For a time she had continued to live alone up on Lobo in a log cabin near the Lawrence ranch; the "Tower Beyond Tragedy," Robinson Jeffers called the Lobo cabin. The hard life was too much for her, and she had moved down to Taos to live in an upstairs studio room renting for $40 a month. Having no stairs, she was obliged to climb up an outside ladder to it. Then Mabel installed her in one of her many houses, a one-room building named the Studio.

I was then living a stone's throw away in a big studio room above the garage in back of Tony House, so called because it lay on land belonging to Tony Lujan on the Indian reservation across the irrigation ditch. Neither of us had running water and plumbing; we shared a common wooden privy. Brett didn't mind the discomforts in summer, for Mabel was not charging her any rent. But in the winter "the roof leaked and the room was on the chilly side, 60 degrees." She installed an oil heater and a cook stove to replace the electric plate I loaned her. This expense averaged $18 a month, and financially the shoe was beginning to pinch her. She had her own small income from England, but with the approach of war her remittances were cut in half.

Mabel usually invited her to dinner. When she didn't, Brett's British arrogance asserted itself. One evening she stormed into the Big House. "Why should you people have a big, hot dinner and I have nothing? Why haven't you invited me?"

Mabel was just as stubborn. "You weren't invited tonight, Brett. The table has been set only for eight. You can't be accommodated." And Brett returned home for toast and tea.

What frequent fusses like this there were between Lawrence's "Three Fates": impoverished Brett; wealthy Mabel; and Frieda, who on the ever-increasing royalties from Lawrence's books had built a new house a few miles from town and was living in it with the Italian Angelino Ravagli, whom she later married.

Through all this, Brett was steadily painting. Yet she was unknown and unrecognized, and her canvasses were ignored by other artists. To make ends meet she began doing "potboilers," small oil sketches she sold for $5 each. When I was away, she wrote me in March 1941 that she had sold seven since Christmas. A few days later she wrote again. "Just hearken to this! I sold NINE paintings to Edward James. Six $5 ones and three ranging from $25 to $100. Now what do you think of that? I am still slightly intoxicated from it. Counting *all* I have sold since Christmas I have made $250. Not bad! The oil heater was a mighty expense, but will not be so expensive as the damned thing didn't work and I had to throw it back to Ilfeld's whereupon he produced a secondhand one, an ugly one which WORKS. It is leaking right now, some screw needs a washer, but that can be fixed."

The "potboilers" continued to sell in driblets to her neighbors—housewives and workers, the butcher, baker, and candlestick maker. There was no doubt about their universal appeal when their owners were induced to bring in their little treasures for public display. The occasion was formally labeled Dorothy Brett's Retrospective Exhibition at the Stables Gallery of the Taos Art Association.

The time was decidedly inauspicious—the blustery night of January 7, 1967, when everyone was grumpy with winter doldrums, cabin fever, and the usual seasonal feuds. One pushed open the door as if hesitant to confront still another of the constant art showings in Taos's fifty galleries. Instantly all the grumps, groans, and doubts of the worldly life outside vanished. One found oneself in another world of joy and laughter evoked by the touch of a magic brush. Ninety-two loaned paintings covered the walls: pictures of the fat rump of a horse; fairies decorating a Christmas tree; Navajo women riders bucked from their horses, their feet up in the air and their full skirts ballooning out like parasols; birds, fish, flowers; anything, everything. All composing one vast mural, in morning colors, of freshness, love, and pristine beauty.

During World War II I was away in Washington, D.C., and New York. Brett wrote me regularly, wherever I was, from 1939 to 1960. All her letters, typed and single-spaced, covered two or more pages and were seldom paragraphed or punctuated. They were bursts of feelings, spontaneous as her paintings. In rereading the huge stack of them now, they seem to record the life of a small town as well as the development of a new and unique painter.

What a catholic taste she had; how sensitive she was to the many diverse influences upon her! For a time she painted rainbows, then fishes. "Fat round hideous fish looking like jewels swimming in a blue-green sea. This morning they played all the low down tricks they could on me. The colors leaked out of the airbrush and made splotches where no splotches should be, the masks weren't cut straight and so on. But in spite of that in the afternoon they became radiant again. They are getting more and more fascinating to work on."

The war upset her, with letters from home about the air raids on London, men from Taos going into the army, women leaving to work in war plants. She wanted to become a welder, a riveter, or "something tough" like that, but she was deaf and too old. So every day she folded bandages with the other "old hens and young ones too. Ye Gods! It was difficult to play the woman's role peacefully!" But she made it down to the airport in Albuquerque, where for several days she watched the planes—B-24s, Flying Fortresses, a huge blue transport, fifty Lockheed bombers, and beautiful swift Lockheed Lightning planes with twin-slim bodies. Then she began to paint a series of bomber planes.

"What I'm trying to do," she wrote, "is to get these bombers 'in lovely flight,' the feel of turning and curving in the air, of the fluttering movement of planes one against the other. I have one now of two Douglas bombers diving down a tunnel of cloud, through a hole in the tunnel lies Italy, Sicily, and the blue sea."

To heighten their dazzle and glint as they darted through cloud and sunlight, Brett added sparkles of glass and shell. Surely no one before had painted the strength and speed of airplanes like this. There was a terrible reality about them, yet they created a dreamlike fantasy. For in many of the paintings appeared angels with sparkling wings. In one a mother angel and her child were seated on a cloud while the father angel drifted above them. The child had caught one of a flock of bombers and held it out, small as a butterfly, to his mother. In another a couple of Indian angels were playing in the sky, entangling their shining wings. This Otherworld dimension, with the assurance that higher powers were helping the Allies to win the war, gave to her paintings a curious significance when they were given a showing at the Museum of New Mexico in Santa Fe. Mabel in her perceptive review pointed out how Brett with passion and intensity had translated her war pain into the beauty of purity and impersonality. Brett's most striking canvass of the series, *Round the Clock,* created a stir in Santa Fe. A Dutch woman rode the bus up to Taos, tremendously excited by the symbolism and wanting to know if Brett knew what she was doing. Brett could only answer that she didn't know; she was only painting planes.

But in a letter to me she expressed the idea that painting must become more interpretive because the camera records life more literally than the artist. Take for example her neighbor Howard Cook, who had been sent overseas as a war artist. He could not help being too factual and literal.

> When I think of his opportunities, the barrage balloons, the planes flying around the ships, the things he *must* have seen, yet he had to *illustrate,* isn't it a pity to think I can't get near any of this activity because I'm an old woman! But I would rather paint a half-a-dozen real good ones, than dozens of illustrations. . . . Painting can be anything, from the purely literal to the fantasies of the mind. One has to lay a finger on the hidden life. I take my planes into the air. It's not the planes so much, but the movement of the planes and their magic against the clouds, seas or mountains. A plane in itself is a marvelous object, one of mechanical and building wonders,

but that is not the wonder I am after, I am taking the life of the plane as it flies, and that is a JOB.

During a visit to Malibu, California, Brett stayed at the beach estate of Carl Hovey and his wife, Sonya Levien, MGM's top writer. Every Sunday some fifty notables gathered for lunch, including Greta Garbo and Leopold Stokowski. Brett was "knocked all of a heap by his amazing appearance," and promptly embarked on a "Symphony Series" of portraits of him. He refused to sit for her but allowed her later to stand in the wings of the concert hall while he was conducting the orchestra. None of her eleven paintings were actual portraits. Like everything else she did, she transmitted reality into fantasy. His platinum-like hair became a rose-colored nimbus haloing his coaxing hands, those hands of which he was so proud and which he took such exorbitant pains to exhibit. And in the painting of him conducting the "Liebestod" from Wagner's *Tristan and Isolde,* he appeared only as a ghostlike manifestation with a sickle moon and effulgent planes of periwinkle blue.

Brett was broke and hoped to sell one or two of this series to Stokowski's bride, the young heiress Gloria Vanderbilt, when they drove through Taos some time later. Mabel concocted a scheme to help her. All of the paintings were hung on the walls of an upstairs bedroom in the Tony House. Mabel would invite the couple for dinner. Then afterward, while Tony, Brett, and I entertained

Stokowski in the living room, she would take the young heiress upstairs and sell her some of the portraits.

The couple duly arrived for dinner. It was tough going from the start. "Did you enjoy your drive from Los Angeles?" asked Mabel. "Very much," answered Stoki, as Brett called him. "Gloria and Stokowski stayed in humble little motels along the way, like ordinary folk." Always referring to himself in the third person, he embroidered this theme by relating at dinner his enthusiastic receptions during a concert tour in South America. "People everywhere were wild about Stokowski and his music. Why, when he was in Brazil the crowd followed him to his hotel in Buenos Aires and stood outside shouting 'Stokowski! Stokowski!' until he showed himself at the window of his suite!" I could not restrain myself from perversely asking, "But Mr. Stokowski, when was Buenos Aires moved from Argentina to Brazil?" In deathly silence we adjourned to the living room. Then Mabel coyly beckoned to the young bride and led her upstairs.

The rest of us endured an agonizing wait of a half-hour. Brett kept pointing her ear trumpet, Toby, toward the stairway, expecting at any moment to see Gloria rushing down with wild enthusiasm to announce her purchase of the entire "Symphony Series." Tony was elaborately dumb, as always. And Stoki, angry at my rude remark, said little. He kept squirming in his seat and constantly changing chairs. Putting on weight around the middle, he wore a corset so tight he could only sit upright on a straight-backed chair.

Finally, Mabel and Gloria came down. Mabel looked glum. The bride was politely complimentary, but it was evident that the paintings didn't impress her enough to buy one.

None of Brett's excursions into "potboilers," rainbows, fishes, bombing planes, and the Stokowski series interfered with her steady paintings of Indians. Indians of course had been the stock-in-trade subjects since the arrival of the first painters who had made Taos famous as an art center. Most paintings of them were romantic and sentimental, such as those of Couse and Phillips; ethnological depictions, such as those of Imhof and Sharp; or character portraits such as those of Fechin—to say nothing of the hundreds of picture-postcard canvasses turned out for the tourist trade. Brett's paintings were like none that ever had been painted before or since. In them we see in full perspective the Yellow Indian of her childhood, as reflected from her own Otherworld perceptions.

If a mystical streak was inherent in Brett's character, its development was perhaps aided by her deafness, which shut off much of the outside world and turned her toward her own inner being. It became more pronounced in her later years as she became more familiar with the spiritual Otherworld. She wrote me,

> It is strange, but I have a Protector, some mighty being who comes to me in a dream and tells me what to do, who lifts me up, and there is no beauty so beautiful, no

> wonder so wonderful, no greater ecstasy than this, this meeting with this great BEING. For days, for weeks, I am beyond the pin-pricks of this world. Would that I could remain forever in this world beyond worlds. But each time the downward drop is less and there remains a strange glow. Perhaps this accounts for my painting, why I can touch the secret life of the Indian, the world of light and dark of the plane, so that airmen cannot believe I've never flown. These things are not conscious in me, I do not know what I am doing. My mind is not conscious of making a plan, or trying to be symbolical or mystical. Some other part of me unconsciously sends out these rays. Perhaps I have lived a singularly unworldly life, I think I have, and I am not worldly, not very clever in everyday life. Yet I seem to know so much more than these worldly people know.

It was natural that Brett's intuitive and mystical awareness of Indian life coincided with the mystical Indian world about her, dominated by their Sacred Mountain and sacred Blue Lake high in the Sangre de Cristos; a world of great religious ceremonials, races, and dances, of swirling feathers and tossing deer heads. No people are more mystical than Indians. Behind their everyday life, dressed in begrimed Montgomery Ward blankets as they work in their fields, there lie secret ceremonies in the kivas and pilgrimages to Blue Lake. These were the Indians Brett painted. "The life behind the life of the Indian. Yes, their own life, behind the life they have to put on living here.

There's the Indian living the life that this community produces, you see, and then there's the Indian living his own life, his own way of living and thinking."

One of Brett's charming paintings depicts a tiny baby having its bath in the morning sunlight, the mother giving it a shower from a watering pot. Another is an ethereal painting of a woman in a white blanket with pale stripes. She is mounted on a white horse and holding her baby in front of her; a man leads the horse. All the colors are pale: "an early dawn with a huge setting moon, a pale apricot, the sky dull mauvish gray, with darker hills, and the pale trunks of aspens. It's beautiful but somewhat difficult owing to the horse. I am having the hell of a time with its shoulders, the anatomy balks me, but it's coming."

With many other simple pictures there came large canvasses depicting ceremonial scenes and dances like the Sundown Dance on San Geronimo eve. A row of dark-faced men swathed in bright-colored blankets look like a horizontal band of the complete color spectrum. They are dancing in a slow shuffle to the beat of a drum and gently waving above their heads the first branches of aspen to turn yellow. In the light of the setting sun everything shimmers, everything moves.

"I have watched trees dancing," Brett wrote me. "They dance before rain, did you know that? And their dance is like the Indian dancing. You remember when the men dance with the golden branches of trees during the San Geronimo Fiesta, and if you watch the rhythm that those small branches make as the men dance, that is also the rhythm of the trees dancing."

Her ceremonial paintings became larger, more complex, more mystically evocative. The Buffalo Dance with sixty-three men wearing great buffalo heads, and the Buffalo Chiefs dressed in white buckskins and carrying bows and arrows . . . two huge canvasses of the Deer Dance, masses of waving antlers . . . the Blessing of the Mares . . . the midsummer Women's Dance . . . the great Corn Dance at Santo Domingo Pueblo . . . the delicately beautiful Zia Corn Dance . . . the Relay Races at Taos . . . the Feather Dance.

The difficulties these great paintings posed is hard for a casual observer to understand. The Indians permitted no photography, no sketching, no note-taking of their ceremonial dances. It was necessary for Brett to memorize every detail. She was also aided by Trinidad, who as a young Pueblo boy had worked and danced up at the Lawrence ranch and became her lifelong friend. He loved her paintings, helped to authenticate details. In order to protect him, she pretended that her paintings came to her in dreams.

Trinidad also told her legends, folk tales of the past, which she painted. One of them is about a young Pawnee warrior from the Great Plains who has been captured while trying to raid horses. There he stands in a circle of Taos warriors in war paint, holding their bows and arrows. The Pawnee gives a shrill death cry and begins to dance. Admiring his courage, the warriors silently watch him. Then they begin to shoot arrows into him, until one at last pierces his heart, and he falls. "But think of it," wrote Brett, "think of the courage, the beauty of this man dancing to his death. I have him, with a great rainbow behind him, dancing in the cornfield, through the golden stubble. This beautiful figure dancing, naked and war-painted, with his peculiar haircut. Lovely. A hell of a lot of work, tho."

Another painting, the *Golden Men,* evokes the secret ceremony held up at sacred Blue Lake during the annual pilgrimage. No white man ever has witnessed this ceremony; all trails up the mountains are carefully guarded during the pilgrimage. Nor did Trinidad describe it. But what he guardedly said about it stirred Brett's imagination, and she conceived it as a Sun Circle of Golden Men—the Yellow Indian again.

She developed a passion for moons. "New Moons, Full Moons, and the last painting is beautiful, it's a huge New Moon setting in a sunset, and before it are three Indians singing to the Moon. They look like strange birds, their backs to us, with the long flowing feathers of their war bonnets hanging down their backs. It has that strange Indian quality of peace and reverence for the world the Indian still has."

As I wrote in an early book named *Masked Gods,* Brett is the only painter I know who has caught the mystical component of Indian character. And it is this series of ceremonial paintings that finally established her reputation. They hang today on the walls of major galleries, museums, and private collectors: Tate Gallery, London; National Portrait Gallery, London; Metropolitan Museum of New York; Boyer Gallery, Philadelphia; Denver Art Museum; Dallas Museum of Fine Arts; and dozens of others. There will be no more like them; for with the attrition of traditional Indian values by modern technology and commercialization, the rituals and dances are disappearing, and the Indians themselves are changing. As Brett said, "We will pass off the scene, but we have seen the heyday of Indian dancing." And that heyday is framed in her gorgeous paintings.

It was natural, perhaps, that no one knew what to make of them at the time. They were too nebulous, too unusual, too colorful, too big. There was only one notable gallery in town, and it was largely monopolized by other professional painters with established reputations. "The Museums have no money," Brett complained, "and the Foundations don't know a real Indian from a Cigar Store Indian, and it makes one sick." So she kept turning out her marvelous little "potboilers," which did sell, but were often criticized for being only decorative. "People don't know how to look at paintings, how to make them part of themselves," she wrote. "They should hang them in their bedrooms where they can watch the light, the moods of the day and night. Instead of that, they hang them over a dining room mantelpiece and never get to know them. Then suffer from the criticism of friends and guests. But a painting should be a personal experience a secret experience, like a tree against the sky outside one's window."

The Brett was flat broke again. Her one-room studio was running down: the wall crumbling, the roof still leaking, the heater still giving trouble. At times she felt it was "too tough for me, I just can't go on." But with her indomitable British spunk she gave vent to an expression of her independence of spirit.

> I am sure, as you say, that New York is dying. I would rather see New York dying than many other places coming to life. Death to me is very fascinating. There comes a refinement to a thing which is giving up its ghost, whereas the other is liable to be gross and vulgar and brutal. It seems to me that to deny it, to put such a consuming faith in the other, is to cut your being in two. As a matter of fact, and this may seem to you a frightful confession, but this new world in the making—this Brave New World—fills me with disgust and boredom. The era of the common man simply means the era of the stupid man, because I'm never impressed by anything which is common. I have never cared for the poor as such. I have only liked them individually and when they have been humble. In their humility they become superior beings. As soon as they take on airs, I despise them. It seems to me this whole war is a kind of triumph of materialistic progress. We are fighting Nazism purely in the spirit of survival, because we are not fighting mate-

> rialism. Our future world will still become a battle between trade unions fighting for higher wages and capitalists fighting for bigger profits, and everything else is squeezed in between. As for us writers and artists, our only hope is to try to create our own heroes out of our own imagination, if we have any. They will call it escapism, but there is no more degrading escapism than the one in which the artist deliberately and even frantically plunges into the crowd, and no surer way to accomplish the complete obliteration of your immortal soul, if you have one. No, I think the artist has no choice but to stand on a very high pinnacle.

There came a break in Brett's luck, another tiff with Mabel to top off her discomforts in the run-down Studio. It was quite clear she had to move, and a number of her friends decided she should have a house of her own. Frieda donated a piece of land off the highway about four miles north of town. Eleanora Kissel, a well-to-do painter, organized a raffle for her, adding to the money Brett could raise. And a newcomer, Joe Vanderbilt, constructed a small house with the help of her Indian friends.

How exhilarating were the months when the walls went up, the roof was put on! But how depressing they were, too. For between Joe, a sensitive man, and herself there developed a close friendship. It was marred by his jealous wife, Ollie, whom Brett regarded as an upstart, cruel, and vulgar snob. Ollie created scene after scene and malicious gossip in town. Brett wrote me,

> So I'm in the soup up to my ears, and the only thing that hurts me is in hurting Joe, for in that way I also hurt my own heart, so I am doing just absolutely nothing. But somehow it becomes boring, damned BORING. It's better, tho this may make you howl, to be a man's mistress than to have all this plaguey business with the wife. If I had been thirty years younger, at a reasonable, seasonable age, that is what I would have done, but ye Gods, it's all too late for that kind of escapade. Friendship with a man, such as the kind of friendships I have always had, have always ended in this same mess. But Lawrence never believed tales about me, never, and that is the difference between him and Joe. Lawrence of course was such a terrific person you can't compare them. He was like a flash of light, Joe is a very good man, simple, honest, good, but no flash of light.

Throughout her life Brett had developed crushes, strong, emotional attachments to one man after another: her father, Reggie; Chinese Gordon; John Middleton Murry, Katherine Mansfield's husband; Stokowski; Lawrence. That she was not a naive virgin, as popularly believed, is revealed in John Manchester's biographical sketch of her in the reprint of her book. One cannot include Joe Vanderbilt among her possible affairs; nevertheless, her friendship with him was close and crucial. As she wrote me,

I think I have missed a lot by not having the experience [of marriage]. It is a natural part of living and as such one should experience it. I feel a blank in my life, in that way. My experiences with men have never been successful, never been happy ones, simply because of a default in me. I am what I read in books as "cold," whatever is precisely meant by that, but I have a sort of hunch that is what is wrong. I have been too bullied by men to ever warm up to them, tho I get crushes. But always at the final issue my old fear returns and the crush ends in panic and disaster. Queer, isn't it? Because I think I could have made a very good wife!!!

This bothered her. She wrote again:

Friendships, marriages, triangles, just pile up the complications. The pattern here I have been through twice before. It all resolves down to this. What is love? What is friendship? They are both entangled, intermixed. There can be no friendship without love, but I am a queer bird, and I have the unholy fear, and that is contained in one small word, MY or MINE, I dread worse than the plague. The possessive spirit, to be possessed, or worse still to possess another, seems to me horrible beyond words. So my love finally comes to rest, knowing that I love the loveliness of the other, in itself the true path of love. . . . There is an enduring friendship between us, and when it comes to this problem of being the third party I do my best not to be the bug in the carpet. Two people living in disunity, inharmo-

> niously, always seek a buffer. Lawrence did, and in those days I was more enthusiastic than wise!! Today I am more wise than enthusiastic. . . . If I were twenty years younger I would have yanked him away from her, but I am older than he is, so I do nothing.

Things quieted down when the house was finished in the winter of 1946. The Vanderbilts left Taos, and Brett settled into her new home. "I am Lord of all I survey! I have my piece of land, my Own House, the mountains standing by, peace and quietness. I can start the gasoline engine and hope to understand the hot water heater. I love coming back in the evenings, lighting the fire in my bedroom, and the lamps, and getting into the most comfy bed I have had for twenty years, and reading my murder. I have all my paints arranged and ready, and I'm going to start painting. So much to do, I hardly know where to begin. Big Ceremonials, strange Indian tales, so many moods of sky and mountain."

So now with the help of her Protector, the mighty BEING who came to her in dreams and told her what to do, Brett entered the period of her greatest productivity.

Slowly her paintings began to sell. *The Blessing of the Mares* for $350, the *Relay Race,* and the *Navajo Woman and Children.* During the last month of the 1956 season the Stables Gallery sold $1,800 worth of her paintings. Some of them were sold for monthly payments as low as $10, bringing her an income of about $100 a month. A Mrs.

Porter commissioned a painting of Lawrence, Mabel, Frieda, and herself, paying $25 a month for a year. Also the National Portrait Gallery in London began to negotiate for a painting of Lawrence, the only ones in existence being Brett's.

After this turn of her fortunes, she bought a car to replace her decrepit old one. It was a DREAM OF BEAUTY, a PRIMROSE YELLOW STATION WAGON, which had been driven only nineteen thousand miles but looked like new, and cost $1,900. How she managed to get it "was a miracle, just one of those things." The Higher Powers worked it out through three businessmen in town: Frenchie, the owner of a restaurant; Brandenburg, the banker; and Harper, the local Ford dealer. They arranged for her to buy it for a $323 down payment and $50 a month.

What a difference a reliable car made in her life. She could drive on the icy roads of winter without fear of constant breakdowns. It was roomy enough to carry big paintings for showings in Santa Fe. In it she could sit at the Pueblo to watch the dances. And perhaps more important, she could take Indian boys fishing up the canyons. Brett was an accomplished fisherwoman, the best in Taos Valley, always bringing home her limit.

The Indian boys with her would laboriously follow the turbulent white-water stream up a steep canyon, jumping over fallen trees and climbing around boulders, casting and casting in quiet pools. Brett meanwhile would remain with her car at the mouth of the canyon. She would sketch or paint, meditate, doze a bit, throw her line into the water. And when the boys returned late in the afternoon, worn out, with a few fish, Brett would show them her long string of "trouties." She never cooked and ate them herself but would distribute her catch to neighbors.

This was her life: painting, sketching, and becoming more and more introspectively familiar with the mysterious, mystical Otherworld. How swiftly the years passed by. Her voluminous letters to me of twenty years ceased in 1960 when I settled permanently in my own home on the mountain slope above Arroyo Seco, ten miles from Taos. Brett's house I passed by every day, and I stopped in to visit her frequently. What a mess it was! She kept successive dogs—Reggie, Sweetie Pie, and others—whose great gnawed bones littered the floor. A new painting was always on the easel, and esoteric books filled her shelves.

Frieda died, and her new husband, Angelino Ravagli, left for his old home in Italy. Mabel and Tony died, and other old friends in Taos. Then in 1963 a new and major influence entered Brett's life in the person of John Manchester, "the Lawrence of her later years." He was a man of many talents: the inventor of a new stove; gifted designer, interior decorator, and architect; writer; and painter. Immediately he recognized the enduring values in Brett's art. He bought a small house near her and remodeled it into a large building that served as his own home and the Manchester Gallery. Here he took over the exclusive showing of Brett's paintings.

High-priced as they were now, they did not have ready buyers. Very little money was sent Brett from her family in England. She was getting more deaf despite new hearing aids; and, with steadily failing eyesight, it was getting more difficult to paint. She was nearing her eightieth birthday, and "this getting old was a bore, a DAMNED BORE."

Manchester took her in hand with her paintings. He managed her affairs, cooked dinner for her every night, and gave frequent parties for her. One of the most memorable was a reception and a showing of her work never before presented to the public, on her eighty-eighth birthday, November 10, 1971. Another occasion came on March 31, 1974, celebrating her fifty years of painting in New Mexico. Jamison Galleries in Santa Fe gave an exhibition of her paintings; and at the second of the Manchester Galleries in Taos an autograph party marked publication of a new edition of her book, *Lawrence and Brett, a Friendship,* with new material written by Manchester.

Throughout these affairs Brett was affable and cheerful, enjoying her glass of brandy. She welcomed the constant stream of visitors who came to photograph and interview her or to plague her with silly questions about Lawrence. Her one vociferous denouncement was directed against the police authorities who refused to renew her driving license, forcing her to give up her car. Although it was becoming difficult for her to walk, she kept threatening to buy a bicycle. What an indomitable spirit she had!

But more and more she became engrossed in the other-dimensional world she had always glimpsed since childhood. This mystical spirit world was as real to her as the world of mountain, mesa, and desert she saw outside her window, and she familiarly referred to it as the "Upstairs."

What held her from escaping into it, as she wanted to, was her close relationship with John Manchester. There seems little doubt that she transferred to him the deep feelings she had had for other men in the past. He embodied for her the images of father, lover, husband, and son. This attachment grew more compulsive when she was forced to give up painting and was confined to a wheelchair. Manchester engaged a woman companion to live in the house and take care of her. Some time later, when the two women did not get along, he brought in another. Both, I thought, were loyal, forebearing, and hardworking, for it was no picnic to dress and bathe and cook for an aging woman, nor was it pleasant for Brett to have another woman in the house after living alone all her life.

Manchester was caught in the middle of their frequent bickering. When he did not side with her, Brett became angry; when he failed to visit her every day, she grew moody and depressed. Her emotional demands on him drained his nervous energy, and he became ill. To add to his worries, he was having financial troubles of his own. It was necessary to close his second, small gallery in town, and his large house was too expensive to maintain. There was only one way out of this bad situation: to sell his house and gallery and move elsewhere.

The prospect threw Brett into a mounting turmoil. Every time I stopped to see her, her frantic questions were repeated. "Do you think John will really sell his house? Is he going to move away? Where will he go? When?" Emotionally dependent upon him completely, she could not bear the thought of losing him.

How little we know of the devils and fears that lurk unseen in the depths of our unconscious selves! For now the fear that she had once confessed to me leapt out with naked cruelty—"the unholy fear contained in one small word, MY or MINE, I dread worse than the plague. The possessive spirit, to be possessed, or worse still to possess another, seems to me horrible beyond words."

She said, she wanted, she truly believed it would be best for Manchester to sell his large house and move to another town where he could use his talents and find new friends. But unconsciously she could not let him go. The Otherworld kept beckoning her; she wanted death to release her into a greater, truer life of the spirit. Yet she was held back by her possessive grip on Manchester, the last straw to worldly life she clutched so desperately.

Brett was never a moaner or whiner. Spunky to the core, she sat uncomplaining in her wheelchair, the sunlight making a halo of her rumpled white hair and a mosaic of her wrinkled face. She watched the changing colors on the Sacred Mountain, the flights of birds and butterflies, and from her bed at night the slow wheeling of the stars above. All the entities of nature were as alive and meaningful to her as to the Indians. She talked of what it might be like Upstairs, how wonderful it would be. Just the same, she thought it would be delightful to come back to Earth on a short visit to see what had happened to the pueblo, the whole world, during her absence.

Underneath raged the conflict within her, which always surfaced for me, a trusted friend of nearly forty years. How agonizing was this last battle between worldly life with Manchester and a greater life of the spirit beyond death.

It seemed to me then that this tragic conflict would be resolved only by Manchester's departure. Only then would Brett be finally released from her fatal attachment.

In 1977 Manchester finally sold his house, and on July 27 transported all his furniture and Brett's paintings to Las Vegas, Nevada. Here he bought a new house and was soon established as a designer and interior decorator. Exactly one month later, on August 27, Brett died peacefully in the Taos hospital, to which she had been taken the night before. She would have been ninety-four years old on November 10.

It is impossible for me, of course, to append a tidy epitaph to her passing. Nor can I render tribute to our close friendship of forty years. Brett was an indomitable, forceful character. She existed as an original in her own right, without being pinned down like a butterfly by the

Lawrence legend. Her rambling letters are a literary record of both her early struggles for recognition as a painter and a crucial period of development of the town of Taos.

As a painter she looms uniquely alone among the hundreds of artists who since the turn of the century have established Taos's reputation as an art center. One cannot compare her to the other painters whom I regard as its most distinctive. Her work was not sparse of line and well controlled like the evocative landscapes of Dasburg, who helped to introduce modern art to America. She took no pains, as did Gaspard, to render in sensual detail the texture, design, and color of her subjects' dress and surroundings. Unlike Fechin, Brett was not a painter of realistic portraits, nor did she possess his compassionate vision of earthy humanness and his superb draftsmanship. She was never able to paint the feet of a horse.

None of this mattered to Brett. Always her objective was "to lay a finger on the hidden life." The life that lay hidden behind the objective realities of everything she saw—rainbows, flowers, fishes, birds and animals, bomber planes, angels, and Indian legends and ceremonials she had never witnessed. The pulse of life itself, that is what she had her finger on. And that is what gave her paintings, even her small "potboilers," movement and beauty, joy and love, and everlasting wonder.

It is this apperception of the Otherworld that contributes a new dimension to Brett's paintings. That it coincides with the mystical Indian view has resulted in a unique body of work, for traditional Indian life has passed its heyday, as Brett noted. But her pictorial record of it will always remind us who have never known Indians of that spiritual essence common to us all, which is forever immune to the worldly encroachments of the changing aspects of modern society.

7
THE HOUSE OF FECHIN

The first painting by Nicolai Fechin I saw was in Ralph Meyers's trading post. It was a small oil of a burro, a "Pikes Peak Canary." As a boy in Cripple Creek, I had seen hundreds of them patiently dragging cars of ore out of mine tunnels. They were everywhere throughout Mexico, and a dozen of them loaded with firewood still plodded through the streets of Taos. Fechin's small painting struck a sympathetic chord in my heart. It seemed an intimate portrait of the meek little beast of burden that had carried all mankind and its civilizations throughout history.

Who was the man who had painted it?

I then met the painter's divorced wife, Alexandra Fechin, familiarly known as Tinka, an abbreviation of Katinka. A small, nervously alert woman with a strong Russian accent, she lived alone in their big house not far from the plaza. After we became friends, she invited me to tea and showed me the exquisite wood carvings Fechin had made, as well as his luminous paintings on the walls. How proud of him she was! "A great artist he is! Everything he touches comes alive!" she said, laying her hand on a smooth lintel. "See. Hand-rubbed!" Pointing out a full-figure painting of herself and several small portraits of her daughter, Eya, her voice seemed impacted with the strength of love. Gradually she related the Fechins' dramatic life in Russia, and Nicolai Fechin began to emerge from his work.

He was born in Kazan in 1881. The son of a talented wood carver and icon maker, he followed his father's profession. When the Art School of Kazan opened, offering a six-year course, Fechin was enrolled at the age of nineteen. Completing the course, he passed the examinations for admission into the great Imperial Academy of Art in St. Petersburg.

There was then nothing like it in the world. The academy was under the supervision of the Ministry of the Imperial Court of Czar Nicholas, and its purpose was to develop art throughout all Russia. Only the most talented applicants were selected. All their expenses were defrayed, but every half-year their work was graded. During the last year each student was required to paint a picture for competition. The exhibition of these competitive paintings was a great occasion attended by prominent visitors, officials of the academy, and often by the czar himself. Prizes were given, the coveted degree of "artist," and traveling scholarships.

Fechin worked hard. For his examination in anatomy alone he made more than three hundred drawings to win the highest grade. During the summers he made several trips: to visit his uncle at Kushniya in the wild country of the pagan Cheremis tribes, to their native village of Lipsha, and up the Yenisei River into Siberia. In 1909 his painting for the final competitive exhibition won him his official degree of artist and a traveling scholarship through Europe.

With high heart he traveled through Italy, Austria, Germany, and France. But in Paris, the mecca of all artists, he became homesick for his dark Slavic forests and native villages. He fled back to Kazan where he was appointed a teacher in the art school and given a private studio.

Success followed him. Invitations to show in exhibitions held throughout Europe began to come. He received a gold medal in the International Exhibition at Munich for one of his paintings, and his work appeared in America at the International Exhibition held by the Carnegie Institute in Pittsburgh. Among such distinguished contemporaries as Claude Monet, Camille Pisarro, Gaston Latouche, and John Sargent, he was greeted with acclaim as a "*moujik* in art," the "Russian Dareist," and "Tartar painter."

In 1913 he married Alexandra Belkovitch, the young daughter of the founder of the Art School of Kazan. She gave birth to their only daughter, Eya. But peace did not last.

World War I came, then the Bolshevik revolution, which destroyed the imperial order of the czar. Fechin moved his family to Vasilievo in the forest along the Volga River. Years later in her charming book of memoirs, *March of the Past,* Tinka recounted their frugal life with their faithful cow, Krasavka.

In 1919 famine and typhoid reached their crest on the tide of poverty and starvation. Fortunately, there arrived members of the American Relief Administration. Also a letter from W. S. Stimmel, the Pittsburgh art collector, urged Fechin to come to America.

Worn out, Fechin decided to leave his homeland. Immigration papers arrived and finally permission from government authorities to leave Russia. At last, in 1923, and as second-class ship passengers, the Fechins saw rising the fantastic skyline of New York.

Settled in a large studio apartment overlooking Central Park, Fechin began work at once. Commissions for portraits began to come in: from Lillian Gish, the movie star; Willa Cather, the novelist; W. L. Clark, founder of the Grand Central Gallery; John Burnham, son of the noted New York architect; and Ralph Van Vechten of Chicago. In 1924 Fechin was awarded the Proctor Prize at the National Academy of Design, and in 1926 he received a medal of award at the International Exposition in Philadelphia.

As in Europe, the city palled; his peasant yearning for the countryside reasserted itself. He first sought relief in Pennsylvania. The next summer, wealthy John Burnham took the Fechins to California as his guests. The third year

Nicolai Fechin

Fechin went to Taos, New Mexico, upon the urging of John Young-Hunter, another painter who lived across the street from him in New York. Here Mabel Luhan provided the Fechins with a house and introduced them to a small group of notable painters who were making the village famous as an art center. Back in New York, Fechin became seriously ill and was advised to leave the city. So in 1927 he moved his family to Taos.

From the first, Fechin felt at home. Perhaps the vast sage-green desert reminded him of the steppes of Russia and the high pine slopes of the Sangre de Cristo Mountains of the forests along the Volga. In the Pueblo Indians he found a reminder of his native Cheremis, Chiuvash, and Mordva tribes; and the simple Spanish farmers seemed much like Russian peasants.

Skillfully blending Russian, Spanish, and Pueblo architectural features, he designed and built a large two-story house on a home site of seven acres. In back of it he then built his own commodious studio, a swimming pool, and servant quarters. Forty-six years old, he now began his period of greatest productivity as a mature artist. All his feelings and faculties came into full play.

The period lasted scarcely six years. Fechin and Tinka were divorced in 1933. Eya allied herself with her father and accompanied him to New York and then to Los Angeles. Heartsick and lonely, he traveled through Mexico with four students. In 1938 he went to the Orient with Milan Rupert, a collector and dealer of Oriental art. They sailed on a Japanese freighter to Japan, then on a Dutch freighter to Java and Bali. Already the fingers of Japanese domination were closing over the archipelago, and under the clouds of World War II Fechin returned to Los Angeles.

The following summer of 1939, I finally met him while walking through his back pasture. He was watching a Spanish workman trim the hooves of Eya's filly. Of medium build, with high cheekbones suggesting a Tartar ancestry, protruding forehead, wide mouth, and quick eyes, there was no doubt who he was. I was not prepared to meet so unexpectedly such a famous man. Unassuming and friendly, he invited me back to his studio, where he gave me a cup of tea with a spot of rum in it. Our several meetings afterward founded our long friendship.

I also met Eya, who was staying with her mother in the large house, and went riding with her. She explained that she and Fechin were comfortably settled with Dane Rudhyar and his wife, Malya, in a large house in La Crescenta above the smoke and fog of Los Angeles, and they had returned to Taos only for a few days so Fechin could pick up some of his belongings. The divorce settlement, she said, had provided that Tinka have ownership of the house and Fechin retain his studio.

This surprised me, for I felt that Fechin had not wanted the divorce and rather hoped for a reconciliation. The attitudes of Tinka and Eya clearly showed this was impossible. Contrary to the deep pride and feeling for Fechin that Tinka had shown me earlier, she was now vociferously resentful of his presence. "I can't walk out of the house without seeing him! Why did he come to bother me so?" And Eya's relationship to Tinka just as clearly betrayed a deep-rooted antagonism against her mother as well as idealism for her father. What a mysterious tangle of emotions in these three friends whom I liked!

Fechin and Eya returned to Los Angeles, leaving Tinka alone in the big, empty house.

One could sympathize with her, too. Her years of hardship during the Bolshevik revolution and the difficulties of beginning a new life in America must have been most trying. The differences in character between her and Fechin could not have made things easier. Fechin was older, taciturn, unsocial, and wholly absorbed in his work. Tinka lacked the companionship and gaiety her own nature craved.

Having no car, she welcomed every opportunity to go driving with her few friends and to attend picnics. During fiestas she was the life of all gatherings as she danced the Beer-Barrel Polka, the *raspa* and *varsovianna* with untiring abandon. Periodically, she developed crushes on younger men, many of them homosexuals. She enjoyed their companionship and the attention they showed her until they became frightened of being deeply involved and ignored her. Then she pursued them, waiting at their parked cars until they showed up, hanging notes on their locked doors. These pursuits reduced her invitations to homes whose hostesses feared that the presence of Tinka and her crushes might result in upsetting scenes.

Nevertheless, being a stable friend, I enjoyed her company and the many stories she told me about Fechin. When they first arrived in New York, Tinka had learned English much more quickly than Fechin and was a great help to him while he painted portraits. He never said a word, depending upon her to instruct the sitter how to pose and to make small talk so the subject would not become nervous.

One of his commissions was a portrait of Commodore Oliver Perry for a Commodore Perry Hotel. Perry, of course, was the historic naval hero of "We have met the enemy and they are ours" fame. Fechin was disgruntled, for he always liked to paint from life. "How can I paint a dead man? Who was he? What did he look like?" Tinka thumbed through history books and rented a naval uniform of the period. In this she dressed and posed for Fechin. Needless to say, Fechin did not regard the portrait as among his best.

My favorite painting in the house was of eggs cooking in a frying pan. One could not properly call it a still life. You could see the grease sizzling in the pan, a wisp of smoke rising, air bubbles forming around the edges. It had been painted in Vasilievo during the revolution when Tinka had been dreaming of fresh eggs. "Never mind!" said Fechin. "I'll paint a picture of eggs for you to look at while you're eating potatoes!" He had no canvass left, so he painted the picture on paper. It was one of the few they brought with them to America, duly stamped by customs officials. In Taos, they backed it with canvass and hung it in the dining room.

Many years later it and a smaller canvass were mysteriously stolen from the unoccupied house. Evidently the thief knew how to get in the back door, passing by other paintings to remove only these two. The egg picture was then valued at about $20,000, although it was too precious to Tinka to set a price upon it; the other was of lesser value. The egg painting was not insured and could not easily be sold, so well was it known. It has never been recovered.

That winter I spent in Los Angeles and resumed my friendship with Fechin and Eya, who were living with Dane Rudhyar and Malya in La Crescenta. An older man, Rudhyar was an acclaimed astrologer, amateur pianist and composer, painter, and writer of philosophic books. Erudite and pedantic, he seemed to me rather dull.

Fechin was invited by Madame Ganna Walska for lunch with her in Santa Barbara one Sunday, and he asked me to accompany him. We stayed overnight in the lovely little town of Ojai. Getting up early, we listened to doves and quail in the chaparral and took a long walk before breakfast. What a delight it was for Fechin to get out into the countryside!

During our drive to Santa Barbara, Fechin eagerly anticipated a quiet lunch and a discussion of his paintings with the well-known and wealthy Madame Walska. He hoped she would buy one of his paintings.

Ganna Walska's name had been familiar to me during my boyhood. An extremely wealthy Polish woman, she had been married several times. Her husband at the time had bought at the mouth of Queen's Canyon near Colorado Springs the great manor house of Glen Eyrie, which General William J. Palmer had built as a replica of the Duke of Marlborough's Tudor castle in England. It comprised sixty-seven rooms, twenty bathrooms, and a hall big enough to seat three hundred people. It was surrounded by a moat across which we boys on moonlight nights would throw stones into the windows of the great castle. Madame Walska's husband, a furniture manufacturer in Grand Rapids, Michigan, had brought her as a bride to occupy this great edifice. We heard that he immediately ordered all the massive hand-carved furniture replaced with modern Grand Rapids furniture. Apparently, she was a shrewd businesswoman. According to reports, she later was associated with the company manufacturing the popular Black Narcissus perfume. One could obtain a squirt of it by putting a coin in a machine in any public washroom and pushing a button.

Her present estate in Santa Barbara was not as impressive, but it was magnificent. When we arrived for our quiet lunch, it was only to discover throngs of people strolling across the vast lawns and through the immense house. Madame Walska we could not find, but soon there sounded the blast of a long Tibetan trumpet calling us to attention. Gathering before an improvised podium, we listened to her explain the reason for the lunch. Madame Walska had become fascinated with a young man, Theos Bernard, who had studied occult lore in the monasteries of Tibet, had written the popular book *Penthouse of the Gods,* and had come to America to start a school of Tibetan Buddhist teachings. It was Madame Walska's intention to provide suitable quarters for it on her vast estate, and she offered to us all the opportunity of contributing money to this project.

Another blast from the Tibetan trumpet summoned us to lunch. There were three types of lunches served in different locations: Tibetan, East Indian, and American. Fechin and I wandered from one to another. We met Madame Walska briefly to thank her; but no mention was made of Fechin's paintings, and completely disillusioned we drove back to Los Angeles.

A few days later, Fechin asked me to sit for a charcoal sketch. It was disconcerting to watch him studying me from all angles, then setting the pose—head down and looking up sideways at him. Abruptly, he attacked the easel.

Tinka had told me this was his usual approach. He would stand off from his easel, minute after minute, studying his subject with the cold, detached stare of a surgeon. Then, suddenly, he would lunge at the canvass with his brush.

"Why do you paint like this?" one of his sitters had gasped.

"A brush is a painter's only weapon," Fechin had answered brusquely. "With it he must attack the canvass without hesitation. He is the boss, not his material."

That morning Fechin threw down his charcoal after working for some time. "That wasn't a natural pose for you, or you wouldn't have kept moving. Come back tomorrow."

Next day I returned for another pose, looking straight ahead. It was very tiresome, but I felt guilty about having fidgeted the day before. Fechin worked swiftly and decisively. The paper he always used was imported from China, light beige in color, thin in weight, but with an irregular surface or texture that accentuated his charcoal strokes. When he finished the drawing, he jerked it off the easel and stood it up against the wall. Then he brought out a new paper and swiftly sketched another portrait. Neither one of them did I see until several years later.

I began to know him better. He was as sparse of speech as of line. He preferred to paint and draw simple people, loved the outdoors and picnics. He abhorred cocktail parties and regarded nightclubs as first-rate places for fourth-rate people. Confronting a picture-postcard sunset, he looked at the stark outline of an old gnarled tree. Caught in a crowd, he followed the wrinkled face of age and suffering. He neither smoked nor drank. He relied mainly on the three primary colors, which he applied one upon the other instead of mixing them; and his diet was as simple as his palette. He always painted from life and drove his car at breakneck speed through the crowded streets.

Rudhyar divorced his wife and married Eya, and they moved to Colorado Springs. Fechin moved into a small Los Angeles apartment and usually ate dinner at the Onstine Cafeteria on Vine Street. I met him there one evening shortly before Pearl Harbor and the entrance of the United States into World War II. It was necessary to tell him that the publishers of my novel *The Man Who Killed the Deer* had rejected the reproduction of one of his paintings for the cover jacket. It was the only oil he had ever made of a Pueblo Indian ceremonial, a beautiful painting that I loved. Fechin was greatly disappointed, for he had hoped its reproduction would stimulate popular interest in his work. His fame had been established in the art world, but he was not well known enough to the general public to ensure a steady sale of his paintings. He hoped now to publish some time a book containing reproductions of his paintings, a brief biography, and his notes on art. Perhaps, he thought, I might help him with it. After dinner we went to a movie which neither of us liked.

I then entered the army and did not see him for some time.

My service in the army was brief. I was discharged at the request of the Office of Inter-American Affairs in Washington, D.C., in order to prepare briefs and propaganda analyses. After D-Day, I was released from full-time work although I was on call as a consultant.

January 1946 opened a busy year. I had managed to complete the manuscript for a new book, *The Colorado*, which Rinehart and Company was to bring out in its Rivers of America Series and which I wanted Fechin to illustrate. Fechin too had found a publisher for his book and asked me to write the biographical text. Fortunately, I was called to Los Angeles to discuss a movie assignment; and with these two projects in mind, I called on Fechin.

Rinehart had consented to use for *The Colorado*'s cover jacket a full-color reproduction of Fechin's painting of an Indian ceremonial—the same painting the publisher had refused to use for *The Man Who Killed the Deer* a few years before. Fechin was delighted. I then presumptuously asked him to do five charcoal sketches illustrating the different geological levels of the great stepped Colorado Pyramid, as I perceived it, and also a title-page drawing of an Indian pueblo rising to a peak through five levels.

Fechin, always practical and representational, balked. "Pueblos may be multistoried, but they don't reach a peak."

"Do it anyway!" I insisted. "Just to get the idea over."

Fechin did it: a beautiful charcoal like the other five. Rinehart was enthusiastic, suggesting he send others.

Hence, Fechin sent a dozen more drawings and lithographs to illustrate my book. He was immensely pleased by their acceptance. This was the first book he had ever illustrated, and he hoped it would bring more popular appreciation of his work.

He also had found a publisher for his own book, which would contain twelve full-color reproductions of his selected paintings, fifty black-and-white reproductions, and an autobiographical text that he had written and wanted me to rewrite. The publisher was to be Merle Armitage, a character in the art world. He was an entrepreneur who imported ballet groups and managed theatrical tours; a gourmet cook; an art connoisseur; and a publisher of books. Usually he met his publishing expenses by serving as a "vanity press"—either finding a sponsor or requiring the author to pay for publication. As it turned out, Armitage requested Fechin to pay $10,000 to produce one thousand copies, and the deal was called off.

Fechin later wrote me about a new project. One of his art students in Los Angeles who was in the advertising business, a man named Northridge, was undertaking to print a portfolio of sixteen Fechin drawings and lithographs. At Fechin's request I wrote for it a short text, which he approved; but Northridge wanted to write it himself. The portfolio came out with excellent reproductions, although Northridge's introduction was quite inept. The portfolio was priced at $15 and sold slowly. Today it sells for $1,000 or more, with individual prints bringing $100 or more.

Next spring we both suffered a severe disappointment. The full-color reproduction of Fechin's Indian painting for *The Colorado* was excellent, but we were shocked by the travesty made of his other work. His drawings, like all his work, were based on tone values. The reproductions took account only of line values. As in cheap newspaper work, large areas were routed out, leaving blank white spaces. None of his other drawings was accorded a full page as promised. They were instead inserted within the text in small sizes. It was unbelievably cheap work.

Fechin characteristically wrote me a single sentence very much to the point: "I am very surprised that the publisher would economize so much on the reproductions, and at the same time spend extra money to entirely spoil drawings on which I put so much time and care." He did not add that he had not charged Rinehart a cent for the use of his work.

His own long-envisioned book was still uppermost in his mind. He had reread my biographical sketch, finding it well written and needing only a few corrections and additions. He now asked me to write his biography the next time he was in Taos. The time came soon, for Eya wrote me from Colorado Springs that Fechin was planning to visit her and Rudhyar. On his way back to Los Angeles he intended to stop in Taos for a few weeks so he could work with me on his biography. She requested that I make Fechin's stay as pleasant as possible, without contributing to his nostalgia for Taos.

She also wrote Tinka. The prospect of Fechin's return threw Tinka into a turmoil. Her chief fear was that once he was back in his studio, he would want to stay. From this springboard she launched into the horrors of seeing him walking in the driveway, diving naked into the swimming pool, and of her being unable to sleep at night knowing that he was so close to the house, even though the doors were locked and bolted.

"He's a savage! He has no feelings at all!" She went on to relate that once a shot from next door tore through a window of the house. Tinka came running into the studio. "They're shooting at us!" Fechin did not look up. "Get out of here! Can't you see I'm working and can't be bothered? Go to the sheriff or somebody else!" The incident recalled another. One morning when she opened the studio door to tell him someone had come to see him, Fechin without a word jerked off the easel the canvass he was working on and hit her over the head with it.

Both of these incidents may have been greatly exaggerated. To me, Tinka's resentment against his presence seemed to echo the old adage of "methinks the lady doth protest too much." Nevertheless, the picture of Fechin hitting her over the head with his canvass somehow made me laugh. "Now, Tinka! You know a man doesn't want to be disturbed while he's working!"

"Pagh! You'll be just as bad! But you just keep him out of my sight!"

The strained relationship between them placed me in an awkward position. I was devoted to both of them and sensed a deep feeling between them that had never been resolved.

When Fechin arrived, we agreed to work in my room rather than in his studio in order to avoid any possible meetings with Tinka. I was living that summer in the big studio room above the garage in back of the Tony House. My studio was a great room with a huge picture window, a corner fireplace, and a wood-burning cookstove. There was no plumbing; I used an outdoor privy and bathed in the irrigation ditch behind it. The building, however, lay directly across the Mother Ditch separating the Fechins' seven acres from the reservation.

On the first morning of our talks I glimpsed Fechin coming through his apple orchard and back pasture. He was not hurrying, but his short, compact body swung forward with a simple directness and animal quickness of movement. As usual, he was bareheaded. He ducked through the barbed-wire fence, jumped the irrigation ditch, and climbed the wooden stairs outside.

Wasting no time in preliminaries, he merely thumped a loose window sill that he noticed immediately and looked up at the pine *vigas* overhead with their lattice work of aspen *lattias.*

"The ceiling is a little low for such a big room, no?"

He then lifted a straight-backed chair from its place beside my work table in the center of the room and set it in front of the big window. He sat down on it stiffly.

"You have posed for your portrait. Now I sit for mine. One hour, two. Ask me what you want."

Fechin was not joking. He was as simple, as direct as that.

So it began. Promptly at eight o'clock every morning he settled himself on the stiff chair to answer questions and relate more incidents for his biography. A slight breeze ruffled his thin, straight brown hair. The sun highlighted his wide forehead, high cheekbones, and wide mouth. Under the protruding ridge across his eyebrows, his quick eyes brightened. His dark face kept changing mood. He spoke softly.

Writing his biography should have been a cinch. I had his own autobiographical notes, numerous brochures, and clippings. I also had a copy of a letter Eya had written him, saying, "It is almost necessary for Frank to have some *more intimate* stories that can be worked into something colorful . . . some adventuresome, exciting, and *more intimate* episodes to work with." These would be his experiences during the revolution and in Siberia, travels in Europe, episodes of student life, and impressions of America.

Despite all this, I ran into trouble from the start. As I began rewriting and expanding the material, I included some of the entrancing stories Tinka had told me about him. But Eya disputed them as inaccurate or untrue, insisting that only she knew the true basis of the alleged incidents. It was quite true that since her parents' divorce she had been her father's companion and confidante. Yet I couldn't believe that Tinka's stories, especially of their years in Russia when Eya was a small child, were wholly imagined. My feeling grew that Eya wished to completely erase Tinka from Fechin's life and art.

Fechin himself was of little help. He stood in the way of his own biography. He wanted to rewalk through his life with the same simple directness that he walked through his pasture. Dates, the places he had lived and visited, the names of the persons he had known and painted. Statistical facts. No more.

"Look here, Mr. Fechin," I protested, "we don't want an obituary. We want a biography."

He loosened up enough to relate the trip he had made with a geologist and another friend up the Yenisei River in Siberia to a gold mine being developed by exiled prisoners. Their chief relaxation was watching the antics of bear cubs they had tamed and breaking wild Mongolian horses. This adventurous time he regarded as the most memorable of his life, and he recounted it well. Years later in America he visited Jim Williams, the noted Western cartoonist, on his K-4 ranch near Prescott, Arizona. He ate and rode horseback with the hands, intensely interested in watching them break some broncs. He compared the Siberian and American methods of breaking a horse to the saddle. Such stories were colorful and exciting, and they revealed his keen observations. But he was gun-shy of observation pointed at himself.

"Mr. Fechin! You're giving me a photograph. Any stenographer could snap it. I want a portrait!"

Still, every morning the paradox built up. Here was one of the greatest colorists of our time objecting to the slightest dab of literary color, a man whose art carried a powerful emotional impact. Yet he balked at revealing his own emotional responses to those persons, places, and events that had deeply influenced his life. A portrait artist whose discerning vision laid bare the soul of his subject, but who resisted the probing of his own character. It was not my wish, as I think he knew, to pry into the recesses of the heart where we all keep hidden those things most dear and sacred to us. At first puzzled by his deep-rooted aversion to revealing any intimate glimpses of himself, I began to understand him as a man who identified himself with his art, not with his own person.

But how, I wondered, could he be highlighted against the international backgrounds and emotional crises that had played so dominant a part in his life? We gave up our somewhat formal sittings and took walks together. How he loved the pine slopes and canyons of the Sangre de Cristos. I asked no questions, content to let him talk. He lost his shyness, remembered an incident, then another.

Often we went on picnics to Fechin's favorite spot up Hondo Canyon at the site of the abandoned old mining camp of Twining. It was a magnificent setting, a high, open meadow flanked by thick groves of slim, white-trunked aspens, and enclosed by towering forested mountains. The old mine lay high up a rocky slope. A mill and several log cabins rotted below. Fechin later wrote me of his "lasting memory" of one of these picnics, which "cleansed me of the depressing influence of big city life. For the first time in years I feel again like a human being."

Inevitably we ran into Leon Gaspard and had a short visit with him. He and Fechin were old friends, but there was no rapport between them; they were poles apart.

It always seemed strange to me that these two men had been brought to the little town of Taos by the same queer destiny. Gaspard, too, was a Russian and an artist who had gained fame in Europe. Despite these remarkable parallels in their lives, their irreconcilable differences threw Fechin into better perspective.

Fechin was shy, reticent, and aloof. Gaspard was outgoing and effusive; he loved cocktail parties, holding friends and visitors spellbound with his famous stories—stories that, as I have written elsewhere, were often highly exaggerated and untrue. Fechin loved simple, peasant peoples wherever he was: the Indians and Spanish villagers in Taos, the peasants in Russia, the peons in Mexico, the native peoples of Java and Bali. Gaspard was widely traveled, but restricted his trips to Asia and Europe. He had no feeling for Indian and Latin American peoples. A man of the world, he always took care to mention the names of the important persons he had met.

The characters of the two men were reflected in their work. Fechin was primarily a portrait artist. The few portraits Gaspard painted were usually full figures set against unique backgrounds. With his Jewish love of texture and Asiatic color sense, he rendered with exquisite detail their rich silks, brocades, and embroidery. His best canvasses were genre paintings of crowds in Russian squares, processions across Volga bridges, cavalcades riding through Mongolian forests. All these made for gorgeous depictions of the once barbaric Asia he had known, and which justly gained him fame.

I have already mentioned how savagely Fechin first attacked a canvass in order to master it. Gaspard, in contrast, carried on a leisurely manner of painting; and unlike Fechin, he often used pastels. How slowly and meticulously Gaspard worked! No sweeping broad brush strokes of paint, no dabs with thumb or palette knife. But a mark of the crayon that he rubbed out again and again, for the substitution of another color.

There is no standard by which one can compare two artists. Each must be accepted on his own grounds. Nor can any style or technique be regarded as exclusively right. In the wide spectrum of art, from primitive wood carvings to the most modern abstractions of contemporary art, there is room for all. They demand only the creativity of the workman who follows his own star and presents to us a new portion of the whole.

Mabel Luhan, of course, was eager to see Fechin; and I went with him to visit her. She served tea outside her Big House on the gazebo set across the irrigation ditch. Fechin kept staring at a small hilltop to the south. On the way home we walked over there. It was a beautiful location flanked by huge cottonwoods, overlooking the apple orchard and the smaller houses she had built.

"A good place for a house," Fechin said shortly, without further comment.

What he had in mind soon became obvious. Ever since he had become uprooted from this relatively unspoiled countryside chosen as his home in America, he had been pining for Taos. His return, as Eya had prophesied, had evoked his strong nostalgia. Obviously, Tinka would prevent him from ever occupying his own studio again. Hence, he wanted to buy Mabel's hilltop and build a new studio upon it. He had painted a large, striking portrait of her, which she admired. This he offered her in exchange for the land.

Why Mabel refused his offer was difficult to understand. Besides the Big House there were five small guest houses on her property. Fechin's portrait of her would have been an invaluable addition to her collection. But Fechin had given her an idea. Years later she built on the spot a large, modern two-story house into which she moved to spend her last years.

Thus ended Fechin's last hope of returning to live in Taos. How tragically sad was this last visit! Packing up all his belongings and turning over his studio to Tinka, he left for Los Angeles. With his departure ended another phase of his unfinished biography.

The large Fechin house was too expensive for Tinka to keep up, yet she refused to rent it and move into the studio. In 1950 there came a break for her and for me.

I had bought a small ranchito above the Spanish village of Arroyo Seco, ten miles above Taos. As the old adobe house did not yet have electricity and plumbing, I could not live in it during the winter. Tinka therefore rented me the studio and her back pasture, and I brought down my two horses and a ton of hay for them to stand at.

No wonder Fechin had loved his studio! I felt at home in it immediately. Beautifully constructed, exuding a curious Russian feel, it comprised a lofty room with a full-sized north window in front of which he had painted, an alcove bedroom, tiny kitchen and bathroom, and a small unused storeroom. I was always conscious of his presence, feeling that he would walk in any minute.

Things had picked up a little for Fechin in Los Angeles. His paintings still weren't selling widely, but a former woman student had bought several. Also, he taught in a school for a time. He then bought a large studio with living quarters in Santa Monica. He still had been unable to find a publisher for his longed-for book, "the seemingly eternal Fechin Problem," as Eya called it. The Bollingen Series and the American Artists Group in New York, to which I had written, were not interested; Fechin was not well known.

My query to Charles Allen, editor of the Stanford University Press, brought the answer that Fechin's book might be included in the press's Stanford Art Series if his work was approved and if Fechin would provide a partial subsidy. Fechin was delighted. He could raise the subsidy. He then sent Stanford a collection of color reproductions of his paintings, a folio of charcoal drawings, and an album of photographs. Stanford rejected the book because Fechin's work was "not the kind which would appeal to artists, art critics, art teachers, or students." Also "it was problematical whether Fechin would occupy an important place in the field of painting," Stanford being convinced that "Fechin has very little of value for the professional, whether he be a painter, critic, or student."

I then proposed that the University of New Mexico include Fechin's book in its New Mexico Artists Portfolio Series. They were interested and began preparing estimates of its cost. Fechin perked up, writing me, "I hope something works out. It would be very nice if the University of New Mexico Press prints some of my work. To tell the truth my art belongs to this country more than to any other."

Negotiations bogged down when a big, bluff, and aggressive man burst into my rented Fechin studio. He was Homer Britzman, who had attended my high school in Colorado Springs and was now head of an oil company in Los Angeles.

Britzman was a character. Years before, while scouting for oil in Montana, he had happened upon some paintings by the yet unknown Western artist Charles Russell. These he bought immediately and began hunting for others. Hearing of Trails End, the house Russell had built in Pasadena just before his death in Great Falls, Montana, he found that Russell's widow had recently died and the executor of the estate was putting the house and all its Russell paintings up for sale at auction. Britzman and another buyer agreed not to outbid each other but to draw lots for each painting. Britzman in this manner acquired some forty paintings, a collection that eventually sold for $140,000. By another lucky draw, he also got Trails End.

He then organized his Trails End Publishing Company, which published an expensive limited edition of reproductions of Russell paintings. With the available color plates, he then issued a cheaper trade edition. He also promoted a Russell spread in the colorful *Arizona Highways* magazine.

Meanwhile, he had become just as enamored with Fechin's work. Perhaps more so, for he had sold some Russell paintings in order to buy a few Fechin paintings. The purpose of his visit to me, he explained, was to promote

Fechin as he had Russell. To begin with, *Arizona Highways* had agreed to give Fechin a similar spread with eight full-color reproductions of his paintings, several sketches, and a text condensed from my long biographical sketch. I agreed. The Fechin spread finally appeared in the magazine's issue of February 1952. It was most impressive, reaching *Arizona Highway*'s 450,000 paid subscribers. Fechin's reputation was greatly extended, and my biographical sketch long remained the only available source on his life.

At the moment, however, Britzman was exploring the possibilities of finding a publisher for a complete Fechin book similar to his Russell book. I wrote the University of New Mexico Press, suggesting that if interested they could use the existing color plates to reduce the expense of publishing the book. The press approved publication provided that Fechin contribute $3,000 toward the expense of reproducing his paintings.

Now began a continuous exchange of letters between Fechin in Santa Monica, Britzman in Pasadena, Eya, then in New York, and the University of New Mexico Press in Albuquerque. Fechin insisted that the $3,000 subsidy be used only to reproduce the paintings belonging to the donor, while Britzman demanded that his own paintings be used, which would enhance their value. Arguments over copyrights and other matters came up. "Poor Nick just doesn't understand how much is involved in putting out a fine art book," Britzman wrote me.

The project finally blew up when the press cancelled publication because Fechin was not listed in the Art Index and *Who's Who in American Art,* and objected to Britzman's efforts to control the project for his personal benefit.

Britzman now proposed to publish an edition of 750 copies himself, providing Fechin two hundred copies as full payment and me fifty copies. The remaining five hundred copies he would retain for sale at $20 apiece to cover the $10,000 cost of publication. Eya's husband, Rudhyar, recommended Fechin's acceptance on astrological grounds.

Fechin rejected the proposal after inspecting a dummy of the proposed deluxe first edition; the paper, he said, could not take suitable reproduction of his paintings. Hence, he gave up hopes for publication of the book he had long desired. Three years later he died in his studio in Santa Monica.

It's not strange that his longed-for book never appeared during his lifetime. Though Fechin's work had received international acclaim, the interest in it was circumscribed by art circles. Commercial publishers declined to issue a book on his art because he was not widely known to the general public.

Art, too, has its gross aspect. It is Big Business. To be successful it relies on prestigious galleries and critics to promote its wares and to publicize the idiosyncracies, antics, and preposterous declarations of its artists. It is a big game played for big stakes with big names and big investments. Shy, taciturn Fechin was never a player in this game. He was devoted only to the aspirations of art itself.

Tinka in Taos was having tough sledding. Seldom cooking a full meal for herself, she would walk at noon to the lunchroom in the large Kachina Motel for her only meal of the day. The motel and the immense estate nearby were owned by Ed Lineberry and his wife, Duane Van Vechten of the wealthy Van Vechten family of Chicago, whom Fechin had previously met. Periodically, Tinka would give them a painting to pay for her meals, enabling them to acquire a collection of expensive paintings.

She related to me that one day, after selling an expensive painting to someone else, she walked into the bank. "Ah, Mrs. Fechin, you've come to see what can be done about the unpaid interest on your mortgage?" she was asked. "No!" she retorted pertly. "I'm paying it all off completely!" Then, she confided, she returned home and burst into tears.

The house kept deteriorating, so she finally moved into Fechin's studio. Then, raising some more money, she hired a Spanish workman and set to work repairing the roof. Up at dawn and working until sunset, she carried up a ladder buckets of adobe, tar, tools, and rolls of tarpaper to the workman on top. Many nights she fell into bed after a cup of tea.

Eya had divorced Rudhyar and married a man named Branham, by whom she had a daughter usually referred to as Fechin's granddaughter. Fechin's death was timely for Eya and her husband. Neither had a job or income. They moved into Fechin's big studio and assumed ownership of the great backlog of paintings, which he had left them.

Soon they came to visit Tinka in Taos, offering to take ownership of the house, relieving her of the expense of taking care of it but allowing her to live in it. Tinka was still indignant when she told me of her refusal. "What do you mean coming here with such an idea!" she told them. "Taking over all my property. Giving me permission to live in my own legally owned house. I don't need your permission or anyone else's. I'll stay here and take care of it without your help!"

So she continued her struggle to maintain the empty, deteriorating house with an increasing sense of possessiveness. It seemed to me that if Fechin, with his complete absorption, identified himself with his art, Tinka identified herself with the house, while Eya identified with her growing compulsion to serve as the spokesman for her idolized father and his work.

Six years after Fechin's death appeared the first book on him. Copyrighted by Hammer Galleries in New York, it was issued during a Hammer exhibition of Fechin paintings. Harold McCracken, director of the Whitney Gallery of Western Art in Wyoming, was commissioned to write the text. The book was essentially a catalog of more than three hundred paintings left to Eya. Her husband, Branham, an amateur photographer, photographed the paintings. The reproductions were scarcely an inch square and of poor quality. Fechin, I think, would have been greatly disappointed by the book, but it showed the enormous backlog of work that could be profitably sold if popularly exploited.

In the Cowboy Hall of Fame in Oklahoma City, Eya arranged after her divorce from Branham a showing of fifty-three paintings from her collection. The Cowboy Hall of Fame was an affluent and curious institution, founded primarily to glorify the role of the American cowboy in "winning the West." The large, impressive building housed all kinds of Western Americana, art, furniture, and memorabilia. Especially featured were portraits of famous movie stars, such as John Wayne and Joel McCrea, who had played leading cowboy roles in Western films. Annual awards were given to current film actors, artists, and writers whose work contributed to the theme. These events were social functions that equaled Hollywood's premiers.

Dean Krakel, the Hall of Fame's director, had fallen in love with Fechin's paintings. His initial showing, as he later wrote, was a flop despite the martinis served. Fechin was not well known, and many viewers couldn't see why his work was exhibited in a cowboy museum. But the prices were comparatively low: a few canvasses under

$7,000 and a few above $15,000, prices soon to be increased tenfold.

Krakel was particularly impressed by the large *Corn Dancer*, then priced at $45,000. Later it was bought for $65,000 along with fourteen others as a gift from a wealthy donor in Colorado Springs. In 1971 Krakel bought twenty paintings from Hammer Galleries and acquired the beautiful canvass *Summer* for $60,000.

To display this collection in a studio setting, the Fechin Studio in the Cowboy Hall of Fame was established in 1972. Mrs. A. S. Krebs of Wilmington, Delaware, then donated the large Russian canvass *Bearing Away the Bride*, appraised at $150,000.

Carrying Fechin's ashes for burial in his Kazan birthplace, Eya now went to the Soviet Union. About the same time Forrest Fenn, then owner of the Fenn Galleries in Santa Fe, arranged in Moscow for the Russian loan of early Fechin paintings to be exhibited in his retrospective showing of Fechin's work. The great showing was held in November 1975. Almost two thousand visitors attended the opening.

Released for the occasion, twenty years after Fechin's death, was his longed-for book, a handsome monograph published by Northland Press in Flagstaff, Arizona. Amply financed, the book reproduced some sixty color paintings and black-and-white sketches. The text by Mary Balcomb of Washington was a somewhat academic appraisal of Fechin's art through many periods, with a foreword of personal comments by Eya. The general impersonal tone of the book affirmed Eya's comment that Fechin did not want "a book full of 'human interest' anecdotes, spiced-up stories to amuse and titillate." This was a decided about-face from her former exhortation to him to supply "*more intimate* stories that can be worked into something colorful . . . some adventuresome, exciting, and *more intimate* episodes to work with."

The book marked not only the climax of Fechin's long wish but the beginning of the anticlimax to the story of the three Fechins. Tinka was not brought down to attend the great showing at the Fenn Galleries, and soon afterward Eya moved her from her home into a retirement home in Albuquerque.

This left Eya in sole possession of the Fechin property in Taos. From the lucrative sale of Fechin paintings, she was comfortably settled in Albuquerque and bought a ranch adjoining the historic D. H. Lawrence ranch on Lobo Mountain near Taos. On this ranch she erected a new building in which to present dance therapy programs. Nevertheless, the big Fechin house became the focus of her interest.

Her promotion of it began with a photographic spread of its beautiful architectural features in the 1979 issue of Cowboy Hall of Fame's *Persimmon Hill* magazine. Two years later she announced the formation of the Fechin Institute, centered in the Fechin house, which was registered as a state historical site. She then began to restore it. Her published writings on Fechin's paintings, drawings, wood sculpture, carvings, and opinions on art began to appear. And at the institute were held workshops and classes in art.

The Fechin Institute, now a showplace in town, attracts hundreds of visitors. It is also a memorial to Fechin's obsession with art, Eya's obsession with promoting his reputation, and Tinka's obsession with the preservation of the house through so many lonely and frugal years.

8
ANDREW'S HARVEST

A few mornings after I'd moved into Mabel's house in Placita, a car drove up; I watched a middle-aged man with a large, noble head and a severe limp hobble with his cane to the door. "I'm Andrew Dasburg," he said. "Mabel told me a new young man had come to live in town and hadn't yet made any friends. So I've come to call."

This wasn't exactly true. I had many friends among the gambling and sporting fraternity but had not made any among what Doughbelly Price called the Silk Stocking set.

Dasburg declined to come in but invited me to a small gathering of friends in his house that Sunday evening. Who he was I didn't know, but I appreciated his welcome to an unknown stranger. Thus began my friendship of some forty years with a notable painter, a man so shy, uncommunicative, and outwardly colorless that it was difficult for me to reconcile his appearance with what I learned of his life and work.

His large adobe house lay in Talpa, a few miles southeast of Taos. It stood back of the road on a long driveway marked by a huge cottonwood. When I arrived there Sunday evening, it was filled with other guests awaiting dinner. For an hour or more we still waited. Finally Dasburg's wife, Marina, came in. Immediately the room came to life. She announced that a beautiful spread was waiting on the buffet. When we finished eating, she set out a gallon jug of cheap bourbon whiskey and began playing albums of classical music.

These Dasburg Sunday evenings all followed the same pattern: an interminable wait for dinner, for she was always late for everything; hours of her playing on a concert piano or playing recorded music; and all this garnished with that gallon of bourbon. For a town dead in winter, devoid of tourists and entertainment, these evenings were greatly enjoyed.

Marina was a sturdily built woman much younger than Dasburg. She was an enchanting character; she was so delightfully vague. Her father was Owen Wister, whose famous novel *The Virginian* was a Western classic and who had written a biography of President Theodore Roosevelt. Marina lived on the Wister estate in Bryn Mawr, near Philadelphia. After her marriage to Dasburg, she spent several months of the year in his house in Talpa. She had written several volumes of verse, but her two loves were music and horses. An accomplished horsewoman, she transported to Talpa one of her jumpers, now too old and lame to ride. She was immensely proud of him and fed him apples on every occasion.

In contrast to her vivacity, Dasburg seemed withdrawn and colorless; but his background was no less interesting. He had been born in Paris in 1887. His father had died when he was an infant, and his first memories were of living with his mother in the German village of Nittel on the Mosel River near the Luxembourg border. When he was five years old, his mother brought him to the United States and settled in the Hell's Kitchen district on West 38th Street of New York. Here, after falling into an excavation, Dasburg suffered a broken hip that permanently disabled him. Nevertheless, he attended a school for crippled children that recognized his talent and recommended his enrollment in the Art Students' League.

In 1909, when he was twenty-two years old, Dasburg went to Paris. Here he met Picasso and Matisse, and saw Cézanne's work. Their revolutionary style of painting, Cubism, and other forms of abstract art so impressed him that they influenced his own work. The following year he married Grace Mott Johnson in London. Their son, Alfred, was born a year later in Yonkers, New York.

For the International Exhibition of Modern Art, commonly known as the Armory Show, as it was held in the Sixty-ninth Regiment Armory in New York, Dasburg exhibited three paintings and one sculpture. The Armory Show has been called the most important exhibition in the

Andrew Dasburg

history of American art. Its purpose was to present not only showings of contemporary American art but the first American showing of avant-garde paintings from Europe. European paintings imported for the occasion included those of Cézanne, Picasso, Matisse, Braque, Gauguin, Van Gogh, and Duchamp, whose *Nude Descending a Staircase* roused a storm of controversy. Almost four thousand guests attended the opening on February 17, 1913. The exhibition opened the way for modern art in America and established Dasburg's importance in the new movement.

He was still influenced by Cubism, writing for *The Arts* magazine an article entitled "Cubism—Its Rise and Influence." But he was slowly developing his own awareness of art as a revelation of the basic rhythms and structure of matter. Then came a series of chance meetings with several persons who influenced his personal life and led to his coming to New Mexico.

He was exhibiting at the McDowell Club when John Reed came up and introduced himself. Reed was a character whose reputation still lingers. A noted correspondent who covered both domestic and foreign fields, he championed the cause of workers. Later he went to Russia, wrote a book on the revolution, *Ten Days That Shook the World,* and was buried in the Kremlin. A former lover of Mabel Dodge, he now invited Dasburg to an evening party at her home.

Mabel was of course already well known for the gatherings in her salon at 23 Fifth Avenue. She was now about to be married to Maurice Sterne, a prominent Russian-born artist and sculptor whose work had been exhibited in Paris, Berlin, London, and New York. Mabel wasn't present at the evening party, which prompted Dasburg to title one of his paintings *The Absence of Mabel Dodge.*

Later he did meet Mabel, who invited him to work for a time at her Finney Farm up the Hudson River at Croton. Mabel's son, John Evans, joined the group and wrote a novel about Dasburg entitled *Andrew's Harvest.* For several years Dasburg lived in New York, teaching at the Art Students' League, at Woodstock, and Provincetown, while continuing an intimate friendship with Mabel. He also became friends with Robert Edmond Jones, the leading stage designer on Broadway.

It was not long before these highly colored individuals were brought together by strange circumstances to participate in bizarre happenings that changed their lives.

Late in December 1917 Mabel and Sterne, now her husband, arrived in Taos for a quick look. Just why Mabel came on one of her sudden impulses she perhaps didn't know herself, but she was tired of old, worn-out Europe and the overcrowded cities of America stifled by materialism. Her overnight look at the plaza crowded with Spanish-American villagers and Indians swathed in blankets was enough. This was the place to make her home! Next morning she rented a large house just off the plaza from a disreputable man named Arthur Manby, who reserved for himself a small apartment.

Things began to happen, as they always did when Mabel was around. She became interested in the Indians occupying the ancient pueblo nearby, especially a big, handsome man named Tony Lujan, who helped her to lay out a large house of her own on the edge of the reservation. She also persuaded Sterne to resume his work on three-dimensional forms instead of confining himself to two-dimensional representations with brush and charcoal. His resulting wax bust of an Indian named Pedro became one of the best pieces Sterne ever accomplished. But Mabel fell in love with Tony Lujan and divorced Sterne, who left Taos.

That summer she imperiously wired Dasburg and Bobby Jones to come to Taos: "It's a wonderful place! And bring a cook! Am sending three train tickets."

Dasburg and Jones arrived—with a cook—and took up quarters in her rented house. Manby, they learned, was a cultured Englishman who had stolen here from its rightful owners a Spanish land grant of 61,605 acres and then lost it. Obsessed by this loss, he became dissolute and mentally unbalanced. Dasburg, however, discovered him to be something of an authority on native Spanish arts: the old figures of Christian saints painted on wood or carven in the round called *santos*, and the embroidered *colchas*. With increasing appreciation, Dasburg began collecting *santos*.

Manby also took him and Jones on trips throughout the valley, pointing out the uneven lines and planes of the adobe houses and the crooked crosses on the roofs and in the graveyards. Jones as a stage designer was so stimulated that after returning to New York he designed settings for *Macbeth* and the Metropolitan Opera's production of *Til Eulenspiegel* that reflected the sometimes fantastic aspect of these handmade mud structures built with walls out of plumb, doors and windows askew.

Dasburg too was deeply impressed by the small box-like villages that reflected the shapes, textures, and colors of the surrounding mesas and mountains. There seemed to be an organic structure and movement common to both. Unlike Jones, he was struck not by the picturesque surface aspect of what he saw but by the underlying patterns of mass and space.

From the vast, rugged landscape of New Mexico he received an emotional impact and new impetus for his work that he had not experienced in New York and Paris. Every year he returned to spend a few months in New Mexico. His interest in old Spanish *santos* and Indian arts and handicrafts led him to organize the Spanish and Indian Trading Post in Santa Fe with several friends, which took him to all the pueblos.

In 1922 he became a naturalized U.S. citizen. That same year he and Grace Johnson were divorced, and he began living with Ida Rauh. She was a woman of many talents—an actress, poet, painter, and sculptor; her portrait bust of D. H. Lawrence was for many years displayed in the Harwood Library in Taos. Slowly but surely, Dasburg was putting down roots in a new homeland. His paintings reflected it. In the Carnegie Institute International Exhibition of 1927, his painting won third prize, with Matisse winning the first prize.

The following year he married Nancy Lane, whose father had served as President Wilson's secretary of the Interior, and made his home in Santa Fe. Their marriage lasted only four years. Divorced, Dasburg then married Marina and finally settled permanently in the large adobe house in Talpa where I first visited him.

The small, backward town of Taos was drawing other artists besides Dasburg. The founders of its art colony, *Los Ochos Pintores*—Blumenschein, Phillips, Sharp, Couse, Berninghaus, Higgins, Ufer, and Dunton—had been followed by the two Russians, Gaspard and Fechin, and two English painters, Young-Hunter and Brett. Other artists with established reputations—John Marin, Marsden Hartley, Robert Henri, and Georgia O'Keeffe—were coming for short periods. What most of the artists painted, with notable exceptions, were representative depictions often romantic and sentimental. Aspens and Indians! Hence, their work was sometimes derogatorily called the Aspen School.

Dasburg didn't fit into any category. A mature man whose severe limp necessitated his use of a cane, he seemed too retiring and shy to voice decided opinions. Although he painted both people and land, his portrayals were neither picturesque nor strictly representational. All reflected his search for the subjects' inner reality. He explained this himself, shortly before his arrival, in the catalog issued at the Forum Exhibition of Modern Painters in New York, a quotation often reprinted:

> I differentiate the aesthetic reality from the illustrative reality. In the latter, it is necessary to represent nature as a series of recognizable objects. But in the former, we need only have the sense of emotion of objectivity. This is why I eliminate the recognizable object. When the spectator sees in a picture a familiar form, he has associative ideas concerning that form which may be at variance with the actual relation of the form in the picture: it becomes a barrier, a point of fixation, standing between the spectator and the meaning of the work of art. Therefore, in order to obtain a pure aesthetic emotion, based alone on rhythm and form, I eliminated all those factors which might detract the eye and interest from the fundamental intention of the picture.

If his paintings were not popular, they still carried a compelling sense of strength and inner vision. While I was more attracted to the colorful Asiatic scenes of Gaspard and the portraits of Fechin, I was drawn to Dasburg by his friendship, his objectivity, the cool logic behind his emotion. He was a man to talk with; he knew what he was doing.

How full of life Marina was, whether playing on her immense concert grand piano, putting on records of symphonies, showing off her lamed jumper, or opening that jug of cheap whiskey. And when she let me read some of her published poetry, I saw underneath her vivaciousness a deep awareness and sensitivity. But Dasburg had contracted Addison's disease. He painted less and less and spent more and more time with Marina in the Wister home at Bryn Mawr.

One time I visited them there, an amusing experience. I was living in New York for a time, when Mabel came on one of her short trips and telephoned me. She had been invited to spend the weekend with Dasburg and Marina, and I was invited to accompany her.

Marina met us at the train and drove us through a countryside I hadn't seen before. What novel and historical sites there were! A stone bridge over which George Washington had crossed, Valley Forge, an ancient cemetery, a wonderful crossroads tavern said to have been established by the Hessians. When we arrived at the large Wister house, we were just in time for a lunch served for several guests.

"I told you I didn't want to meet a lot of people!" Mabel said crossly.

"But they want to meet you," said Marina. "You won't like it, and neither will Frank. Andrew's not here, but I've got something arranged Frank will like afterward."

What this was she announced after the luncheon guests had gone. "Frank, you're going riding!"

"I don't have any clothes to ride in!" I protested. "I only brought my pajamas and a toothbrush."

"No matter," answered Marina airily. "The maid will give you some of my younger brother's."

The maid conducted me upstairs to my bedroom, where she had laid out riding trousers and a pair of boots. The riding trousers came down only to my shins, and the boots didn't fit. So I came down the stairs, like a curious Ichabod, wearing trousers that didn't reach by far my street shoes.

"Good!" said Marina. "Let's go!"

She bundled me into her car and drove to her riding academy, a tidy compound of corrals, barns, and jumping courses maintained for her socialite, horse-loving neighbors. Here we were met by a gracious woman neighbor whom I understood to be a countess and who didn't blink an eye at my appearance. Marina introduced me, saying casually, "Frank is from Colorado, so of course he must ride Colorado."

"Quite so," agreed the Countess.

In a few minutes a groom brought up Colorado, a big, well-knit bay which was being trained as a jumper. The groom looked me over with obvious distaste and asked curtly, "Can you ride?"

I could only mutter, "I've been on a horse."

"Mount, then, and ride down to the far stable and back."

When I returned, Marina said, "I told you so. Now, Frank, put him over one."

The groom led me to a hurdle and backed away. I let Colorado nose and measure it, or whatever he did, reined him back on the course, then gave him a boot. I had never jumped before. Nor had Colorado yet been trained sufficiently. By all the rules, untrained and with a strange rider, he should have balked at the hurdle. Instead he took it in one muscular leap. For an instant I felt as if I were flying through the air. Then suddenly I came down on the flat English saddle with an impact that nearly jolted out my teeth. But miraculously I found myself still on Colorado.

What an achievement it was! Inordinately proud of myself, I trotted Colorado back to Marina, the Countess, and the groom. "What did you think of that? How'd I do?"

Said Marina sadly, "Frank, your elbows were out."

She and the Countess then took me out into the countryside to watch them ride. How marvelous they were! Dashing hell-for-breakfast through open patches of forest and brush, clearing fence after fence in rhythmic soars. What a horsewoman Marina was! Erect in the saddle, as if a part of her mount, she looked like a Valkyrie—a picture of her I'll never forget.

That evening the Countess and her husband gave a dinner in their impressive home. From the greenhouse, plants and flowers had been brought to fill the hall. The dinner was formal, with silver and crystal place settings for some twenty guests. Andrew and I were seated next to each other. Such was my introduction to English saddles, jumpers, and an aspect of life far different from that in New Mexico.

Two mornings later came a decided anticlimax. We had risen early in order to catch the train back to New York and had time only for a cup of coffee. But when we went to open the door, we found it stuck. "Fix the lock, Andrew," said Marina. "Or unfix it." It wasn't the lock, declared Dasburg. The night had been cold and damp, and the wood had swelled. We all rushed to the back door. It was stuck, too. Mabel by this time was in a dither. "A beautiful house, but nothing works." Replied Marina cheerfully, "Just like New Mexico, dear!"

"Are we all to be imprisoned until hot weather comes?" asked Mabel. "Do something, Andrew! SOMETHING!"

He looked at me glumly. It was Marina who did it, breaking a pane of the window beside the door. Andrew then stuck his arm through the opening and jiggled the lock while I pushed on the door. Miraculously, it opened. Mabel dashed out.

"But you can't rush off like this," Marina said cheerfully. "We must all have a stirrup cup. A hot toddy!"

"Not if it's made with that vile Taos Lightning you always drink at home!" grumbled Mabel.

Marina laughed and fixed our drinks. Then, in high humor, she drove us to the train.

Dasburg seemed out of place at Bryn Mawr. With his illness and physical disability he couldn't ride, and I think he wouldn't have liked to had he been able. Nor did he appear to feel at home in the impressive house, obviously preferring his own New Mexico adobe. The animated talk of the neighbors about social events and horses left him high and dry in his own thoughts. Marina on the contrary, was in her element. This was her family home and the life she had always known.

Their difference in character seemed not to bother Marina during her summer sojourns in Taos. She seemed to enjoy her life there, too. Still, I began to feel that she was drinking too much of that bourbon dubbed Taos Lightning.

The Second World War broke out. For several years I was away. When I returned to Taos, I heard depressing news. Marina had gone to live at Bryn Mawr. Some time later, suffering a drinking problem, she was confined to an institution.

Dasburg was left alone in his house. Apparently he had discovered a new treatment, injections of adrenal extract, which helped him. Nevertheless, he gave private lessons to young painters. He had the unusual ability to bring out a student's own personality and ability, rather than teaching him his own technique. Under his guidance Earl Stroh, Cady Wells, Kenneth Adams, and Howard Cook became successful painters.

When he again took up his brush, it was to turn out an amazing range of work. One of his favorite subjects was the view from his studio, a separate building behind his house. Talpa lay on the high northern edge of the arroyo dividing Talpa and Llano Quemado. One could look down upon the patchwork fields on the floor of the wide arroyo and the straggle of adobes on its opposite high bank, or, looking northward, see the clustered villages of Talpa itself and Taos at the foot of the Pueblo's Sacred Mountain. All these views he recast in oil, pastel, or line drawings to reveal their relationship of line and form.

His perception was shown when Spud Johnson and I were commissioned to edit a series of articles for *New Mexico Magazine.* The subject of my own assignment was "Indian influence on Taos art," which of course included architecture. Perhaps no other building in New Mexico had been painted as often as the church of Saint Francis of Assisi at Ranchos de Taos, dating from the early 1700s. It was a monumental adobe of curious structure. Fechin's painting of it from the front depicted the twin bell towers. Most other painters showed the massive back structure with its great retaining wall. Dasburg, when I asked him about these different aspects, explained that the front of the church reflected Spanish influence, the two towers reaching toward heaven symbolizing the Christian, masculine influence. The back, with its downpressing solidity, reflected the Indians' allegiance to the feminine earth.

During these years he suffered a financial setback. His work was not selling widely, and the injections for his disease cut into his living expenses. Moreover, his old car was on its last legs and ready to give up the ghost. It was a great day when Mrs. Wurlitzer of the Wurlitzer Foundation bought him another, presenting it to him in the presence of Earl Stroh, one of his former students. Andrew could now drive into town without fear his old car would break down at any moment.

Every Friday we had lunch together at El Patio, whose special for that day was fillet of sole, which Dasburg loved. Later, we both ate lunch in the small Northtown Restaurant at Placita, which served cheap home-cooked family-style meals. Everyone shared tables, and Dasburg enjoyed the company of friends and their gossip. Going out to lunch became one of his invariable customs. It was his one full, hot meal of the day, as he prepared his own simple supper. During a later period he always invited to lunch at La Doña Luz restaurant his "Friday Girl," Tally Richards, who owned an art gallery. During his last years, when he became unable to drive a car, his chief delight was being invited to dinner at Casa Cordova in Arroyo Seco. He always finished his meal with a scoop of ice cream covered with strawberry preserve, a dessert long listed on the menu as a "Dasburg Special." Irrelevant as these details seem, the places where he had lunch mark for me the course of his advancing years.

In 1963, during a brief, hectic marriage, my wife, Rose, invited several guests to Thanksgiving dinner. They included Dasburg, my visiting New York agent, Barthold Fles, and the popular Arizona artist Ted De Grazia. As Fles was new to New Mexico, I drove him out to see Taos

Pueblo. When we returned late that afternoon, all the other guests were assembled. As we entered the house, Rose, inordinately jealous of all my friends, hurled the cocktail shaker at me. Before I could recover from this surprising welcome, she rushed to the oven, removed the browned turkey, and flung it on the floor. She then dashed outside the house and threw stones through the windshield of my car in the driveway. What an exhibition; what a mess it was! Broken glass and spilled liquor over the living room, turkey and dressing spread over the kitchen floor! Dasburg and Fles fled to the Taos Inn, where they ate their Thanksgiving dinner.

I joined them there, contrite and embarrassed. Bart Fles, whose wife had just left him, shrugged. "You're no different from the rest of us, Frank. It happens to us all." Added Dasburg, "Wine and women! You and I've had no luck with either of them, Frank!"

Late in January 1970 came the tragic announcement that Marina had burned to death in a two-story cottage on the Wister estate at Bryn Mawr. According to reports, the building was observed to be engulfed in flames shortly after midnight. Firemen reported hearing screams but were unable to make their way inside. Later they found Marina's body lying just inside the door on the first floor.

The news shocked and saddened all of us in Taos. Dasburg had nothing to say. What could he say?

He was now eighty-three years old, a broad-shouldered man with a rugged face, wide mouth, high forehead, and wispy white hair. Fortunately, life was made easier for him when his son, Alfred, and his wife moved to Santa Fe and came up to see him often. His neighbors Joe and Lucille Mondragon, who had done household chores for him for some forty years, came in regularly.

Indomitably, he continued painting, relying more and more upon line drawings to reveal his vision of the inner patterns of the landscape. His favorite subject was the Sacred Mountain of Taos Pueblo. Winter and summer, a friend drove him out to the mesa for a clear view of it. Here he set up his easel to draw or sketch. None of these paintings quite pleased him, and he would return to do another. "I still haven't got it yet!" he often said. "A mysterious mountain."

Nevertheless, his late work was judged to be among his finest. It was so widely appreciated that his canvasses were spoken for even before he had finished them.

A Collectors' Show of fifty-five of his paintings from 1927 to 1965 had been given in the Stables Gallery, Taos, in 1966. In October 1975 a "mini-retrospective" showing of his oils, watercolors, pastels, lithographs, and drawings was held at the Governor's Palace in Santa Fe. Two years later an exhibition in the Santa Fe Armory for the Arts featured a still life painted in 1913, reminding viewers of his participation in the famous Armory Show of that year. Important museums throughout the country had acquired his work. Dasburg had been granted a Guggenheim Fellowship, awarded a doctorate of fine arts from the University of New Mexico, and give a special award from the governor of New Mexico.

None of these honors, I think, impressed him. He continued working until April 1979, when he was briefly hospitalized. One Sunday in August he listened to a radio replay of the Taos Music Festival concert. When it was over, he mentioned Marina, according to one account, and said, "I think I want to go."

He died peacefully at home on Monday, August 13, 1979, at the age of ninety-two. With him were his faithful neighbors, the Mondragons, and his nurse, Esther Ackerman.

A memorial service was held on August 18 in the St. James Episcopal Church. The church was so crowded with people from throughout New Mexico and the East that late arrivals had to stand in the back behind the pews. The service was interrupted by a member of the New Mexico Arts Commission, who read a proclamation from the governor of New Mexico designating this as Andrew Dasburg Day. The service was too long. Dasburg would have liked something more simple, I believe.

Preparations began for a comprehensive Andrew Dasburg Retrospective Exhibition, which opened in November at the Fine Arts Museum in Santa Fe. The catalog prepared by the museum's director, Van Deren Coke, listed ninety-six works from 1908 to 1979. Many were on loan from museums and galleries, private collections, and individuals. The National Endowment for the Arts provided partial funding of the exhibition, scheduled to travel to Arizona, Colorado, Texas, and Nebraska, with a final showing at the Santa Fe Fine Arts Museum.

Andrew's harvest! How abundant it was! His seventy years of painting had established him as one of the leading exponents and innovators of modern art in America. Much has been written about his work, but little about the man. Even Van Deren Coke's biography, chiefly discussing Dasburg's work, only mentions that his economical drawings deal with the psychological problems of balance and energy.

This observation might well apply to Dasburg himself. Throughout his life, he had psychological problems, which he never attempted to solve or even spoke about. He always held a tight rein on the horses that pulled his chariot. It seems clear, however, that Dasburg always regarded his personal life as less important than his paintings. And he expressed his own vision in the simplicity of line and form with the objectivity that was an essential part of his character. He was not concerned with the cosmetic beauty of the earth's surface, the yellow aspen groves and the flowering chamisa, the dark green pine slopes. But, like a surgeon, he probed the skeletal structure of bone, ligament, and integument that integrated mountain and mesa in a living whole.

It seems odd to me now, as a layman who knows little about painting, that these sketches of mine include so many painters. Yet these painters were also characters unusual in every way. And it was as gifted individuals and close friends that they appealed to me. So it was with Dasburg. My long friendship with him, from the morning when he first knocked on my door, was with the man, not the artist. There was nothing abstract about it. To me he was warm and understanding, without being demonstrative, and was always direct as his paintings—a rare combination I cherished.

9
THE LAST OF THE MAYAS

The wind and the rain of time and change have worn away the ancient civilizations of Indian America, but there still remain focal spots where one feels their lingering energy. Places like Tihuanaco on the receded shore of Lake Titicaca in Bolivia. Machu Picchu and the present city of Cuzco in Peru. Teotihuacán in Mexico. Of all these and many others I've known in broadening out from Taos my lifetime studies, the ruins of the Classic Maya temple cities and a small jungle village of Mayas lying along the Usumacinta River seemed to interconnect more closely with our own ancient ruins and contemporary Indian societies in the Four Corners.

The northward-flowing Usumacinta marks for much of its length the boundary between Guatemala and the Mexican state of Chiapas. One of the longest tropical rivers on the continent, it cuts through a dense rain forest of towering mahogany, ceiba, sapodilla, and palm trees choked with growths of bamboo, ferns, vines, and brush.

In it lie the temple ruins of the ancient Maya civilization. This also is the homeland of the Lacandones, the last surviving full-blood descendants of the Classic Mayas.

To get here would have been difficult for me without the help of Gertrude "Trudi" Blom, widow of the archaeologist Franz Blom. She operated *Na-Bolom* ("at the Sign of the Jaguar"), the Centro de Estudios Científicos, in San Cristobal de las Casas, Chiapas. In 1950 the couple had established their home here, gradually adding rooms to accommodate archaeologists and anthropologists who came to study the Mayan ruins and the Lacandones. During my visit twenty years later, it was the most unusual guest house in town. With an excellent library and Trudi's collection of color slides, it offered ample facilities for research and study. Meals were served family style at a table seating twenty to thirty guests. At its head presided Trudi, as we called her, fluent in German, French, Spanish, and English, and shouting and cursing in either.

Trudi, then about seventy, was a character. *Na-Bolom* she ruled with dictatorial aplomb, even to prescribing our disposal of used toilet paper. Her secondary role was that of the Great White Goddess of the Lacandones. It was generally constructive. She took them medicines, helped to sell their bows and arrows, and beleaguered the Mexican government to establish this jungle homeland as a reserve. Hence, if any visitor wanted to see the Lacandones or the Maya ruins, Trudi, wearing her baggy pants and stout boots, took them.

When I was there, a few of us asked her to arrange a trip. There were five others besides me. I will give them these names: Edgar Smith, a photographer; middle-aged Professor Jones and his wife; and the younger Brown couple, both teachers. Preceded by Trudi and the Browns, the other four of us took off in the plane Trudi usually chartered, a four-passenger Cessna 180. A "jungle pilot" often has to wait hours for the mist to clear from the dank *selva* before taking off. We were fortunate; the morning was clear. The earth below spread out in rolling wooded hills dotted with small clearings in which stood tiny villages of a dozen huts. Then, below a sea of cumulus clouds formed by the rising mist appeared the rain forest, a growth so dense it looked like a blanket of moss. Soon I glimpsed a tiny silver rivulet curving through it: the Usumacinta. To travel through the jungle by horseback would have taken two days or more. But in an hour our little plane ducked down through an almost invisible opening to a narrow landing strip in a small clearing beside the river.

Nearby stood a cluster of several partly ruined adobe buildings occupied by a family of caretakers. Trudi and the Brown couple were waiting for us. Trudi was shouting and swearing at a boatman readying a long dugout canoe on the riverbank.

This was Agua Azul, formerly a *central* for mahogany cutters and *chicleros* who gathered chicle, the sap from the *zapote chico,* or sapodilla, for making chewing gum. From here the massive mahogany logs were floated downriver to Tenosique, where they were tied into rafts and floated on down to the Gulf of Mexico for shiploading. B. Traven in his well-known "jungle novels" described the inhuman operation of such camps. Indians were enslaved, marched through the jungle, and forced to fell the great mahogany trees, which often reached a height of 150 feet. When they failed to cut their allotted number of tons, Indians were hung up by the thumbs or staked out overnight to be mangled by jaguars.

The mahogany dugout canoe prepared for us was long and sturdy and contained an outboard motor. When we had loaded our baggage and seated ourselves, the Mexican boatman started the motor and pushed off downriver. The Usumacinta unwound before us, wide, deep, and placid, but with a strong current. It seemed like a narrow swath cut through an impenetrable forest whose hundred-foot height walled us in on each side. Lofty mahogany trees, giant umbrella-shaped ceibas sacred to the Mayas, red *palo mulatos,* palm and rubber trees. Clumps of bamboo, dense undergrowth entangled in huge ferns and poisonous *matapalo* vines. Orchids, waist-high begonias, flowers of every color grew everywhere. Each turn of the river revealed a new aspect of lush splendor. We caught glimpses of long-tailed parrots, always flying in pairs, and tiny spotted deer. Over all brooded an unbroken silence, the hot hush of the noonday sun. Immobile and silent ourselves, we seemed implanted in a newly created virgin earth.

After a few hours the dugout beached on a sandy spit on a wide turn of the river below a twenty-foot-high bank. Up this we climbed to a clearing containing a two-family compound of six or seven *chosas.* All these huts were roofed with thatchings of palms; one had walls of bamboo poles. This center *chosa* was one big room with a four-foot-high, flat-topped fireplace for communal cooking. Children, dogs, pigs, and chickens roamed loose through the compound. Hanging our hammocks in two empty *chosas,* we ate supper by lamplight, balanced ourselves in the hammocks under mosquito nets, and lay listening to the monkeys.

The jungle encroached to the edge of the small clearing. One dared not walk far alone. The ruins of Yaxchilan lay hidden, and next morning we began to seek them. First it was necessary for the head man, who was their caretaker, to cut a path through the dense growth with a machete. Within a few weeks, he told us, it would be overgrown again.

Yaxchilan, embraced by the wide curve of the Usumacinta and isolated deep in the rain forest, must have been, like Palenque, one of the loveliest of all Mayan temple cities. Why it hadn't been preserved and restored like lesser sites is a mystery. The Spanish explorers saw the ruins in 1696. Teobert Maler mapped them in 1897; and many later archaeologists studied them, only to leave them to be swallowed up by the jungle, with some of their precious stelae snaked out by thieves. Maler's map shows forty structures rising on terraces to the Acropolis Grande and nearby Acropolis Pequeno.

Now it was almost impossible to detect the architectural plan. The encroaching growth was destroying all temples. Huge trees not only enveloped all buildings, but tree-sized roots and branches grew through roofs, walls, and subterranean chambers, tearing apart the cut stones. Even so, one saw how lovely they must have been. The pyramid temples were not high, but their upper facades and roof-combs were beautifully ornamented with figures in stone and stucco. The stone here is said to be especially hard, so the sculpture was among the best. Yaxchilan is famous for its stone lintels carved in exquisite bas-relief. Lintel 8 records a Calendar Round date of A.D. 755. The huge stelae were equally magnificent. Most of them had fallen and were covered with moss. Others that have been studied had been turned face down to prevent their inscriptions from weathering.

The great temple on the highest terrace was most imposing. In front of the middle doorway lay the decapitated statue of Hachakyum, the god of the ancient Mayas who made heaven and earth. Here the Lacandones still make pilgrimages to burn copal and offer prayers for the time when the head and body will be reunited. It will mark the destruction of this world and the beginning of a new era, with the rebirth of the old gods and a final flowering of the ancient Maya culture.

The Lacandones also make pilgrimages to Palenque and Bonampak, not far away. Palenque is easily accessible. With its majestic Palacio, its small and exquisite temples, and its pyramidal Temple of Inscriptions containing its underground tomb, it is the finest and best preserved of all the Classic Mayan ruins. Bonampak, hidden in the jungle, was not discovered until 1946 and was still accessible only by chartered plane when I was there. Credit for its discovery is given to Giles Healey, a United Fruit Company scout; but he was led to Bonampak by a Lacandon who promised to show him a sacred Lacandon shrine in the ruins. News of Bonampak's existence spread rapidly.

When I saw it, it was deserted save for a caretaker. The two main structures lay on a hill overlooking a great plaza in which stood a large stela carved in bas-relief. The temple on the right comprised three rooms, all of their walls covered with the now famous fresco paintings. The roof was covered by rusty tin sheeting to protect the murals from drippings of limestone or calcium. The scenes depict preparations for a battle, torture of prisoners, and the dance of victory. Warriors are wearing jaguar skins and towering headdresses of quetzal feathers; ladies in white robes are drawing blood from their tongues; an orchestra is performing with long trumpets, drums, and rattles; a severed head lies below. The temple has been reconstructed and the gorgeously colored paintings faithfully copied in the great national museum in Mexico City.

Lacandon Indian

Yet of these three Usumacinta ruins—Palenque, Yaxchilan, and Bonampak—it was Yaxchilan that struck deepest into my heart. The crumbling ruins of a holy city, a tarnished jewel of classic Maya civilization, a place of brooding mystery.

A few days later we left the jungle clearing at Yaxchilan shortly after midnight for the return trip upriver to Agua Azul. The early start was necessary, for our dugout canoe would be bucking the current, requiring much longer for the trip. From the moment we started, we could feel the strong undercurrent below and the spray in our faces. And now began for me a passage that seemed at once vivid and unreal, timeless as a dream.

The trip down in daylight had revealed at every turn the lofty walls of the rain forest on each side, the dense undergrowth and the profusion of brilliant flowers, glimpses of long-tailed parrots, a tiny spotted deer. How alive was all this lush splendor! Now in the dark we could see nothing but the pale glint of the river under a quarter-moon that hung suspended over the high, dark walls on each side. How silent it was! An all-pervading silence seemed to muffle the put-put of the outboard motor behind us. Silent, we sat immobile, engulfed in unbroken stillness and darkness. There was no sensation of movement. The river kept unwinding before us as if we ourselves were becalmed. Nor did we move through time. Midnight gave way to dawn like an image on a screen. And now in faint light the silvery-gray curtain of mist shrouded the forest.

With sunrise there appeared the tall, bare trunks of the ceibas, the shapes of the great mahogany trees. The colors of flowers screamed forth. Two parrots flew overhead; a jaguar raised its head from the riverbank. It was as if we were witnessing the creation of an original and resplendent new world.

"Pee stop!" yelled Trudi suddenly.

Obediently the Mexican boatman steered the dugout to beach on a gravelly island in the river. We all got out to relieve ourselves and to stretch our cramped legs. It was then I noticed a flower growing on a sandy spit farther out in the river. A single, tall-stemmed, exquisite, lilylike tropical flower whose name I didn't know. Nor did it matter. For something about it struck deeply into my heart. In a few weeks the rainy season would begin. The Usumacinta would swell into a raging torrent that would submerge the sandy spit and the life of this fragile and isolate flower. Perhaps no other human beings had seen or would ever see it again, but its impending fate was of no importance. Proclaiming the fullness of its present moment, it stood there proudly affirming the transcendent life and beauty given it without the need of any human admiration. Like lovely Yaxchilan, it would stand for its own hour before being erased by the wind and the rain of worldly time. And that, I suddenly realized, was enough to justify the brief life of this fragile blossom, and of Yaxchilan.

So somehow this single flower on a sandy spit in the great Usumacinta epitomized for me the essential meanings of the whole Maya civilization and the organic lifetime of our own technological Western civilization. Each undergoes its own cycle of growth, death, and transformative rebirth. Only our recognition of this universal pattern makes it easier to accept the completeness of our own life cycles.

The plane was waiting for us at Agua Azul. Professor Jones and his wife flew back to Las Casas. His sightseeing evidently was too much for him. Whatever his illness was, he had been falling asleep continually: on the plane, in the canoe, whenever he sat down to rest, anywhere, at any time. The rest of us—Edgar Smith, the Browns, and I—remained with Trudi. Having guided us to the ancient Mayan ruins, she was now going to show us the last surviving descendants of the Mayas.

There were two settlements of the pitifully few hundred Lacandones. The southern settlement of Lacanja lay along the tiny tributary of that name, not far from the ruins of its ancient ceremonial center, Yaxchilan. Its members had been converted to Christianity by a resident Baptist missionary and were adopting modern dress, gadgets, household utensils, rifles, and liquor. Naha, the settlement to the north, lay on the shore of beautiful Lake Naha, closer to its ceremonial home of Palenque. It contained the religious leader of all the Lacandones who adhered to traditional Mayan beliefs. This dichotomy between the northern and southern Lacandones appeared to duplicate the division between the Traditional and Progressive factions of the Hopi tribe in my own Southwest. And, as I learned later, it was to have the same tragic consequences.

In a nearby clearing Trudi had established her jungle camp. In the center stood one long, open *chosa* with a thatched roof, which served as a community room. The cook stove was a solid mahogany table with a clay top on which a fire was built. From an iron rack hung pots and pans. Surrounding this room, and tucked into the edges of the forest, were four other small *chosas,* also open on all sides, with stout posts containing hooks on which to hang our hammocks.

How pleasant this little camp was in the daytime. Edgar, a photographer, was never still. Loaded down with color and black-and-white cameras, pouches of film, and lenses, he seemed to snap everything in sight. An authority on orchids, he identified twenty varieties growing on one tree, giving the botanical name for each. The two Browns kept busy taking notes on the tropical birds flashing in and out of the forest backdrop. The nights were not as pleasant. The constant dripping of water from the great trees sounded like rain and produced a clammy cold. Also, sleeping in a hammock was an art I hadn't acquired. The hammock was so constricting I couldn't turn over without danger of falling out, and I kept getting tangled in the mosquito net over me.

Next afternoon a file of Lacandones came to pay their respects to the Great White Goddess. Trudi welcomed them with hot chocolate and cookies. These were the first Lacandones I'd seen. At the head of the file was Old Chan K'in of Naha, the eighty-year-old religious leader of the northern Lacandones. Except for his erect, commanding presence, he differed little in appearance from his followers. All were short, well-built men with tangled black hair falling loose over their shoulders; they had pleasant childlike faces. Their eyes were slanted, accentuating the epicanthic folds of the lids. All wore only white, loose, knee-length gowns from which protruded their broad bare feet. Gliding noiselessly out of the forest, they looked like ghosts or sleepwalkers in nightgowns. That they could make the long barefoot journey through the dense jungle growth to Yaxchilan or Palenque seemed incomprehensible. Speaking Spanish, they talked with calm assurance, enjoyed their cookies, and lit short cigars of home-grown tobacco. Contrary to the wild stories about them, I found in them more warmth and responsiveness than in the primitive Tarahumaras of the Barranca de Cobre in Chihuahua.

Old Chan K'in invited us to his home in Naha, which lay on the southeast shore of Lake Naha. The community comprised small compounds of thatched huts, called *caribels,* scattered in clearings among the forest. His own *chosa* was like the others, a long hut with a thatched roof. He had three wives, each having her own cooking fire built on the earthen floor. Also, he had three married sons and eight unmarried children.

While we talked, one of the wives was busy making *posole* in an iron pot suspended over her fire. Corn was the staple diet, and its preparation was an arduous job. The kernels were first softened by soaking in lime made from snail shells, then ground into meal on a stone *metate*. It was then mixed with water, chile, or honey for cooking into a porridge, or rolled into balls, and wrapped finally in banana leaves.

How busy all the women were with their never-ending chores: cooking, tending children, making baskets and hammocks, gathering bananas and pineapples. A primary task was weaving home-grown cotton into cloth for their white tunics. Several of them were working at their back-strap looms tied to a tree. Another was beating mahogany bark into a pulp. This, we were told, was dyed red and woven into the headbands worn by men during ceremonies. The women were shorter than the men, very shy, with placid Mayan faces. Each wore her black hair braided into one long pigtail hanging down to her waist. Tied to the end of this braid was a bunch of clear yellow parrot feathers.

Old Chan K'in, despite his age, worked as hard as the rest of the men. He tilled his own land, burned patches of forest, and planted corn, squash, and beans between the blackened stumps. Their method of planting was the immemorial way of the ancient Mayas and the early Hopis back home: simply punching holes in the earth with a sharpened stick to receive the seeds. To add to their diet, with bows and arrows the men hunted wild pigs, deer, monkeys, pheasants, and parrots.

Old Chan K'in's *milpa* lay across the lake. To show it, he instructed K'in and Young Chan K'in to paddle us across the lake in their mahogany dugout. On the way he pointed out the great, fallen tree from whose trunk it had been laboriously hewn out. The branches of the huge tree, he explained, had been fashioned into tables, benches, and household articles.

Lake Naha was exquisitely beautiful. Enclosed by the towering rain forest, it lay like a great, still, clear blue pool fringed with water lilies and brilliant flowers. Curiously enough, there lay not far west another small lake, Alligator Lake, edged with swamps and bamboo growths, its water brackish yellow and full of alligators. But Lake Naha was clear as glass. Unable to restrain ourselves from diving in for a swim, we began stripping off our clothes. Mrs. Brown modestly hesitated. "Go on!" demanded Trudi. "You don't have anything more to show than standard equipment, do you!" So Mrs. Brown too stripped and plunged in.

Such was the simple life that must have been followed by the ancient Mayas. With the mysterious collapse of their great Classic civilization and the abandonment of the resplendent temple cities in the ninth century, the people most likely dispersed to live in small outlying settlements. Seven centuries later came the Spanish invaders, destroying the ruins of the old cities, burning all the remaining records of their history, pillaging, and massacring the surviving Mayas. The Lacandones fled into the depths of the great Usumacinta rain forest to escape massacre.

Here they have remained for centuries. Isolated and inbred, uneducated, and living a primitive existence, they lost all the brilliant knowledge of astronomy, astrology, mathematics, hieroglyphic writing, and religious philosophy of their Mayan ancestors—a heritage that may stem back to the preceding Olmecs of 1200 B.C. or earlier. And yet in the stories and religious ceremonies conducted by Old Chan K'in, the *t'o'ohil,* or religious leader and prophet, many of their ancient beliefs and traditions have been preserved.

Lacandon religion involved a hierarchy of innumerable gods. Chief of them was Hachakyum, who made the world and all upon it, he whose decapitated statue lay in front of the great temple at Yaxchilan. They were all represented in the "god-house," which Old Chan K'in permitted us to enter. It was a long, open hut with a shelf extending under the thatched roof. Here stood a row of "god-pots": pottery incense bowls marked with red and blue stripes, and shaped like heads of birds and animals. Each represented a god in the pantheon. Here anyone could come to burn incense and chant prayers for the birth of a child, for safety on a journey. While we were there, a man performed a curing ceremony for his ill wife. Squatting down in front of a god-pot, he sang in a low voice.

Burning copal, he smoked a green wand in the incense, then left to touch it to his wife's head and throat.

The renewal of the god-pots was a major ceremony. It occurred every eight Earth years, or five cycles of Venus, a cycle once sacred to the Mayas, and lasted forty-five days. All participating Lacandones slept in the *chosa,* remained continent, and constantly drank *balche.* The drink was made from the fermented bark of the *balche* tree and had mild hallucinogenic effects. To the Lacandones, it was a holy drink made by the sun and moon; it had the power to wash away all evil.

According to Robert D. Bruce, an anthropologist who has studied the Lacandones for twenty years, this renewal of the god-pots perpetuated the ancient Mayan "renewal of the idols in the month of Pop," as described by Fray Diego de Landa in the sixteenth century. There are other correspondences between Lacandon religious beliefs and practices and those described in Mayan codices and inscriptions. Bruce further asserts that Old Chan K'in could name the tutelary gods of all the temples in Palenque, and Trudi stated that he knew of the burial crypt below the Temple of Inscriptions long before it was discovered by archaeologists. Lovely Palenque was the birthplace of all the gods. Then Hachakyum instructed the young corn god to build a new city for the gods to dwell in. This was Yaxchilan, with its temple-home for Hachakyum himself. Old Chan K'in seemed to regard Yaxchilan with more awe and reverence then Palenque.

The stories he told as he lay in his hammock and smoked cigars were earthy and often humorous. Most of them were of the creation of the world by the gods as well as the interdependence of men, animals, trees, stones, and stars. He was not reluctant to tell these stories to us outsiders, nor was he self-conscious about his easy, intimate relationship with all living things in heaven and earth.

One of his stories struck me as being especially significant. Whenever a tree is felled, a star falls from the sky. Hence, a Lacandon before chopping down a great mahogany asks permission of the forest and of the stars above. So too do the pueblo Indians back home in the Southwest ceremonially ask the great pine they are about to cut for permission to sacrifice it.

This Lacandon belief explained Old Chan K'in's fear of the growing interest of Mexican officials in the mahogany trees of the Lacandon rain forest. Accompanying this threat were Lacanja's abandonment of traditional beliefs and adoption of Christianity, the steady influx of modern gadgets and cheap whiskey, and increasing numbers of visitors like ourselves.

His concern about these incursions from the outside world was shared by Trudi. She kept badgering the federal government of Mexico to establish the Lacandon homeland as a national reserve. To arouse interest in the endangered Lacandones, she later made a speaking tour of the Southwest; I attended her lecture at the University of Arizona.

Another exposition of Lacandon life was the publication of Christine Price's poetic *Heirs of the Ancient Maya: A Portrait of the Lacandon Indians,* illustrated by Trudi's striking photographs. I had met Price at *Na-Bolom* in San Cristobal, from which Trudi had taken her to Naha. She was a writer and illustrator of books for young readers. Small, perceptive, and courageous, she was a world traveler who had visited Mexico, Egypt, Afghanistan, Africa, and the Pacific Islands to record the arts of wood sculpture, pottery, weaving, and dance. After we became friends, I induced her to visit New Mexico and took her to the great Corn Dance at Santo Domingo Pueblo. She later gave up her home in Vermont and settled in Albuquerque. Here she began work on a book of early Spanish colonial churches of the Southwest, but tragically died before completing it. Her moving book on the Lacandones, however, is one of the best portraits of a people in the last full moon of their ancient culture.

The book *The Last Lords of Palenque: The Lacandon Mayas of the Mexican Rain Forest,* by Victor Perera and Robert D. Bruce, recounts the tragic events that have taken place since I was there. Trudi was successful in persuading the Mexican government to establish the Lacandon homeland as a reserve. But the Department of Forestry had given permission to a lumber company to harvest its giant mahogany trees, the very lifeblood of the Lacandones. An enterprising Christianized Lacandon of Lacanja then induced the government to appoint him as the official representative of the Lacandones. He promptly authorized the cutting of 444 marked mahogany trees and appropriated for the Lacanja settlement the nominal payment by the logging company, which was earmarked for the benefit of all Lacandones.

Cutting of the great mahoganies, some of which had been growing since before Columbus discovered the New World, began in 1978. The results were disastrous. The mahoganies for centuries had supplied the Lacandones with their dugouts for transportation across Lake Naha, with ceremonial "canoes" in which *balche* had been fermented for drinking during religious rites, and with furniture and household articles. More important, they prevented the rain forest from drying up. Once the trees were felled, the jungle was being reduced to low growth and weeds, the streams were dwindling, and the topsoil was washing away.

Through the devastated area loggers bulldozed a road to Palenque, one hundred kilometers away. This necessitated moving the settlement of Naha, including Old Chan K'in's home and the god-house, as well as Trudi's camp at the upper end of the lake. Lacanja experienced a burst of prosperity from the logging company's payments. It was reflected by a new, primitive hotel, more modern innovations, increasing drunkenness, and a growing influx of tourists. Naha faced extinction in the midst of the destruction of its rain forest.

More and more apparent to me was the striking similarity of the tragic life pattern of the Lacandon Mayas and the Hopis. They were both isolated for centuries, one tribe in the impenetrable tropical rain forest, the other in the arid desert of Arizona. Both carried on the ages-old traditions of their people, until the coming of the whites introduced a new way of life. Then occurred among the Hopis a tragic schism between the Traditionalists and the government-sponsored Tribal Council faction, like the conflict between the Lacandon settlements of Lacanja and Naha. The Mexican government established the Lacandon homeland as a reserve, as our government marked the Hopi land as a reservation. But exploitation of natural resources soon followed: the cutting of mahogany trees, the strip-mining of vast deposits of coal. These brought in new roads and modern customs, resulting in alcoholism and a breaking down of traditional customs and rituals.

The Lacandones, as we know, were direct descendants of the ancient Mayas. Could the Hopis also have been related to the Mayas in the far past? Their migration legends relate that the Hopis first arrived on this new Fourth World somewhere in the tropical south. Several clans settled at a red-earth place. Here they were instructed to build a city by the *kachinas,* who were guiding spirits in human form. The city was a resplendent ceremonial center where the Hopis were taught the laws of world creation and world maintenance. In time evil entered, and the Hopis abandoned the city to continue their migration north.

The Hopi name of this mysterious "Red City of the South" was Palatkwapi. No one knows where it might have been. Some Hopi elders believe the legendary city, the birthplace of the Kachina Clan and its rituals, was the imposing Mayan temple city of Palenque in Chiapas, the birthplace of the Mayan gods. There is no anthropological evidence to support the Hopis' vast body of legends that they migrated from the south. Yet as I have suggested elsewhere, there seems no doubt that the vast pre-Columbian civilization of Mayas and Aztecs was gradually extended north to southwestern United States. Perhaps the people who later called themselves Hopi were a small Mayan branch, possibly a religious cult, which migrated north to the Four Corners area of our own Southwest.

In any case, the similarities between the Hopis and the Lacandon Mayas can't be ignored. They are brothers in belief, custom, and spirit. This deep-rooted empathy takes voice in the Lacandon and Hopi prophecies that the world will soon be destroyed because of its prevalent evil. If the cutting of the mahoganies was not enough to confirm this prophecy, another catastrophe occurred.

In April 1982 the volcano El Chicon in southern Mexico erupted with a violence exceeding that of Mount St. Helens in the U.S. Northwest. The eruption dissipated gas and sulphuric acid droplets over the entire Usumacinta rain forest and ejected volcanic ash that blanketed the walls of the majestic ruins of Palenque, Yaxchilan, and Bonampak. This catastrophe, following the felling of mahogany trees and the destruction of the rain forest, seemed to confirm Old Chan K'in's prediction that the *Xu'tan*, the End of the World, would come in A.D. 2008.

The time is phenomenally close to the date of 2011 predicted by the great Mayan Calendar more than a thousand years ago. Although the Hopis set no date, their well-known Hopi Prophecy announces the imminent end of our materialistic civilization. These predictions, stemming from an ancient and an alien mode of thought, sound our own feeling that we are on the verge of the greatest change in our way of life in world history.

Whatever may happen elsewhere, the end of the Lacandon world seems certain. For some time plans have been projected to erect a series of large dams along the Usumacinta, whose backed-up waters would submerge not only the Lacandones' present homeland but the great ruins of the Mayan cities of the past. An alternative proposal has been agreed upon by presidents of Mexico and Guatemala. They envision joint creation of biosphere reserves to protect their shared forests and a national park to preserve some of the great Mayan ruins, such as Piedras Negras and Yaxchilan. Which of these two conflicting plans will be eventually accepted is still undecided.

The Hopi homeland here in the U.S. is also marked as a "sacrifice area" by industrial interests that would develop its coal and uranium deposits. Meanwhile, the Hopis are gradually being assimilated into the mainstream of modern life. It is possible that the few Lacandones may also survive as isolated individuals and families. Yet as an integrated tribe, they have become another of the countless peoples whose native culture, traditions, customs, and religion have been eroded by the wind and the rain of time and change.

10
THE FOUR CORNERS

Our own root culture and spiritual home is the great hinterland heart of America, the Four Corners region. The name derives from the only point in the United States where four states touch: New Mexico, Arizona, Utah, and Colorado. The region extending from it is the high Colorado Plateau, walled on the north by the lofty male Rockies and bounded on the south by the Little Colorado River. Two greater rivers mark its eastern and western boundaries: the Rio Grande on the east; and to the west the mighty Colorado, which cuts through the world's greatest chasm.

This rugged upland desert defines seemingly illimitable space instead of measurable place. Its sea of juniper and sage breaks into crests of forested mountains and subsides into a floor of sand slashed by rocky canyons, dry washes, and arroyos. From it rear flat-topped mesas, tall graceful spires, and squat ugly buttes. One comes first to an ancient forest whose massive trees lie level, petrified into stone, then to a lake of black frozen lava. All these shapes and textures of the land are distorted and magnified by the clear, thin air. And on them the salmon pink of dawn, the blinding white of noon, the livid reds of sunset, and the lilac dusk—all the kaleidoscopic spectrum of color with its changing tints and shades—cast still more cloaks.

A mystical realm of the fantastical unreal. But a living land. And a sacred land to those who always have known it as their homeland, its boundaries marked by four sacred directional mountains giving them spiritual strength to endure the harsh realities of their simple lives.

The Four Corners may have been one of the oldest habitations of animal and human life in our America. The footprints of four-toed dinosaurs made two hundred million years ago are still imprinted in the rocky floors of remote canyons. Human artifacts date back twenty-five thousand years or more. And there is evidence that wandering hunters and gatherers of wild seeds began to settle as early as 1000 B.C. in this inhospitable region contrasting markedly to the lush river valleys beyond. From the first arrivals, the incoming groups of wanderers must have felt the Four Corners to be a center of power, possessing a high degree of psychic energy. Succeeding tribes down to the present so regarded it. They still hold many places in special reverence: mountains, springs, valleys where healing plants are gathered, canyons that supply colored sands for ceremonial sandpaintings, and shrines where spirits have manifested themselves.

Here in the Four Corners were established the first patterns of our indigenous civilization.

The first one developed in Chaco Canyon, in northeastern New Mexico. By A.D. 500 the earliest arrivals had settled down here in pit houses, rude shallow pits roofed with branches and mud. Archaeologists now name them Basket Makers for the fine baskets they wove from yucca fiber.

About A.D. 700 a phenomenal change began. It was as if the Basket Makers were somehow enlightened by a concept of a new and greater mode of life. It took shape as they began to build permanent surface structures of hand-hewn rock whose many rooms housed the entire community. In these communal buildings the people achieved a closely knit society that replaced their independent existence in individual and family pit houses. For later archaeologists the people also took on another name—Anasazi, a Navajo word meaning "Old Ones."

Their communal buildings still included as separate features the cylindrical pit houses. These now became kivas, large underground chambers used for ceremonial purposes. The ever-enlarging, massively built communal structures became known as *pueblos*, or "towns" in Spanish; and their builders were called the Pueblo Indians.

By A.D. 900 Chaco Canyon was the hub of a population center, reaching an estimated number of seven thousand or more people in 1100. In this small area, scarcely eight miles long and two miles wide, existed twelve large pueblos surrounded by seventy outlying smaller communities.

The largest was Pueblo Bonito. Semicircular in shape, with walls of perfectly fitted cut stones, it was five stories high and contained over 650 rooms. Popularly called the first apartment house in America, it remained the largest until one was built in New York in 1887, nearly a thousand years later. Its inhabitants were far from being a primitive people eking out a precarious existence from wild game and patches of corn and beans. Their artistic talents matched their superb architectural skills. They wove cloth from native cotton, made fine baskets, fired beautiful pottery, and fashioned jewelry and ritual objects inlaid with turquoise. In addition to their lavish use of turquoise, they loved seashells and parrot feathers, which were brought up from Mexico by traders who traveled over an established trade route.

Their priesthood conducted frequent and complex rituals in the great circular kivas. There were thirty-five kivas in Pueblo Bonito alone. One of the largest, in Casa Rinconada, was sixty-four feet in diameter.

Aerial photographs today reveal a network of four hundred miles of roadways connecting more than thirty pueblos. Running straight as strings, 125 miles to the north and 125 miles to the south, they cut through sandstone outcrops and cross causeways built over low spots. They suggest that Chaco Canyon was a trading center and a ceremonial center for religious observances.

Evidence that solar astronomy was included in Chacoan ceremonialism came to light in 1977 when Anna Sofaer discovered a celestial calendar on top of lofty Fajada Butte at the southeast edge of Chaco Canyon. It was formed by three great upright stone slabs resting against a cliff wall and two spiral petroglyphs carven upon the face of the cliff. Shafts of sunlight cutting through or beside the spirals were observed to mark summer and winter solstices, spring and fall equinoxes, and the nineteen-year cycle of the moon.

News of this ancient "Sun Dagger," as it was called, spread widely and gained immediate acceptance. *Science 80* publication hailed it as an astronomical and geometrical marvel ranking with Stonehenge, and an Oxford symposium recognized it as the only known sun and moon calendar in the ancient world. Whatever its status, this marker leaves little doubt as to the cosmological orientation of Chacoan society.

Why the great pueblos in Chaco Canyon were abandoned about A.D. 1200 is not known. Prolonged drought, deforestation, and soil erosion are conjectured as causes. Nor is it known what happened to the people, although it is believed that many of them migrated east to the Galisteo Basin in central New Mexico. Yet in a scant three centuries, within one of the most arid and harsh areas of the

Southwest, they founded what may justifiably be called the first prototypical civilization in the United States.

During the decline of the Chacoan pueblos, another and much different group of people straggled into northern Arizona, not far west from their predecessors. We know these pueblo Indians today as Hopis. Eventually they built nine permanent pueblos on the tops of three high mesas. Oraibi on Third Mesa, the largest and most important, was founded in A.D. 1150, or earlier, and is still inhabited. This establishes it as the oldest continuously occupied settlement in the United States.

The Hopis adhered to a conceptual life pattern they had had since their creation. It is expressed in a rich body of myth, legend, and religious ceremonialism. Wholly religious, their worldview is abstract and metaphysical, difficult for rational Western minds to accept. Yet its universal meaning deserves a close look. A brief outline will reveal its salient features.

To begin with, the Hopis assert that they lived on three successive worlds before this one. Each world was destroyed when the people became greedily materialistic, ignoring the laws of their divine Creator. A minority survived and moved to the succeeding world to start life anew.

This creation myth conflicts with the Christian myth that the world and mankind were created only once, at a

John Lansa—Hopi Badger Clan

definite time. Nor is this four-world concept uniquely Hopi. It is held by contemporary Zunis and Navajos and was common to the ancient Mayas and Aztecs, although they believed the present world was the fifth. The idea is found in Greek mythology and Zoroastrianism. It is a main tenet of Buddhism, which expounds in depth man's evolution through four stages. With the imprint of its cosmology and cosmography upon so many diverse peoples, the four-world tradition is universal. It seems to me that the cataclysmic destruction of the Hopis' three previous worlds should not be taken literally. They may be dramatic allegories for the stages of mankind's evolving consciousness, symbols of psychic changes relating the inner world of man to his outer material world.

The Hopis, then, voyaging across the ocean of the unconscious after the destruction of their Third World, arrived on this present Fourth World. According to legend, they landed literally on the western shore of southern Mexico or Central America. This region's guardian spirit, Massau, gave them permission to stay but did not permit them to wander freely over the virgin, beautiful continent. He directed them first to make orderly clan migrations, or *pasos,* in four directions to where the land meets the sea. Only then would they find their permanent home and carry out the divine plan of the Creator.

Following these migrations, we now encounter an intricate maze of clan legends, archetypal images, symbols, and ceremonial interpretations—a vast compendium of orally preserved history and religious myth.

Obeying Massau's instructions, clan after clan during many generations made *pasos* to the north, west, south, and east. Upon reaching the extremities where the land met the sea, the leading clans turned right before and after retracing their routes, thereby forming a swastika rotating counterclockwise to symbolize the earth, which they were claiming for their people. The other clans turned left, describing a swastika rotating clockwise with the sun, which symbolized their faithfulness to the supreme creative force. This is the origin of the swastika and sun symbols still painted on the gourd rattles used during ceremonies. During their journeys the clans left everywhere behind them countless ruins, petroglyphs, pictographs, and clan signatures inscribed on cliffs and boulders to mark their passage. All these constitute what the Hopis now call their title to the land.

Completing their migrations, all clans returned to the Four Corners region, between the Colorado and Rio Grande Rivers. Here they gradually collected at *Tuwanasavi,* the "Center of the Universe." They regarded it not as the geographic center of the continent but as the magnetic earth-energy and spiritual center lying at the junction of the north-south and east-west arms of their great migrations.

Whether we view the migrations as forming the pattern of a cross or a swastika, their meaning is much the same. The cross is one of the oldest and most universal symbols known to man. The center point always has been profoundly significant. For if the four arms of the cross extending in opposite directions represent division and conflict, their point of intersection signifies reconciliation and unification. Regarded another way, the horizontal arms represent linear, secular time, the vertical arms represent durational, eternal time. At their intersection they merge into one unbroken timeless time. The center point, in effect, is the meeting point between the conscious and the unconscious.

The swastika, a variant of the cross, adds movement to this static pattern. For the *pasos* represent psychological journeys to the limits of the vast ocean of the unconscious, where the land meets the sea, and back to the center of consciousness. The *pasos* are spiral in effect rather than linear, as suggested by the rotational movement to left or right indicated by the swastika. Great concentric circles draw inward ever closer to a transcendent center. This is still the inner movement of all humanity, the continuing search of every human soul for its spiritual center.

So at *Tuwanasavi* the Hopis found at last the center of their inner universe and their permanent homeland. It mattered little that it was a harsh and inhospitable plateau without streams to irrigate their little patches of corn, beans, and squash, without a mild climate to make their life easy. They would have to depend upon scanty rainfalls evoked with prayers and rituals. But here they could reestablish the life pattern of creation. Their one high purpose was to help maintain harmony among all forms of life: great breathing mountains, talking stones, birds and beasts, cornstalks, and pine trees, all possessing spiritual essence as well as physical form.

Hence, for more than eight centuries the Hopis dedicated every phase of their austere life to the preservation of their religious pattern. Their annual cycle of nine great ceremonials, with their countless rituals, prayers, recitals, songs, and dances, dramatically portrays the creation of this world, the advent of mankind, their migrations, and the life plan they still adhere to against modern political, economic, and social encroachments.

Most rationalistic Western observers dismiss Hopi tradition as nebulous myth, ignoring its psychological meaning. They often include bands of the early Hopis and the dispersed Chacoans under the general name of Anasazi. Yet the Hopis were a far different people than the Chacoans. They did not pattern their small one-story pueblos after the monumental Chaco structures. Their kivas were rectangular, not circular. Nor did the Hopis develop a road system between their settlements. And unlike the unity and cohesiveness of Chaco, each Hopi pueblo maintained its secular and ceremonial life separate from the others.

Just who were the Hopis? Where did they come from? Orthodox anthropology defines them as members of the Shoshonean branch of the Uto-Aztecan language family of Mongoloids, who migrated to America across the Bering Strait sometime between twenty-five thousand and fifteen thousand years ago. These homogeneous ancestral people are said to have spread gradually southward throughout all the Americas and developed their culture from scratch. This theory is no longer tenable. Research shows many later migrations from Asia by boat across the Pacific, forces exerting Chinese and Buddhist influences upon Mayan and Aztec iconography.

Hopi culture supports the idea of its Mesoamerican background. Both the civilizations of ancient Toltec Teotihuacán and Classic Maya collapsed about A.D. 750, the time the Hopis say they first entered the Four Corners. If this is so, we can venture the belief that the Hopis, from their myths, were a splinter group that migrated north after the collapse of these great pre-Columbian civilizations. In support of this belief is the cultural baggage they brought with them, including many Mayan traditions and customs they still observe.

The vanished people of Chaco Canyon have left in their majestic ruins the prototype of our modern pueblo architecture and communal apartment houses. The enduring Hopis have given us, instead of rock-hewn ruins, a glimpse into the invisible realm of the boundless human spirit. Their annual integrated series of ceremonials are the oldest, and perhaps the only true, mystery plays in America. Deeply religious and metaphysical, their meaning long has been ignored by rational, materialistic observers. Yet with the universality of their buried truths, they speak intuitively to us of the law of laws still embodied in our hearts.

A third influx of people straggled into the Four Corners, first reported in 1582 by early Spanish explorers making their *entradas* north from Mexico. By 1776 there were reported to be seven hundred families, enough for Fray Escalante to mark that region of his map as the "*Provincia de Navajo.*"

There seems to be no doubt that these *Apaches de Navajo* were Athabascans who had migrated south from Canada. Some of them, later known as Apaches, continued south to settle in the deserts of southern New Mexico and Arizona. The main body of the Navajos remained in the Four Corners.

They were savage, primitive newcomers, but vital, aggressive, and wonderfully adaptable. Raiding Hopi villages, they learned the rudiments of farming, weaving, and other arts. Yet they ignored the architectural art of the Chacoans, even the smaller one-story pueblos of the Hopis. They remained a nomadic people whose homes were adobe-and-brush dwellings called hogans built at widely separated springs and waterholes.

What drew and held them here on this inhospitable upland could have been only its curious magnetism as a focal point of spiritual energy. Nothing else seems to account for their immediate empathy with the region. The

Navajos' creation myth relates that their emergence from four underworlds as the Earth Surface People took place here instead of in their former Canadian home. Their new homeland, sanctified by their Holy People, the Yei, was marked by four sacred mountains, one in each direction.

The Navajo myth psychologically parallels that of the Hopis in recounting their emergence from previous underworlds, but it gives more emphasis to happenings after they arrived. The events are verbally handed down in a series of interconnected myths presented in recitals, songs, prayers, and dances. These ceremonials are known today as "Sings" or "Ways."

Moving Up Way relates incidents in the pre-emergence underworld. Blessing Way recounts the birth of Changing Woman, who is the earth and changes aspect from summer to winter. In Night Way the people move up to the present world. With Monster Way begins the post-emergence myths in which the destroying monsters are killed by the Hero Twins. Their death weakens the vitality of the people, so a ceremonial is needed to destroy their ghosts. Enemy Way serves this purpose. There follow Flint Way, Mountain Way, Night Way, and many more. Each serves as a ceremony for healing specific illnesses. A sand painting is made by the medicine man or Singer trickling colored sands on the floor of the ceremonial hogan. The ailing patient remains seated upon the floor while the Singer recites the myth and sprinkles him with the sand. No other indigenous American art form surpasses the

Navajo sandpainting in unique technique, abstract design, and emotional effect. Each in form is a mandala, like the well-known mandalas of Tibetan Buddhism also designed to create a psychological effect upon the viewer.

While the Navajos were beginning to take possession of their homeland, Spanish settlements were increasing. These the Navajos raided, capturing horses and sheep that the Spaniards had brought into this country. With horses the Navajos could move more swiftly and widely. They raided Spanish settlements as far as the outskirts of Santa Fe. The war between Mexico and the United States, resulting in the annexation of the Southwest in 1848, accentuated the problem of Navajo depredations. For now came a new wave of intruders from the east. They were white people, "Americans," on their westward march of empire across the continent. By now nearly ten thousand Navajos roamed and raided the territory. The inevitable clash began when General James H. Carlson announced plans for an elaborate Navajo campaign. By July 1, 1863, all was ready. The Navajos were given until July 20 to surrender or to be killed or made prisoners.

The campaign began under the direction of Kit Carson. He advanced slowly, running in horses and sheep, tracking down every Navajo family.

Deep snows came. There was no corn in the Navajos' fields. They couldn't hunt or light fires to keep warm, lest they be tracked down. In January Carson led four hundred men to the Indians' last stronghold, spectacular Canyon de

Chelly. Here he destroyed two thousand peach trees, depriving the Navajos of even bark for food. Huddling in icy caves, the Navajos faced starvation, death, or capture. Their surrender marked the defeat of other surviving bands.

In March 1864 began their "Long Walk" to captivity in the Bosque Redondo, 180 miles southeast of Santa Fe. A total of 8,491 Navajos, including the aged and maimed loaded in wagons, struggled past crowds of jeering conquerors.

Bosque Redondo, with Fort Sumner in its center, was part of a military reservation occupying the bottomlands of the Pecos River. The land had belonged to the Mescalero Apaches, and the four hundred imprisoned survivors regarded the Navajos as interlopers. The bickering tribes were set to work planting two thousand acres of wheat and corn, and digging thirty miles of irrigation ditches.

The free-riding Navajos were not accustomed to such menial labor. Each crop planted for three years was a failure. The alkaline water sickened them. They could not eat their rations of wheat flour. Wood was too scarce to burn for heating; they shivered in flimsy shelters of canvass and brush. Finally, they gave in to hopeless despair.

Their captors were equally discouraged. The cost of feeding them had been reduced to about twelve cents per head a day. Each Navajo was now being issued each day only a pound of beef and corn with a pinch of salt. Hundreds sickened and died.

Sent to investigate the shocking conditions in this Indian concentration camp, a congressional committee decided to remove the Navajos to a part of the country as far out of the way of the whites as possible. The area selected was a portion of their own homeland in the inhospitable Four Corners.

Their bondage was over. In June 1868 the remaining 7,118 Navajos were marched home. Here they were issued two sheep and goats apiece and set loose without horses or wagons, cooking utensils, tools or guns, and expected to die out soon without embarrassment to the remote public.

Instead, they increased and prospered at a rate that had no parallel. As they kept multiplying, the government kept enlarging their reservation to a total of sixteen million acres, roughly twenty-five thousand square miles. The offering of the token sheep, which Navajos nursed into flocks totaling a million head, became the primary support of the tribe's growth. Mutton was the usual staple. The wool clip they sold through isolated Indian traders, for long their only contact with the outside world. The women tended flocks and wove woolen blankets on upright looms lashed to cedar posts. Beautifully colored, with a symbolic design, and durable enough to be used as a rug, the Navajo blanket was a work of art distinctive of its time and place. At the same time, Navajo men fashioned jewelry from turquoise mounted in silver melted down from Mexican pesos. Exquisite squash-blossom necklaces, hand-hammered bow guards, rings and bracelets sold widely.

Always adaptable, the Navajos successfully bridged the gap between ancient and modern ways of life. They formed their own tribal government, with an elected tribal chairman and chapter representatives meeting in a modern administration center at Window Rock. Later, financed by royalties from oil, coal, timber, and uranium leases, the tribe published its own newspaper and broadcast radio programs in Navajo; and it became politically powerful enough to make its voice respected in Washington. The Navajo Nation, soon numbering 165,000 members, was the largest and richest Indian tribe, occupying the largest Indian reservation in the country. It is an example of what every tribe in the United States might have accomplished had they been permitted to develop their own cultures in their own homelands, instead of suffering genocide.

Despite the differences between these first native societies, they had one common foundation. All were vertical or religious cultures, in contrast to our Anglo horizontal or secular culture. Geomantically oriented, they viewed the physical world as a manifestation of the cosmic forces of heaven and earth, and they regarded the land itself as a sacred living entity. Both the Hopis and the Navajos believed that four previous worlds had existed in immeasurable cosmic cycles, being oriented to the four primary directions and related to the four elements, water, air, earth, and fire.

This worldview, or frame of reference, as we might call it, was a holistic concept, a philosophy, and a "mystical ecology" by which mankind could keep in harmony with all the forces of nature.

How different was the horizontal or secular culture brought to America only three and a half centuries ago. Pragmatic, inventive, and enterprising, our Anglo ancestors had a remarkable genius, too. The first arrivals at Plymouth Rock were economically impoverished, psychologically repressed people who had forsaken their motherland and now faced an unknown virgin continent. Within a couple of centuries their expanding race possessed this same continent from the Atlantic to the Pacific. A century later it exercised economic domination over most of the world's undeveloped countries, becoming the richest, most materialistic, mechanistic, and powerful nation on earth.

In achieving this superlative role, our Anglo-American culture has given immeasurable benefits to mankind: electricity, telephones, radio, TV, new medicines, heart transplants, jet flights everywhere, and rockets to the moon. But in alienating itself from nature, it has impoverished its spiritual life and mental health to a dangerous degree.

Its outstanding characteristic is its excessively rational mode of thinking. Repressing the intuitive function of our dual nature, we tend to discount cosmological, geomantic, and other metaphysical ideas as impractical. Our predominant Christian religion is founded on the belief of only one world and one life span for humanity, and we consider the earth inanimate property to be exploited at will. President Calvin Coolidge expressed the national ethic best: "The business of America is business." The chief endeavor of our nation is to constantly increase its gross national product by the manufacture of consumer goods.

It was inevitable that eventually our technological civilization would engulf the comparatively small and remote area of the Four Corners. This inundation swamped both the land and its native people.

As mentioned earlier, a reservation had been established in 1868 for the surviving 7,118 Navajos, later enlarged to sixteen million acres, about twenty-five thousand square miles.

In 1882 President Chester A. Arthur by executive order established another reservation for the Hopis "and other Indians the Secretary of the Interior may see fit to settle thereon." It comprised 2,500,000 acres, about four thousand square miles, lying in the middle of the immense Navajo reservation. Living upon it were eighteen hundred Hopis and three hundred Navajos.

The sedentary Hopis generally restricted themselves to their mesa-top pueblos, but farmed small *milpas* below. The nomadic Navajos with their increasing flocks of sheep strayed into Hopi land and settled in permanent homes near springs and waterholes. Despite Hopi protests, the government ignored the fallacy of confining two tribes within one area.

With passage of the Indian Reorganization Act of 1934, the Hopis were brought under direct federal government control by the establishment of a Tribal Council comprising a representative from each pueblo or village. This white man's system of "democratic government" was utterly foreign to Hopi tradition, each village having its own ancient clan structure and spiritual leader, the *kikmongwi,* who directed its religious and secular life. Many villages refused to send members to the Tribal Council, whose function they regarded as merely rubber-stamping the dictates of the Bureau of Indian Affairs (BIA).

The discovery of coal beneath Black Mesa widened the split between Hopis who supported the Tribal Council and those who adhered to their traditional beliefs and customs. At the same time, it aroused the active interest of the federal government.

Black Mesa's area of thirty-two hundred square miles was almost as large as the four-thousand-square-mile Hopi reservation. It was estimated to contain twenty-one billion tons of coal, with other vast reserves of oil, gas, and uranium; it was seen as one of the greatest undeveloped energy-producing centers in the world. Mineral rights were legally declared to belong to both the Navajos and Hopis. Now began a long period of legal jousting by the two tribes.

In 1962 the courts ruled that the Hopis had sole rights to 650,000 acres in the 1882 reservation, thereafter known as District 6. The rest of it, about 1,900,000 acres, was designated a Joint Use Area for both tribes. There was little "joint use," due to the number of Navajo sheepherders on the land. The Navajo tribe had increased to about 100,000 and the Hopi to about five thousand.

The court decision opened Black Mesa to industrial development. In 1966 the Interior Department granted leases to the Peabody Coal Company, a member of the consortium of the country's greatest power companies, which already had devastated Appalachia.

Three years later Peabody began strip-mining eight million tons of coal yearly. Its colossal Four Corners power plant spewed daily into the air more pollutants than New York and Los Angeles combined, pollutants covering ten thousand square miles. The coal was pulverized, mixed with water, and pumped through a 273-mile slurry pipeline to the Mojave generating plant in Nevada. The required water, amounting to three thousand acre-feet per year, was pumped from an underground water table that fed springs and waterholes. This "Rape of Black Mesa," with its devastation of land, depletion of water resources, and pollution of air, aroused a storm of public protest. It was ineffective and forgotten too soon. The following year a Navajo power plant was erected in Arizona, and the eight to ten million tons of Black Mesa coal it processed yearly were shipped by a new railroad as the plant's seventy-story smokestacks poured still more pollutants into the air.

The complicated history of this development reveals devious practices followed by federal government agencies and powerful private interests as well as the greed of individuals for money, prestige, and political power. Documented details, published in reams of reports, make unpleasant reading.

They also involved religious issues and personalities whose mention is unavoidable. The secretary of the Interior who granted leases to Peabody was a member of the Mormon church. The Interior-approved Hopi tribal lawyer was an elder of the Mormon church in Salt Lake City; he negotiated the contract, although he was a counsel for Peabody at the same time, and collected from the Hopi Tribal Council a commission of exactly $1 million. The chairman of the Hopi Tribal Council, a devout Mormon, directed the spending of Peabody royalties on the building of a modern civic center. The contracts for its administration and other buildings were awarded to his brother, who was head of a Hopi construction firm, operator of the Tribal Council's Cultural Center, and publisher of the Hopi weekly newspaper, which derided the Traditionalists as a "quarrelsome dissident faction" holding "outmoded religious beliefs."

The Tribal Council, under the control of the Bureau of Indian Affairs, had matters well in hand. With Peabody royalties, it was employing Hopi workers to build the new civic center, administration building, and high school. Yet a feeling of spiritual bankruptcy permeated all three mesas.

To settle the land dispute between the Navajos and Hopis, the Land Settlement Act was passed in 1974, dividing the Joint Use Area equally between the two tribes. The partition provided for the resettlement by July 6, 1986, of an estimated twelve thousand Navajos occupying Hopi land and about one hundred Hopis on Navajo land. To oversee their resettlement, the act established a Relocation Committee.

Two years later the Navajo population had increased to 165,000 and that of the Hopis to eleven thousand; little progress on resettlement had been made. The one hundred Hopis and perhaps two thousand Navajos had been moved to new houses in Winslow, Flagstaff, and other towns. Unable to speak English and understand city life, many lost their homes to unscrupulous real estate agents and money lenders. Homeless and heartsick, they wandered back to the reservation only to find that their previous home sites lay on the wrong side of a three-hundred-mile barbed-wire fence, a virtual Indian Iron Curtain patrolled by armed BIA guards.

The heart of Navajo resistance was the people of Big Mountain. They cut fence wires and defied military action, asserting they would die rather than be ejected from their ancestral homelands. Declaring that their Tribal Council was not fully supporting them, Navajo elders signed a Declaration of Independence as the Big Mountain *Dine* Nation, upholding their sacred right to their land.

Their stance was aired before the United Nations Human Rights Subcommission on the Prevention of Discrimination and Protection of Minorities meeting in

Geneva, Switzerland, in 1981. Navajo spokesmen challenged the forced relocation as a violation of religious freedom under the First Amendment and accused the United States of violating human rights. The spokesmen asserted, "The pattern is a familiar one. The bottom line in every major Indian removal program to date has been white control of land and resources."

On February 8, 1985, President Ronald Reagan notified both tribes that if relocation was not achieved, the administration would take appropriate action.

Two weeks later the Hopi rebellion came to a head when the traditional village of Mishongnovi formally severed its connection with the Tribal Council, announcing it would support the traditionalist Navajos at Big Mountain in their resistance against forced removal.

It became clear that if the threatened military action took place, Big Mountain would become another Wounded Knee confrontation.

Fortunately, sane minds prevailed. The set date of July 6 passed peacefully. Military action was replaced by a slow process of attrition as individual families' flocks of sheep were so reduced that they were forced to move.

For some years it has generally been believed that the relocation of Navajos and Hopis from this area was caused by the so-called land dispute between the two tribes. A recent published paper by the Indian Law Resource Center in Washington, D.C., presents clear evidence that the Hopi Tribal Council has plans to exploit coal resources in the Big Mountain area. The evidence contradicts the past claims of the Hopi Tribal Council that mineral development plans had nothing to do with their efforts to evict Navajos from Big Mountain.

The evidence consists of a court document, "Statement of Claims of the Hopi Tribe," and two maps prepared for the Arizona Superior Court. It details the tribe's plans for adding more mines, generating stations, and slurry pipelines to a power plant in Nevada. To carry out this development the court is asked to reserve 8,120 acre-feet of ground water per year (about twice that used by the Black Mesa slurry), and twenty-one thousand acre-feet annually for future mineral and industrial developments other than coal.

As all leases involving Big Mountain land and water must be approved by the secretary of the Interior, the federal government will likely approve these plans. Such a program would of course necessitate the removal of all Indians from the Four Corners. For others besides myself whose lives and thoughts have been shaped by this heartland, its devastation and the erasure of its mythical meaning would be an immeasurable loss. It would mark the final dissolution of its first independent societies and the end of the indigenous American culture cycle begun by the Chacoans. It would also conclude the transcontinental conquest by a nation that from its founding has placed property rights above human rights.

Implications of the industrialization of the comparatively small Four Corners jackpot of natural resources have spread farther; they include the entire Southwest. And they reflect a marketplace ideology leading to a worldwide despoliation of land, waterways, and the atmosphere.

Yet we still have time to learn from our pueblo and Navajo neighbors that the living earth is a font of spiritual energy as well as a source of physical energy. The cosmic energy is the same, viewed differently by those taking either an intuitive or a pragmatic approach to its totality. Reconciliation of these two modes of thought, with the realization that matter and spirit comprise one undivided whole, has yet to come. When it does, it will surely embrace the ancient wisdom and spiritual beliefs of the first native societies in the Four Corners.